Readers Love
I WANT A NEW LIFE!

"Beautiful! Michele Poydence breathes faith and life into her characters and leaves you wanting more. You come to know and love these women, and though it's hard to let go, we can take their message with us on our own personal journeys. *I Want a New Life* carves the path. We simply need to have faith and follow it."

~ Ann M. Faust

"I laughed out loud and pondered the idea that getting a new life really *is* possible. This fun book offers wit and wisdom for anyone 'stuck' in life who wants to make a change."

~ Mary Alice Cookson

"*I Want a New Life* leaves me waiting for more – the sequel and the movie. Excellent material for a book club."

~ Tina Stephens Herrmann

Readers Love
I WANT A NEW LIFE!

"It was so much fun and so intriguing to watch these three women take various paths to claim their new lives! I want to see more of these ladies!"

~ Eileen Colianni

"A wonderful read! I recommend it to all women wanting to make changes in their lives."

~ Karen L. Malena

"When I finished this novel, I was so sad that it was over. It's hard to find well-written books with great characters, and with a story that is both inspirational and funny. Oh, how we need more novels like this! I cannot wait to see more from this author."

~ Topaz, Be a Leading Lady.com

I Want a New Life

By Michele Poydence

Copyright © 2012
Anything's Possible Publishing
P.O. Box 85, Oakmont, PA 15139

Printed in the United States of America

ISBN-10: 0-988-48670-9
ISBN-13: 978-0-9884867-0-6

To Mom and Dad for your unconditional love,
and to my family, friends and everyone who believed in me
or loved me along the way.

And to you, my readers…

wishing you abundant blessings, love and joy
on your journey to a beautiful
New Life.

I Want

A

New Life

Michele Poydence

~ Saturday ~

Casey

This is the day.

The words come into Casey Swanson's mind with undeniable certainty, more fully awakening her. It isn't the remnant of a dream, of that much she's certain. It's a kind of inner voice she's never "heard" before, more distinct than spoken words.

A warning? A promise? Was that *God?*

Casey kicks her legs clear of the K-Mart sheets cocooning her and wipes her long hair, damp with sweat, off her forehead. "This is the day" *what?*

Like an instant special delivery message, the image of her getaway bag – a yoga bag from a yard sale, actually – comes into her mind. For three years now she's kept it filled with necessities, just in case she could ever get away. For a weekend. A month. A dog year. Let's be real; sometimes she wants to run away forever.

But first, a walk and talk with the girls.

Is this the day she leaves Skip and the boys?

Eliz

Would someone please explain how I came to be engaged to a man I've only known for three weeks and I'm not sure I like, let alone love?

Eliz Wilding surveys the rock of a diamond on her left ring finger and asks herself this for perhaps the hundredth time in less than twenty-four hours. Considering she was passed out drunk for half of them, that's a lot of asking. She crawls out of bed, wondering what the day will reveal about last night's blackout. Her head pounds like a jackhammer on steroids as she reaches for her pink silk robe.

Please tell me we're not flying to Vegas to be married by some Elvis impersonator in his chubby stage at the Little White Wedding Chapel.

She *does* realize that the whole perfect storm started on her thirty-third birthday. Eliz sprained her ankle dancing and ended up being a patient of Dr. Dwayne Hanson. Apparently she must have laid on a little too much Blonde Charm because now he's her sudden fiancé.

Everything's still too fuzzy in her mind from last night's booze marinade to even try to connect the dots from there, just yet.

Maybe a quick walk with Casey and Amana Anne will

clear the hangover cobwebs from the few brain cells I have left. She heads downstairs, her robe sleeves flapping like the drooped wings of a dying bird.

But let's keep our priorities straight.

Eliz reaches in the refrigerator for what's left of the champagne from last night and grabs a fluted glass from the cupboard.

First, a drink.

Amana Anne

"You know who this is and you know what this is about."

Amana Anne pauses in mid-motion from picking up her landline at the sound of the deep, masculine voice leaving a message. Of course she knows. She sits quietly on her breakfast bar stool, as if making a sound might give away that she's there.

"You have a week to decide, then I'd appreciate your decision." Oliver was always one to cut to the chase. The click of his hang-up is like a closing punctuation mark.

One week to decide the rest of my life, she thinks, staring at the blinking green message light for a long moment. *Which would mean finally sharing my secrets with Casey and Eliz*. Amana Anne drains the last of her green tea and studies the stray flecks that settled in the bottom of her mug as if they might spell out an answer.

Her late husband, Nathan, actually christened her the "Keeper of Secrets" when they were dating, even though he eventually wheedled them out of her. There's still a little, tender twang at the memory of Nathan, even after all these years. That familiar, but now fainter, arrow of pain. Maybe when you have a great marriage you never completely get over the loss. Especially when it ends like *that*.

Don't go there, she tells herself. No time to be getting yourself in a funk. She jumps up and slips into her walking shoes, all the while mentally preaching to herself like her entire future's depending on it. Which it is.

You can't heal what you keep buried. You can't change what you won't confront.

The truth is, she's feeling scared just at the *thought* of what she's about to do. There's no map on where to begin or how. But she knows for the first time in too many years, she isn't going to be the Keeper of Secrets anymore.

Into the Woods

"I want a new life!"

Casey and Eliz shout in unison as they both come over their opposite hills and spot each other in the lushly green Dark Hollow Woods. They laugh because it's as if they're in a childhood game of trying to get first dibs on saying, "You're it!"

This started about a month ago when they spied each other, converging for their weekly walk on the nature trails surrounding the Oakhaven townhouse plan where the girls all live. When Casey yelled in frustration from her hilltop that she wanted a new life, Eliz thought it was hilarious since Casey couldn't even wait to vent until they came together.

By the next week, Eliz had been arrested for a DUI and hefted over her total life savings for the fine. As soon as Eliz saw Casey's cocoa-brown-haired head pop over the hill that Saturday, Eliz jumped the gun on her and wailed, "I want a new life!"

It shocked Casey that Eliz started echoing her. Eliz usually had this open-hearted energy, a high-spirited anticipation about life, exuberance. Normally, you couldn't help but be buoyed by her presence. Ever since the DUI weekend though, Eliz and Casey both shouted their mantra the moment they saw each other, as if the first to yell it would actually *get* the new life.

Casey's still deliberating over whether she should tell the girls she *is* about to get a new life, her mind whirling faster than her feet as she charges down the hill. She decided after a final row with Skip this morning. The specifics of her escape fantasy, quickly becoming a reality, are still foggy. How, where, or for how long are not exactly clear. Maybe she'll just go for a looong afternoon drive, like until she hits Shangri-La. Her feet slow as she approaches the middle of the hill, the reasons not to tell the girls becoming more plentiful.

First, she might have a crying jag if she has to reveal all the whys. Second, what if they try to talk her out of it? At the very least, they might badger her to wait and think things through. A part of her didn't even want to see the girls today because of all of the above, but something visceral in her *needed* to see them one last time before she left.

As though summoned from Casey's thoughts, Amana Anne's head pops up from the southeast hill, her dark strands of hair floating in the wind like streamers behind her. Amana Anne must have heard their shouting because her arm is already up in the air, finger pointing toward the heavens for *her* mantra.

"Believe!" Amana Anne yells, sprinting down the hill.

Eliz yells back, "Okay, I *believe* I desperately want a new life!"

They all laugh, running, to converge on what they named Baby Bridge since it's just six baby steps across the tiny oak bridge. With an emotional pinch, Casey thinks how she'll miss their healing laughter. Their mirth has been her balm these last few years since the three of them chanced upon each other in the woods and started walking together.

The girls found they all shared a biting sense of humor, enjoyed each other's playful banter and wit, and could tease each other with love. They're all smart, but each admits to pockets of brain freeze *dah*: Casey because she's just started going through The Change, Amana Anne because she's in the midst of it, and Eliz maintains her mind just skip-dee-looes off sometimes, usually to daydream about men.

"Hey, I want a new life, too," Amana Anne says.

Eliz high-fives her, glad she took the ring off. The girls surely would have noticed and it's not like she had any semi-coherent explanation for how she got it in the first place.

Casey catches her breath, wishing she could drop the 18-year-old baby fat from having the twins, and be as fit as the girls. "Puuhleeease, Amana Anne, I'll take your life if you don't want it."

"You're practically perfecto, Amana Banana; don't smoke us," Eliz uses one of her many nicknames for Amana Anne, this pet name picked up from Amana Anne's mom.

"The only thing I'm practically perfect at is keeping secrets, which ends today," Amana Anne says. There. It's out.

"Secrets like you missed cleaning a corner of the dryer lint screen once or something equally horrif-ible?" Eliz makes a mock terrified face as she starts walking at a good clip, the prospect of chilled champagne suddenly resurfacing. Casey and Amana Anne know Amazon Woman Eliz'll leave them in the dust if they don't hop-to so they fall in behind her.

"Are you in the witness protection program?" Casey teases Amana Anne, who gives her a gentle punch on the arm. Amana Anne notices Casey's eyes look puffier than normal. *Has she been crying?*

"How are you, Case?" Amana Anne asks gently, putting an arm around Casey to give her a little, caring squeeze.

"I'd be clinically depressed but I can't afford the clinic," Casey says, and they all laugh.

"Maybe we can get a two-for-one deal, Case-mo." Eliz picks up the pace to a speed walk. They're silent for a moment, in sync like a single heartbeat, a bond beyond words in the rhythm of their bodies, the oneness created with their breath, their marching limbs. Amana Anne points up ahead to a couple ducks floating on the brook, their vibrant green heads bobbing. It's a perfect June day. The girls often silently point out wildlife to each other as they walk: whitetail deer, cardinals, wild turkeys, or baby raccoons sleeping high up in the hollow of a tree.

Casey's already lumbering to keep up, being careful not to stumble on the sticks and stones that pepper the path. She always feels like the out-of-shape loser who's the last one picked for a team. Part of it is she's in sweltering exercise pants and a matching navy jacket because it's the only thing she owns that's clean and still fits without cutting her circulation off at the waist like a tied sausage. She hasn't had it on a half hour and yet somehow it already looks like a wailing wall of wrinkles, while Amana Anne and Eliz always appear as if they could sleep in linen and wake up without a crease.

"Get back on point, Bananzo." Eliz is never winded when she speaks, no matter how fast or far she goes. "The Secrets. Pronto. I'm Splitsville in a few for a hot brunch date."

Amana Anne sprints ahead of them, then stops and turns, causing the girls to nearly tumble over her.

"First, I need to ask you girls something, because it's related to my secrets," Amana Anne says. "Would you like to come with me on a one-week journey to a new life?"

"Yeeeeeeeeeeeeeees!" Eliz gives what they've come to call one of her "Elizabethan" screams. When they walk in the woods, she always leaves her "inside voice" at home, and relishes a good bellow as much as any five-year-old.

"Where?" Casey asks.

"It starts as an inside journey," Amana Anne says.

"Ooooooooh, geez Louise," Eliz moans, getting them moving again. "I thought you meant a girlie go-go to Muscle Man Beach or something exciting. *Inside* myself is the last place in the *world* I wanna be."

11

"Yucko." Casey pretends she's tossing her cookies at the idea, which is close to the truth since she ate about a molehill of raw cookie dough last night.

"Come on, yinz guys," Amana Anne cracks them up when she – 'Ms. Proper-pants' as Eliz nicknamed her – resorts to their native Pittsburghese. "I'm not saying it *can't* be an outer journey, too."

A train whistle sounds in the distance, long and low, as if beckoning them. When they're in the exact right spot on what they call Papa Bridge they can glimpse the train through a clearing as it whizzes by on its high tracks. But today they're just now crossing the medium-sized bridge with the lightest-hued, prettiest oak logs in the park.

Amana Anne's over Mama Bridge first and turns to face them, walking backwards for a moment. "You know how a lot of people take a one-week vacation to get away from it all, then their same problems are smacking them in the kisser the moment they get home?"

Eliz mentally sloshes through a slew of singles' cruises. What Bana says is true; Eliz always comes back to the same ups, downs and crazy going arounds because she never found her sea legs in *life*.

"People still have to face the same unchanged challenges and relationships and jobs they hate," Amana Anne continues. "Because their *lives* haven't changed."

Casey doesn't want to admit that her family only takes staycations on Porchville. But when the boys were younger and they got away for el cheapo camping weekends, yes, she always came back to the same old drudge of a life.

"How about taking one week on a kind of inner sojourn to transform our lives?" Amana Anne asks.

"Or Chinese Water Torture would be almost as fun." Eliz's champagne buzz is dimming fast with all this spiritual yak-yak. *Another champagne daycation is all* she *needs.*

"Change our lives in a *week*?" Casey asks.

"Look, God created the whole *world* in seven days,"

Amana Anne says. "Do you have any idea what could happen if we give our lives, I mean no-holds-barred *completely*, to God?"

"We'd be sent to the Congo, that's what," Eliz says. "Bugs, snakes, ants, cannibals."

"Ahhh, Amana Anne...," Casey trails off, not quite sure how to put it. "I always thought you already gave your life ..."

"You thought since I'm a New Life coach and I'm talking it, I must be walking it," Amana Anne finishes for her. "That's the first secret I want to come clean on: I'm a hypocrite. I never completely gave my life to God. I guess because of what happened with Nathan."

Amana Anne seldom spoke about her husband passing on. Fine with Eliz, who has an allergy to even thinking about death and what that might mean for *her*.

"So either this 'God Stuff' works and I prove it or I shut up about it and go back to my old boss, Oliver, and being 'a suit' in a week," Amana Anne says. "Which means I need a breakthrough, immediately."

"I'm gonna have either a breakthrough or a breakdown myself," Casey says.

"Ditto," Eliz agrees.

They each become lost in their own thoughts for a few moments, until they hit Papa Bridge, with the dark, Sweet Birch wood. It takes a dozen long strides to get across, and nearly twenty for Casey's short legs.

"Can we sit two minutes on Papa's lap?" Amana Anne suggests.

Casey's always grateful when Amana Anne knows she's about to bust a gut.

Eliz moans, "Just *two*, Bana." She needs two *drinks*. Pronto.

Amana Anne wipes the bridge floor with several quick strokes and a couple Kleenex she always keeps handy in her pocket. They plop down and dangle their feet over the edge.

13

"What could happen if we really believed?" Amana Anne asks quietly, looking down into the gently gurgling brook. A leaf twirls in half-circles as if trying to decide which way to go.

"Believed what?" Eliz asks. The sound of water rushing over the rocks beneath her gives Eliz a momentary, albeit fleeting, sense of peace.

"That we could be, do or have anything we really want, as long as it's within God's will," Amana Anne answers. "What do you guys *really* want in life?"

Casey throws up her hands in exasperation. "You know how all these successful people say to follow your passion? For me, it's a big ordeal to have motivation just to get out of bed in the morning. I'm clueless." Casey tells herself that's not entirely true. She *does* daydream. Like that she'll have a really cute, comfy clothing line in happy colors on QVC. Or she'll get it together with her weight and exercise, and be some kind of buff, shining example to other women who thought they'd never pass on a Dunkin' Donuts dozen. But *realistic* passions? Not one.

"I, on the other hand, have plenty of passion, buddy-girls," Eliz says. "What I really want..." Eliz taps her finger on the wooden bridge as if to accentuate her resolve, "...is to be my own boss. I'm tired of always trying to dodge the lay-off bullet." She was still the low girl on the totem pole at the ad agency, as a relative newbie at it.

"And Amana Anne?" Casey asks like a school teacher calling on her prize pupil.

Amana Anne throws a twig in the water and says quietly, "I never told anyone, but I've always dreamed I'd be a motivational author and speaker who helps people around the world."

"You'd be fantastic!" Casey says.

"You're already aces at keeping *us* half sane," Eliz says. Amana Anne's the best life coach in town, albeit she mixes in the "God Stuff" a little bit much for Eliz's taste.

"Thanks, but I feel like helping others on a bigger scale is my life's mission, and... I also feel like I'm going to wet myself just *thinking* about public speaking," Amana Anne says.

"That's because you're old enough to be Methuselah's granny and you're incontinent." Eliz can never resist teasing Amana Anne about being in her fifties.

"I hate to admit this," Amana Anne sighs, "but another secret is that I... I... I..."

Eliz gives Amana Anne a whack on the back.

"Okaaaaaay, I don't believe in *me*," Amana Anne spits it out. "I dream bonsai for myself and sequoias for everyone else. I tell my clients they can do anything, but what *I* believe is this voice inside my head that says, 'You'll never do that!'"

"This is weird but... ," Casey trails off uncertainly. "*I* heard kind of an inner voice this morning. Not what you're talking about, Amana Anne, not negative. It was like an angel, or God. *Whoever* said, 'This is the day.'"

Eliz hums the Twilight Zone theme, which earns her a poke from Casey with her elbow.

"Maybe 'this is the day' for all of us, some kind of turning point," Casey says.

"I'm due back on planet earth so *this* is my turning point," Eliz jumps up, her buzz all but worn off.

"Let's *make* it the turning point to start our new lives," Amana Anne extends a hand to help Casey up. "I told you I stopped seeing clients because I wanted to finish my book on how to get a new life. How about if I drop you girls off a copy?"

"Drop away, Bana, but I'm not globbing onto a whole book of the God Stuff," Eliz says.

"Then how about just a quick prayer together before we part?" Amana Anne asks.

Eliz groans like she's being asked to donate a kidney.

"Sure." Casey needs prayers, a lot, for wherever this day

15

is taking her.

"Awwww, what the heck." Eliz figures she has nothing to lose. If anyone needs prayed for, her number's up and waving a red flag, on the off-chance the prayer stuff works.

The girls join hands and form an intimate circle. Amana Anne and Casey close their eyes and bow their heads.

"Lord, we know You can do more than we can ask or think," Amana Anne prays.

Casey feels something like a warm current coming from Amana Anne as she prays. The power of the Holy Spirit? She's heard people talk about experiencing this. In fact, her buddy from church, Toya, felt it twice from pastors praying for her in healing services, but Casey never experienced it. She feels like she's floating on a river of grace.

"We know You created time and that You can do things suddenly, in a moment, so we ask you to transform our lives and give us direction this week, Lord," Amana Anne prays.

Eliz studies the way Amana Anne seems like she really *is* talking to someone present.

"You said, *our* only work is to believe and we believe," Amana Anne prays.

I'll be working on it, Lord, Casey prays silently.

"Thank You, Father," Amana Anne concludes. "And thank You, Holy Spirit, for guiding us with wisdom on our way. In Jesus' mighty name, amen."

Now I'm really confused when she talks about all three, Eliz thinks. *Not to be disrespectful if You're there, God, but I don't know who is whozee or who does whatzee.*

"Amen," Casey says, and gives Amana Anne's hand a squeeze of thanks.

"Same time, same place, next Saturday and we'll see what miracles God has done, okay?" Amana Anne starts to speed walk like a recharged battery.

Casey feels guilty nodding her head in affirmation as if she's absolutely going to be here.

"Lower your expectations for my camp," Eliz starts for

the hill that'll take her home. Eliz and Amana Anne always run up two steep parallel paths that take each of them to their townhouses, and Eliz always races Amana Anne to try to summit the top of her hill first.

Casey never even enters the competition. She always takes the lowest path, the long way, because the hills are too steep for her. To Casey, it seems analogous of their lives, that Eliz and Amana Anne are always moving up into the sun, into the light, and that she's always down where the sunlight barely filters through the trees.

"I'm *raising* expectations to Heaven," Amana Anne calls over to Eliz, gaining on her. "I think something amazing is going to happen to all of us."

"Believe!" Amana Anne shoots her hand up and points heavenward, turning back with a smile to include Casey. Eliz disappears with a wave down the other side of her hill. Amana Anne's heavenward hand is the last thing Casey sees receding over the horizon. Casey wonders if this is the snapshot she'll always hold in her mind of their last walk together.

And if she'll ever see either of them again.

This is the Day

By the time Casey gets back to the relative cool of her bedroom, there are tiny rivers of sweat streaming between her breasts. She's glad the faded beige curtains are still drawn, making her clandestine activity seem less real, surreal almost. As though maybe she's not really doing this.

Casey tugs at her getaway bag in the back of her closet, and a middle-age grunt escapes her, like she's hefting boulders. The bag is buried under piles of clothes in various sizes that she's ballooned into and out of over the years. Outgrowing her wardrobe is another, albeit far secondary reason, she thinks she has to leave. On some level, she realizes this is insane. The jogging suit she has on only fits because she cut all the elastic out of the waistband, and it's irritatingly scratchy against her belly. She cut the size out, too, because it's a bigger number than she'd want the ER staff to ever see should she be in an accident.

She locates her cash stash from under the mattress and stuffs it in her back pants pocket. It's only ninety-two dollars but BTN, (better than nothing) as Eliz would say, when describing most of her dates. Casey takes her driver's license out of her bedraggled everyday purse and puts it in her side pocket. She'll transfer it to the smaller and nicer purse she keeps in her car for church. No point in taking credit cards,

18

since they're all maxed out.

Casey swings the getaway bag over her shoulder and trots downstairs. In their living room, black trash bags (like a myriad of Santa sacks) cover nearly every foot of their worn carpet. She always knows exactly what's in them. They're filled with electronics that don't work, broken toys, smelly clothes, other people's refuse, maybe even bed bugs, for heaven's sake, and Skip *knows* she's got a deathly fear of crawling critters. Their home already has enough junk and discarded clothes to furnish an alternate universe and dress their entire civilization. Compliments of her husband: "The Junkman."

Skip is sprawled in work clothes on their couch, a bag of chips resting on his pot belly, while the boys loll on mismatched but apropos La-Z-Boys with slumped-in cushions. They never *did* look like twins and they especially don't now at eighteen; Wyatt's squat and chubby, Tyler had a growing spurt and he's long and lanky. The boys are eating Skip's idea of breakfast when she's not around to nag them into *real* food; Wyatt swigs Big Daddy Root Beer and Tyler pops a Cheeto into his mouth, then wipes orangey hands on his jean shorts. As usual, they're all in some kind of junk food/TV coma, oblivious to her as she heads for the front door.

Outside, the stench of insecticide from her neighbor Mrs. Amery's ongoing garden war with the insect world assaults her nostrils. Mrs. Amery's sweeping her practically sterilized patio like she's planning to make meatballs on it. She pointedly eyes Casey's leaf-strewn patio, muttering as she goes inside, "Doesn't the woman own a broom?"

Yes, but you borrowed it last night to fly to your witch's coven, Casey wants to retort.

True to her word, Amana Anne's already left the book copy in a lovely dusty-rose cloth bag on Casey's doorknob. Casey deposits it inside her getaway bag and feels a lump in her throat about leaving Amana Anne. *Worse yet, I'm leaving my* kids. *Just temporarily,* she consoles herself. *Just til I find my marbles again.*

At the thought of actually leaving Wy and Ty, misgivings assail her like gadflies and she wishes Mrs. Amery's insecticide could deep six her anxieties away. *How can I be so certain in my heart one minute about doing something and then so uncertain in my head the next?*

She sighs at what passes for their yard on her way to the car. Dozens of dandelions polka-dot the lawn like blonde-headed, slender beings trying to see what's going on over the high grass. On the driveway, there's a dark oily streak coming from underneath her dilapidated Saturn. It may not even make it out of the cul de sac since it's pretty much being held together by duct tape and bubblegum.

The gold Saturn was supposed to be *her* car and the pick-up truck in the garage was Skip's. But inside "her" car, the seats and floors are inundated with the guys' fast food containers, crumpled gas receipts and used napkins. She pulls down the back seat to stuff her getaway bag in the trunk because the trunk push-button stopped working weeks ago and, of course, Skip hasn't fixed it. She'll be darned if she's going to take on being a grease monkey and yard boy when she does every other living thing around here. As Casey heads back inside, she notices that not once do any sad feelings float to the surface about leaving *Skip.*

The guys are still happily mesmerized, now by a tap-dancing Geico Gecko commercial. She can't do anything unusual to tip them off like try to hug them or kiss them or even, heaven forbid, talk to them. Getting any of them to answer her with the TV on was about as easy as flossing a piranha's teeth anyway.

She'll call them later, after she drops the promised cookies at the church social, gets on the road and has time to think. And *Who knows?* she reasons as she grabs the cookie plate, maybe she'll change her mind again and be back before the cows come home.

"Woooo, wooo!" Casey almost drops the plate at the sound of Skip's eardrum-splittingly high train whistle imitation.

"Get on board the Cookie Caboose," Skip announces like a train engineer, jumping up. The man has built-in cookie radar. He throws couch pillows at both boys simultaneously to rouse them.

"Choo-choo!" Skip chugs like a train, grabbing the car keys from the counter as Casey reaches for them. Tyler and Wyatt bound out the door after him.

The guys almost *never* go to extra church functions with her. Now, on top of everything else up in the air, she'll have to wrangle the car keys off Skip.

"Yinz're all hoofing it home," Skip informs them, walking to the car.

What? Casey's stomach lurches as they climb in.

"I'm taking this baby to Zack's for inspection," Skip says, pulling out while Casey's still shutting her door.

"Dad!" Wyatt yells, "I found the moolah from our Colossal Yard Sale Weekend!" Wyatt hands Skip the stash cash.

Casey could strangle Skip because her money must have fallen out when she was bending over to put her yoga bag in that blasted broken trunk.

"I was *wonderin* where I put that!" Skip folds her money into his shirt pocket. "See how God blesses us when we go to church extra?"

"*You're* going to church for a sugar rush, and that's *my* money," Casey grabs for the cash in his pocket, but Skip puts a protective hand over it.

"Ouuu, someone's got a front seat on the bitter bus, boys," Skip says. "We'll let your mother off on the corner of Cranky and PMS today."

"Menopause," Casey testily corrects him, giving up on wrestling the money off him.

"Same dif," Tyler says.

21

"Why is it when women act bad it's hormones and when men act bad it's us?" Skip asks. Casey can see they're on a roll now, yet again, at her expense.

"Know why they call it menopause?" Wyatt asks, not waiting for an answer. "Because it's like, *men – oh – pause* before you get around these crazy ladies."

Their Saturn sputters loudly and jerks forward.

"Whoa, Dad, you're gonna need every nanopenny to get this bomb passed," Tyler laughs, kicking his feet into the back of Casey's seat. This would usually earn him a good nag-yell, but Casey decides that shouldn't be the last thing he hears from her *if* she can wrangle the keys off Skip. Not that it's the last Tyler would *ever* hear from her. Just the last for who knows how long.

"Not to worry, folks," Skip pitches his voice like he's warming up a crowd, "We're gonna make another million moolah this week since it's…"

"Colossal Yard Sale Week!" Tyler and Wyatt yell in unison.

Which is yet another reason Casey feels she must go. Tomorrow starts Skip's, and by default *her*, week-long yard sale. ANYTIME - DAY OR NIGHT, he'd advertised in the Penny Saver for the previous Colossal Yard Sale Weekend. And *who* was awakened every half hour by some night shift yard sale fanatic? Skip and the boys could sleep through a sonic boom. (She actually once tried a Sonic Boom Alarm Clock on them – "If these don't wake you, you're probably asleep for good," their ads promised. Apparently not. They zzzed through it like chainsaws.)

Look, she wanted to say to the night-owl shoppers, *I only get three and a half minutes of sleep most nights as it is, between tsunami night sweats and hot flashes.* Which was the case again last night.

No sleep. No money. Maybe no car. Not a promising getaway start.

Skip pulls up to the Faith Christian Community Church,

Faith 3C as it's known to its members, a homey church of coral-colored bricks, and a white cross on its high, pointed roof. Casey likes the mix of folks from Oakhaven and Wilksburg, the various cultures and colors and incomes. Albeit, Casey and her family are at the lowest income end, but it doesn't matter to anyone there. With one exception. Perhaps every church has one of those members you strongly suspect may be a satanic plant to test people. Skip parks in the ten-minute unloading space and normally Casey would let loose a lecture but she has to somehow sweet talk the keys off him.

When they enter the social hall, they're warmly greeted by church members munching cookies by the door, and the smell of ginger and allspice wafts up from the sweets buffet. The table's loaded with windmill cookies, lemon drop wafers, Funfetti cupcakes and Pastor Warren's signature Black Forest cake. Everyone's milling about chatting, laughing, and partaking of goodies. Spatterings of friends sit at round, white tables, sipping coffee and tea. The foghorn voice of the "satanic plant," Winifred McFurston, accosts them before they're inside a full minute.

"If it isn't our Junkman and Junklady!" Winifred croons from across the social hall, closing in on them. She sports a high lace collar which resembles an air filter around her crinkly neck. Skip and the twins are already plowing down the buffet like anteaters on an anthill.

Winifred clamps her crab-like claw on Casey's arm, drawing her close, so at least *she* won't go AWOL.

"Oh Sweetie," Winifred croons and her garlic breath could take out an entire tribe. "You do look... at loose ends." Dealing with Winifred is the emotional equivalent of slamming your fingers in a car door. Winifred's one of those people who believes if she prefaces insults with plastic concern, she has a birthright to shoot you in the kneecaps.

Casey's always helplessly tongue-tied with Winifred, as if she's prey bitten by one of those predatory animals who paralyze you first with venom before they kill you. When Casey's *alone* she has countless, biting comebacks to what was previously said to her by the Winifreds of the world. Just never in person. Casey can feel another of Winifred's zingers coming on because Winifred's looking perplexed, canvassing Casey up and down like she might be interesting purely on a sociological level.

"Soooo, maybe we'll find some pretty new duds for you at the Colossal Church Yard Sale?" Winifred winks at Casey, a wink saying they both know there'll never be one.

Winifred pulls this shaggy dog story out every few months, ever since Skip promised to do a church yard sale as a fund-raiser.

"We won't call it 'junk' at the sale, we'll call it recycling, going green," Winifred wildly flutters her jewel-bedecked fingers as if they have an independent life of their own, little mini-princesses all competing to tell a story.

Winifred's eyes give Casey a quick flick to dismiss her as a social inferior, then she hurries off to grab the last piece of Pastor's Black Forest cake. Winifred always makes Casey feel like she should be a walking apology. *Okay, no one can "make" you feel anything*, Casey hears Amana Anne say in her mind. But Winifred *does* tend to look at Casey warily, like she's from some repeat offenders' program.

A pretty lady comes up behind Casey to give a friendly elbow nudge and whisper in her ear, "Case, you best give up those oatmeal cookies before you're tempted to use them as ammunition."

Casey didn't realize she was still clutching them. Her friend Toya takes the cookie plate and sets it next to her own infamous white chocolate, cranberry and macadamia nut cookies. It was Toya, in fact, who came up with the idea of having a getaway bag packed and ready, with no apologies about it to her own husband, four kids, or anyone else who may think it was their business.

Toya would mime picking up her packed getaway bag

and taking off, when they'd share about their husbands and kids driving them bonkers. Toya would laughingly ask, "Is anyone sick-ee-poo and can't catch the plane for that cruise?" Then she'd answer herself, "I'm off to the islands as your most accommodating stand-in." She'd conclude with, "If I left home every time I felt like it, the dog wouldn't even remember me, should I return."

But in reality Toya always seems to have it far more together in every area of her life.

For example, today, as usual, Toya's perfectly coiffed and dressed, and smells tantalizingly tropical, like mango, coconut and citrus. She probably just came from her beauty salon, Toya's Tresses, which specializes in haircuts and extensions for black women. Toya's own hair is spunkily short and straight, "afro-tamed" she calls it and she looks like a hair model.

Casey feels like the cavalry's come whenever Toya's at her side with moral support, especially with Winifred, especially today.

"Oh Lord, put a guard over my mouth when certain people are around," Toya chuckles. "Better make it a legion."

Toya picks up one of Casey's oatmeal cookies. "Or better yet, one of Casey's cookies." Her eyes light up with pleasure as she takes a bite.

"Mmmmm yummy, Case," Toya murmurs. She gives Casey a look behind Winifred's back, warning Casey by making a fin with her elbow that the Jaws shark is still circling the water. Casey actually sees Winifred more like an astute hen who innately knows the pecking order with humans. People like Toya wouldn't allow a single feather to be pecked from her, while people like Casey would allow her feathers to be pecked one by one by all takers until she couldn't fly.

There's a sudden whistle from the front of the hall as Reverend Warren Suppleton clears his throat into the microphone up on stage. He's one of the most sincere and compassionate people Casey's ever met, with deep-set black eyes and skin the color of roasted chestnuts. He politely informs people who call him African American, "I'm Caribbean, with all due respect. And yes, I do a mean limbo."

"People!" Pastor Warren's voice is now raised with tinged urgency so Casey takes a seat by Toya as people quiet to hear him. Pastor Warren usually has a leisurely way of talking so his tone itself all but silences the room.

"Listen up, please," Pastor gives a waving motion with his hand for people still yammering – like Skip and the boys, of course – to shush. Skip leans against the wall across from Casey, slouching like a Gumby.

"We just got a call from Arnold," Pastor Warren says. "He's late because he broke his leg and he's on his way to the hospital." Amid the murmurs of concern, Casey recalls that the reason for today's social is to see Arnold Waystetter off on his mission trip.

"Arnold's going to be okay," Pastor Warren motions again with his hands like he's rubbing their collective backs soothingly, for people not to be alarmed.

"He even still has a sense of humor." Pastor Warren glances outside the long, glass windows at the sound of the green Happy Trails bus pulling up into the lot. "He said if anyone happens to have a packed suitcase in their car and can use his ticket…" Pastor Warren trails off with a laugh and members of the congregation chuckle appreciatively.

Good heavens, Casey thinks with a rush, *could this be God opening a door for me? Should I? How much clearer of a message do I need? "Go, Casey!" in skywriting?*

"I'll go!" Casey jumps up like a jack-in-the-box.

A sprinkling of astonished comments rises up from the congregation. "What?!" "You have a suitcase in your car?" "This *must* be a God thing."

Toya's eyes widen with both surprise and kudos, and she murmurs to Casey with a you-go-girl smile, "Why didn't *I* keep my getaway bag in the car?"

Casey can feel Skip's eyes pivot down to her in shock. "I can go!" Casey says to confirm it, not meeting Skip's glare. The congregation spatters applause and cheers.

Skip lets out a skeptical scuff of air she can hear eight feet away. "Yeah, that'll be the day," he says for the benefit of everyone within hearing distance. It's his standard dismissal that's echoed through the years whenever she talked to him about doing something new, becoming something more or dreaming something bigger for her life. Tyler mimics his dad's scoff, but Wyatt looks at Casey with a pained grimace like she just ran over his toes on purpose.

Skip sets down his coffee and snicker doodle number six on the table in front of him, planting his hands firmly in his pants pockets. His stoic look says even if she does mysteriously have a suitcase in the car *he* has the keys and she can fuggetabout it.

The Happy Trails bus beeps loudly and Casey reacts like a Pavlovian dog, rushing outside past Skip, the boys, and her church "family." She runs to the Saturn, mentally noting that they're past the ten-minute unloading time and everyone's going to see.

The Happy Trails driver leans out the bus door, cupping a hand over his eyes against the sun. "You the mission pick-up?" he calls to her.

"Be right there," Casey calls back. *There? Where exactly will "there" end up being?*

She bangs the palm of her hand on the right rear edge of the rusted trunk with a good whack since this worked once before. Nothing. Casey hammers the trunk again with a series of desperate blows that could K.O. a prizefighter. It finally capitulates and creaks open begrudgingly, with an unsportsmanlike groan of surrender. She snatches the getaway bag and slams the trunk.

Pastor Warren, Toya, and several members of the congregation filter out to the parking lot with Skip and the boys. Skip's the first one to her. It's the fastest she's seen him move since high school second-string football days.

"Have you lost your mind?" Skip asks.

"A good chunk of it," Casey says. "I'm leaving in hopes of salvaging the rest." *Maybe sometimes you need to lose some of yourself to find yourself,* she thinks, dropping her bag to run to the boys. Tyler stands ramrod-stiff when she tries to kiss him on the cheek. He leans away from her, like she's a leper, that she would dare to be affectionate in public. There's no way she can kiss his cheek without leaping up for it and the last time she tried that she almost broke both their noses. Wyatt's noodle arms remain loose at his side as Casey hugs him, his face is like dead wood to her kiss.

"I'm on a schedule, lady," the driver calls, going back on the bus.

Pastor Warren gives Casey a warm, quick hug and talks fast. "Go to the US Air counter. We have a contact at the airline who'll straighten things out so you can use Arnold's ticket. Someone'll pick you up on the other end at the airport and take you to the mission church. We'll call your cell if we need to touch base."

No reason to explain that she doesn't have a cell because it broke and they couldn't afford to replace it. The driver revs the motor loudly. She grabs her getaway bag and rushes to the bus, with Skip in hot pursuit. At the base of the bus stairs Casey puts her arms out to hug Skip. He plants his hands on her shoulders, holding her in place at arm's distance.

"That'll be the day when you just up and take off like this, Case," Skip says. "I mean it."

Casey unplies Skip's hands, hoping Pastor Warren and anyone else who may be looking assumes it's an affectionate squeeze versus trying to release a death grip.

She looks Skip in the eyes and says softly, "This *is* the day."

There's a flicker of Skip's confused surprise as she firmly releases his hands and jumps onto the bus. Pastor Warren and the church gang call their goodbyes after her, and Toya blows her kisses. The driver impatiently closes the door in Skip's stunned face, coasting away as Casey's jostled up the stairs. Out the window, she catches a glimpse of Pastor Warren and Toya and the gang still waving. Skip stands, hands on his hips, looking after the bus. The boys are already headed back inside with their friends.

Casey weaves down the crowded aisle, through a river of friendly, animated faces and chatter, to *whoomp* into an empty seat in the back. As the bus rolls away, the thought leadens in her stomach that she has no idea where she's going, what she'll be doing, or *if* she can do whatever mission is before her. *Has* she lost her mind?

She hugs her getaway bag to her chest like a life preserver. *God help me*, she thinks, as the bus roars onto the parkway heading for the airport. She realizes she hasn't, in fact, talked to God in more months than she can count, beyond praying today with Amana Anne and Eliz. Casey closes her eyes and takes a long breath.

Lord, I'm sorry I've been out of touch for so long, and I want to thank You for always being there for me anyway. I'm not sure what *I'm doing, which I guess is painfully obvious. All I know is I'm scared. Really scared. I'm trusting You to guide me wherever it is I'm about to go.*

Because apparently, this is *the day.*

Wowie

Amana Anne snaps off her Playtex gloves, satisfied with her newly-scrubbed, sparkling kitchen sink, and parts the lace sheers above it. A ruby-throated hummingbird flies to her hanging petunias, his wings a blur of happy activity in the quiet serenity.

Until a yodel pierces it. Accompanied by approaching roller skates. Amana Anne cringes because it could only be one person.

It *used* to be a quiet neighborhood before her mom moved into the plan.

"Yoooo hoooo!" Wowie skates full force into the screen door, with a crazily crooked pink helmet covering one eye. "Great news, darling daughter!"

Wowie is ninety-eight pounds of stomping dynamite in jean capris, roller skates and a T-shirt that says *All This & Brains, Too*. She used to be almost Amana Anne's height of five foot five inches, but she swears she's "shrinking into oblivion" at just over five feet.

"Mom, you look like some kook-a-nut." Amana Anne opens the screen door.

"I *act* like a kook-a-nut, so it works out." Wowie adjusts her helmet so she can see. Her hair is white with short layers spiking out around the helmet like a porcupine. They both have the same forest green eyes and high cheekbones, albeit Wowie's are now a bit sunken.

"Momsy, need I remind you, you're *eighty*!"

"What's your point?"

"That I'm getting you a gym membership so you can have a *safe* exercise program."

"I already have a safe exercise program right at home. I go upstairs, I forget what I wanted. I come downstairs, I remember. By the time I trot back upstairs, I have no idea again. All day. Who needs a gym membership?"

"What am I going to do with you?" Amana Anne sighs.

Wowie lowers her voice conspiratorially, "Come out and play. I'd come in but Miss OCD might have a myocardial infarction if I skid her floor with my skates."

According to Wowie, Amana Anne has Obsessive Compulsive Disorder because she cleans like everything's just one molecule away from the Bubonic plague, and irons her underwear.

"Yep, I'm the female Howard Hughes sans the fortune." Amana Anne joins Wowie on the patio, a little posie paradise with petunias, and coral and pink impatiens. She inhales the fresh air sweetened by a neighbor's newly-mowed lawn.

"You wouldn't believe the deal I got on these babies at the yard sale." Wowie turns her varicose-veined ankles from side to side to showcase the skates.

"I hope they threw in a tombstone because you're gonna need one if you keep skating." Amana Anne dead-heads the magenta petunias, careful not to break the tiny, delicate white baby's breath intertwined with them, a pretty accent against the deep violet.

"Why'm I here?" her mother asks.

"Some great news...?"

"Ohhh, right-o. I found that cell phone you gave me. In the freezer."

Amana Anne drops her head in resignation.

"Is that bad?" Wowie asks.

"Better the phone than the cat."

"That's what I love about my girl. Always looking on the bright side. And, by the way, do I *have* a cat?"

"No, and that's why."

"Guess what I *do* have." Wowie twirls on her skates, then holds up her hand as if for silence from a mass audience, her standard cue when she wants to announce something big.

"I'm afraid to." Amana Anne waits for the other shoe to drop.

"Well, what I'm *going* to have," Wowie clarifies. "A boyfriend."

"A *what*?" Since Amana Anne's father went to Heaven a few years ago, Wowie always said he'd be her one and only.

"I decided if *you're* never gonna date again, I'll liven things up for both of us." Wowie skates a few feet down the sidewalk and turns, doing her version of Escapades on Ice, Geriatric Edition. "Since *your* love life is an oxymoron."

"Heaven help me," Amana Anne looks up to the sky pleadingly.

"Not only is Heaven helping you, your madre dearest is," Wowie says.

"What are you talking about?"

"About making your dreams come true," Wowie gives a Queen Mother wave to a befuddled Amana Anne as she skates toward the street. "Be at Golden Horizons, five o'clock sharp."

The Sudden Fiancé

Eliz glances sidelong at her supposed fiancé, Dr. Dwayne, driving his "Beemer Baby," as he calls his black BMW coupe, through Oakhaven. He's a good looking podiatrist with sandy-blond hair and hazel eyes, although his Armani slacks are a bit of overkill for a casual brunch.

At least Dwayne and I are both great dressers, Eliz thinks as she readjusts herself on the smooth leather seat. Her Jones New York sleeveless, gold V-neck showcases her tanned arm "guns," and the JNY white shorts accent her taut legs to full advantage. Since the brunch is "smart casual," white-on-white Nikes complete the ensemble.

Eliz is all too aware that she isn't naturally lovely like, say, Amana Anne. With a slightly Roman nose and smallish eyes, she has to work with the magic of makeup. But Eliz makes sure she whips everyone with her physique. She's tall and statuesque at five-nine, and hard-muscled with drum-tight abs, arms and buns. Her short hair is a stunningly bright "Champagne" blonde, after her favorite drink.

Champagne, specifically, is what got her into all of this: Engaged to a man she finds as exciting as reading a phone book, but whose credentials alone impress everyone else, especially her parents. It raises her "stock" in the eyes of others, which she desperately needs because she's been a monumental mess-up most of her life. Yet *being* with him lowers her spirits to abyss-level and makes her feel like she's selling her soul. It doesn't escape her notice that the "tear drop" diamond now back on her finger seems dishearteningly appropriate.

Dwayne clears his throat to speak and startles Eliz back to her depressing reality. She wishes she could break him from this bad habit of reminding her of his existence.

"You know your eggs're getting older by the minute," he says.

What?! Eliz generally flat lines after syllable one comes out of his mouth because he's fascinated with talking nonstop about himself. She's *hoping* she didn't just hear what she thinks she heard.

"We better hurry and set our wedding date." He cranes his neck up like a flag pole and bends it to each side to crack it. "Are you aware of the stats for mental handicaps with old-egg kids?"

"I have my *own* mental handicap right now, thank you," Eliz says, her head pounding again from the hangover. She turns to look out the window at anything but him.

They're entering Wilksburg, the little town that's right next to Oakhaven, but a world apart. Oakhaven is pristine and picturesque. Wilksburg is rundown, with old buildings and littered streets, where lost-looking kids hang out in front of graffitied, boarded-up businesses, flicking cigarette butts onto the sidewalks. Both towns have their share of Pennsylvania-pretty trees, but that's where the similarities end.

Dwayne sucks air through his teeth, making little tweetie sounds as he stops at a light. He looks around suspiciously at the changing surroundings. It takes everything in Eliz not to catapult out the Beemer sun roof when he does the tweetie noises, which is often. Clearly, she shouldn't marry him. *She's* the one who'd have to live with him, not all the people he impresses. She's just waiting for her head to clear from last night's drunken stupor to figure it all out. On the other hand, in about two minutes, she's about to have a hair-of-the-dog-that-bit-you drink (or six) at Jamaica's champagne brunch. Thank heaven Jamaica's pink brick apartment building's dead ahead.

"Park anywhere," Eliz instructs, and Dwayne scans the multi-ethnic neighborhood like he's arrived on Uranus.

"I thought we were just driving *through* Wilksburg. I'm not parking my baby *here*." He means his car, not her. He says it with incredulity like someone told him to leave a real infant at the curb.

His eyes widen with a dawning realization. "Is this friend of yours… a… a… person of color or something?"

"For your information, Mr. Skinhead-or-whatever-your-problem-is, Jamaica's …"

"*Jamaica*!?" He cuts Eliz off accusingly, like she'd purposely kept some integral clue from him.

"Eeeeliiiiiz," he says, drawing her name out like he's reprimanding a two-year-old who should know better, "*We* don't have friends like…"

"There is no *we*!" In a knee-jerk reaction, Eliz rips off her engagement ring and flings it at him.

Dwayne throws his hands up to shield his face. "You almost hit my eye and I'm a surgeon!"

"You're a *racist jerk*." Eliz opens the door and jumps out, slamming it good-riddance behind her as the light turns green.

A Middle-Eastern taxi driver behind Dwayne blares his horn and Dwayne takes off like he's afraid of the "person of color" as much as he is of Eliz. The taxi roars by her, spewing black exhaust in a fog of fumes. Eliz stands on the curb coughing, in shock over what she just did.

Well, isn't this what you wanted? Out? She jaywalks across the street to Jamaica's, holding traffic at bay with her outstretched hand, feeling a jumble of mixed emotions. The security of having *someone*, especially *now*, with all that's happened in the last few weeks, felt like a paradoxical port in a storm when any harbor would do. And now she blew that, too.

At least there's still the immediate, if temporary, haven of booze at Jamaica's, Eliz decides as she enters the bleak apartment complex lobby. A musty stench smacks her nostrils like the carpet's dank and sure enough, there's a spongy, squishy feel to it under her feet. She bounds up the side stairs three at a time to Jamaica's, and gives the door a rapid-fire series of knocks. It sounds desperately rabid, but the promise of instantaneous liquid anesthesia supersedes social graces.

Jamaica peeps out like it's a police raid. She's wearing a deep apricot tunic that compliments her cinnamon skin, with matching jeweled thongs. Music filters into the hall, a mix between jazz and reggae. Jamaica sips a mimosa with an orange slice perched on the rim. She's a little looped already.

"Hey, Jailbird!" Jamaica greets her, laughing. Jamaica's the only one who knows about Eliz's recent Jail Gig. Eliz didn't even tell Casey and Amana Anne exactly how far south her life has gone lately, just that it tanked in general.

"Can it, Jam!" Eliz eyes their coworkers inside, concerned they might hear, but they seem intent on piling their plates at the brunch buffet.

"What? You think your parole officer's hiding in the hall?" Jamaica teases.

"Knock it off. You *know* I don't have a parole officer."

"Yet. The day is young. Cause you may wanna commit armed robbery after I fill you in on *this* elmore." Jamaica steps into the hall and pulls the door shut behind her. "I don't know if I'm gonna tell anyone else from work because then they'll be bummeranged at my brunch," Jamaica whispers. "But, we're laid off!"

"That's not possible," Eliz says, then can see from Jamaica's serious nod it not only is possible, it's true. Eliz grabs the mimosa from Jamaica and drinks half of it in one long gulp.

"Ed just called to RSVP no show to my brunch." Ed Barr started the small marketing and advertising agency where they work, Rising Star. Or rather, where they *used* to work.

"He chowed with Sal last night," Jamaica tries to grab her mimosa back, but Eliz holds tight, swatting Jamaica's hand away. Sal's their best client. His account alone's been keeping them afloat this past year. "Sal's taking his marketing in-house. Effective immediately."

Eliz puts up her hand for Jamaica to stop. Depressing information overload. She downs the rest of the mimosa and hands the empty glass to Jamaica.

"This is gonna require a *lot* more champagne." Eliz heads back down the steps.

"Bring a case," Jamaica calls after her.

"A vineyard," Eliz means just for herself.

Eliz won't be back. The drop-down kind of drunk she needs to get can't be around *anyone*. It'll need to be more booze than Eliz can consume anywhere but in the privacy of her own home, doors closed, curtains drawn.

"Hey! Where's Doc?" Jamaica leans over the stair railing.

"Finito." No point even getting into the whole one day engagement.

"You wanna check out Mr. Backup, then?"

Mr. Backup's some guy Jamaica's been wanting to fix her up with for months. Well, *someone* was going to have to buy Eliz dinner. She'd planned on asking Ed for an advance on next week's pay just to buy groceries this week. She should have grabbed some food from Jam's brunch, but a drink is the more pressing business at hand.

"Tell him Mulligan's at eight," Eliz calls back, escaping out the door. She could walk to Mulligan's if she got too hammered to drive.

Outside, sudden sunlight breaks through a drift of clouds

and causes her to squint. She curses herself for being too lazy to locate her sunglasses before she left. Eliz waits for a dilapidated car with a loud muffler to pass and jaywalks again across the street. His receding bumper sticker reads, *Due to the current economic climate, the light at the end of the tunnel has been switched off.*

Ain't that the truth? Eliz thinks, starting a slow jog, glad there aren't many people out yet to negotiate around and that Jamaica only lives a short run away.

Thank heaven I didn't eat anything yet today so the mimosa will kick in fast. A sliver of relief washes over her. *It's already starting to work a little magic.* Through the vision of her softly growing mimosa high, the sun sparkles on the sidewalk and even the little stones in the pavement shine cheerily.

Things look sooo much better with a little booze. Which'll be plenty handy because she's already feeling the gnarly hands of panic grabbing at her heels: *You have no money. You have no job. And what exactly are you planning to do about groceries for the rest of the week?*

Before the Jail Gig, she'd always prided herself on *not* being in the seventy percent of Americans she read about, living paycheck to paycheck. Okay, she only had a couple thousand in an emergency fund. *Had* being the operative word here. Since her DUI slammer stint, the hefty fine, a bounced rent check and threat of eviction, her life has been in a financial tailspin.

Don't think about it, don't think about it. She picks up her pace and breaks into a measured run, setting her mind instead on the bottle of cheap, but chilled champagne she always has in the fridge for just such a crisis as this. Now, *that's* an emergency fund.

And very soon, at least for a little while, it's going to take away all her pain.

California!

Not a bad start to a mission trip. Casey ventures past the bright, orange "Welcome to San Diego" sign and joins the airport crowd with mock confidence, like she belongs, heading for the luggage carousel. Almost everyone's dressed in shorts, flip flops, tropical summer dresses, and brightly colored golf shirts. One muscle guy in a tank shirt and shorts has so much hair on his body he looks like a walking Carpeteria Store. *She* feels like a Pillsbury Dough Girl amid all these California Slim Jims and Janes.

Her long-sleeved exercise jacket and pants are making her muggy so she considers taking the jacket off and just having the white tank on, but her cellulited upper arms look like grapefruit peels. Then again, it's a visual toss-up since her jacket has a long, wet drool stain down the front because she was in a deep coma-sleep for most of the flight. For the first time in years she hasn't had her countless cups of java through the day to keep her semi-conscious. She probably slept in sheer relief, too, that the plane wasn't headed somewhere like the Siberian tundra of Yamal after all, and that they even let her *on* the plane. She thought for sure one of the crew would say, *Sorry lady, those bags under your eyes are over the weight limit.*

On the luggage carousel amid the array of real luggage other passengers grab, the getaway bag circles to her. She's hoping to see someone who looks like they're remotely expecting her in the pond of people greeting and hugging loved ones. What was she thinking that she didn't get more information? To say nothing of coming without money or a cell phone. Well, no one could accuse her of over-planning. She feels a growing sense of panic, then remembers she should be praying instead of worrying.

Well, Lord, You brought me this far. I'm trusting You.

Near the automatic door exit, a few limo drivers hold signs: Mr. Monroe, Amin Rach, Xon Tech, Kampanero. She spots an older, scruffily-bearded gentleman at the end of the line, holding a hand-printed sign, "Arnold Waystetter." Casey waves a relieved hello.

His eyebrows knit together. "You Arnold?" he asks with a smile, as if to say, *This is California, I guess anything flies.*

"I'm his stand-in, Casey." She puts out her hand. He shakes it, shrugging his shoulders.

"Barry here. Need help?" He puts his hand out for her getaway bag.

Casey realizes she's again clutching it like a life preserver.

"I'm good, thanks." *Relax*, she tells herself.

Barry motions with a head nod to follow him through the glass doors. He shuffles in worn, brown sandals, his bunions and corns bulging. Outside, the California sun is a bright egg-yolk-yellow. The air smells different... tropical, and Casey wonders if this is the scent of the ocean. She spots her first palm tree planted between two cement buildings, followed by more of the regal beauties studding the entire street, as if they're somehow standing guard to protect her on her journey.

"Right on time now," Barry says as a blue shuttle bus pulls to the curb. The words "San Diego Shuttle" are stenciled in black on the side of the door. Barry pulls it open and motions a gentlemanly "*Ladies first.*"

"That's Pacho," he nods toward the Hispanic driver, who offers her a shy, gap-toothed grin when she waves hello. The only other people on the shuttle are three teens in wild Hawaiian shirts in the back, loudly horsing around and dancing in their seats to music from a Smart Phone.

"We be unloadin' the rowdies down a spot," Barry assures her as he plops into the front seat with a *whump*. Casey chooses a seat midway between the "rowdies" and Barry, who starts conversing in broken Spanish with Pacho.

The shuttle grunts and acts ornery as they exit the airport and weave onto the heavily trafficked four-lane boulevard. More palm trees dot the landscape, solemn and proud amid the panorama of buildings.

Casey can't *believe* she's in California. She'd never been out of Pittsburgh beyond a couple of plane trips to Minnesota, when Skip's parents passed on. Suddenly, here she is on the other side of the country. It *feels* like another world.

She yawns and unzips her jacket, settling against her bag. There's a soothing feeling about being in a back seat, like when she was a kid not having to worry about driving or where she was going. But a worry *is* surfacing now about where she *is* going, which reminds her to instead concentrate on giving thanks that God will continue to guide her.

"Ouuuu, look what Thumper's Nana packed him." One of the rowdies yells and the teens howl with laughter. Casey realizes she must have dozed off because it wakens her with a start. She wonders how long she snoozed. A few minutes? A half hour?

"Traveling's *constipating*." The kids erupt in guffaws as the shuttle pulls up in front of the Red Roof Inn. The first rowdy, in red Nike shorts, runs past Casey and tosses back a bottle of prune juice to the kid behind him.

"Hot potato!" The Nike kid yells and jumps out.

"Hot prune-ato!" The second rowdy yells, planting the

Sunsweet forty-eight ounce prune juice onto Casey's lap. He leaps off with the third kid, both laughing like hyenas.

Barry and Pacho shake their heads after them. "Now ain't that a shame?" Barry says. "Guess they growed up in some barn where roosters had got better sense." Barry puffs his cheeks and lets out a huff of air. "Dress better, too," he adds with a chuckle.

The shuttle eases back onto the boulevard, and Casey realizes she actually *is* desperately thirsty. She slept through the beverage offerings on the plane and hasn't had a thing to eat or drink all day. Ladylike or not, she can't contain herself. Anyway, Barry and Pacho are deep in conversation again already.

The prune juice's yellow lid twists off easily with a click and the juice goes down sweet and thick. It's warm enough to bathe in, but she doesn't care. She swallows several hefty gulps without stopping until Pacho makes a sharp left and a big splotch of the dark juice jumps out of the bottle, running down her white tank top like a muddy river through snow.

"You up next, Miss Casey," Barry calls back to her as she recaps the juice like she could unspill milk.

Casey looks out the window to see modest, middle-class homes lining the street, with neat yards and shady trees. A white, steepled church is on a large corner lot at the end of the street. As they draw closer, Casey sees a few buildings on the lot: a parish house, what may be a social hall, a school, and a closed-off little gated area that's probably storage. A wooden sign on velvety green grass reads Crossroads Church. *Seems like I'm in the right place. If this isn't a crossroads, what would be?*

The shuttle stops in front of the long one-story brick building that looks, at least in part, to contain classrooms. Barry jumps out and opens her door. He hands her a gold key. "You find a note in where you sleeps back in the nursery. We drops volunteers here all the time. We knows the drill."

Casey hops out with her bag, calling back thanks to Pacho.

"Nada," Pacho gives her a little seated bow like he's being congratulated for a performance.

Although they're inland and she can't see the ocean, she can again smell its salty sweetness on the breeze that billows through her clothes and hair.

Barry stretches his long legs as he talks, pulling the side van door shut behind her. "God bless, Miss Casey." He points to the red door. She can see through the low windows it's a children's classroom with tiny, wooden desks and chairs in neat rows. Barry jumps back into the front of the shuttle, calling out the window as Pacho pulls away, "Take care, now."

Casey waves back, feeling like it's *her* first day of school. She slowly turns the knob on the red schoolroom door. And feels like she's entering a future beyond what she could ask for or imagine.

Agent of Change

"Not exactly what you were expecting, and you're patently clueless, right, Kiddo?" Rhodine Katz cracks her gum, and Amana Anne's glad Wowie isn't here to ask, "Are you chewing your cud, dear?" Wowie gave Amana Anne's book to her chum Mrs. Katz when she learned Rhodine, her literary-agent daughter, was visiting.

"Excuse me?" Amana Anne asks politely, her eyes darting around the Golden Horizons Senior Care garden to see if anyone else heard Rhodine. There's only Rhodine's mom, Mrs. Katz, asleep nearby in her wheelchair, lulled by the soft gurgling of the pond and gray clay water fountain next to her, where water spurts from the hand of a fairy atop the fountain.

Rhodine shifts uncomfortably on the ornate metal bench they're sitting on like it's hard on her bottom, and flicks her fingernails. She's got one of those strong faces, not conventionally pretty, but the kind of face your eyes are drawn to in a crowd because there's a laser intelligence there. Her makeup's a little caked in the crinkles just forming around the edges of her eyes. Although she's "kiddo-ing" Amana Anne, she's probably younger than her. Just doesn't look it.

"You have a dynamite book. But no platform, correct?" Rhodine asks like she already knows the answer.

"What's a platform?" Amana Anne has the distinct impression this is something Rhodine thinks she should know.

"Ooooh, boy. Just what I suspected. An unknown self-help author with no platform is about as coveted by publishers as a fly in soup. You're not exactly the female Dr. Phil in potential sales. You understand what I'm saying?"

"All except the platform part."

"Your *platform*, Kiddo," Rhodine enunciates loudly as if Amana Anne's hard of hearing.

Mrs. Katz half-wakes, highly irritated. "*Now* what?" she asks like she's had her skirt tugged yet again by some rascally child.

"I'll be over in a minute, Ma," Rhodine calls, then lowers her voice to Amana Anne, speaking in a tone that suggests *she's* the child.

"A platform is how many speeches have you given in the last year? How many talk shows, radio shows, public appearances?"

Speaking to Casey and Eliz in the woods was Amana Anne's limit so far, and *that* was plenty. Her stomach flip-flops at just the *thought* of speaking to a crowd. Amana Anne glances down at her own "Believe" tote leaning against the bench, as though it's incriminating her.

"So a platform's something you jump off instead of a high bridge when you have to speak in public?" Amana Anne knows it's the wrong lame joke before it finishes coming out of her mouth.

It's confirmed DOA by the patronizing look Rhodine flashes her. "I *hope* you're not an unknown, without a platform, *and* a fear of public speaking cause that would be the Devil's Triangle kiss of death and I'm *really* wasting my time."

Rhodine's cell rings, a no-nonsense tone, like a landline.

45

She rolls her eyes at the name that shows, like she's hearing from them for the kajillionth time.

"Hold," she says wearily into the phone without a hello and continues to Amana Anne. "Your physical package is media ready. You *look* the part of a self-help celeb. Fact, that's why I'm even meeting you. Your mom included a pic. You wouldn't believe the difference between headshots people send from when they were three decades younger and their real present-day mugs. Ugh!" Rhodine makes her version of an "ugh" face, crossing her eyes, simulating buck teeth in a slack mouth and hooding her eyes like she can barely see.

"Just build a platform for a couple years," Rhodine says.

"A couple *years*?" Amana Anne's voice jumps an octave into Minnie Mouse range when she's upset, like now. "Isn't there some other way?"

"Sure. Be an overnight sensation." Rhodine gets up and stretches her lower back like it hurts from sitting on the metal bench. "Lotsa luck, Kiddo." Rhodine cracks her neck to work out a kink, and lumbers toward her mother.

"Thank you," Amana Anne calls after her. *I think.*

Rhodine waves her off, no problem, and sighs heavily into her cell, asking, "Bottom line?" She groans at whatever bottom line she's hearing. Amana Anne sits for a moment watching Rhodine's retreating back like it's the receding of her dream. *A couple* years*? I have a* week.

But there *was* that overnight sensation clause of hope. God *can* do things suddenly. Look at Joseph, who went from being a prisoner in Egypt to prime minister in a day. Like Jesus said to the disciples, your only work is to believe. *He'd* take care of the miracles and doing a "suddenly."

Amana Anne grabs her Believe tote, slips out of her sandals and pulls Wowie's psychedelic skates out. She nabbed them off Wowie's porch on the way here to ensure that her mom wouldn't break her neck. *Yep, I can break my* own *neck,* Amana Anne tosses her sandals in the bag and

46

slips her feet into the skates. Amana Anne tried the skates out on the way over. *Why not?* she thought, rather than carry them. She had taken the skates off a block away from where Rhodine might see her and think she's a flake. No need to worry about impressing her now.

Rhodine's apparently got a long-winded bottom line she's still hearing about as Amana Anne waves and skates by. *How about an unknown without a platform, who fears public speaking, and who* skates? Rhodine watches like Amana Anne's a mental patient on the lam. Mrs. Katz snort-snores herself awake and shakes her head as if to say she's seen it all.

Amana Anne pivots to avoid a pothole and whizzes by the Golden Horizons Senior Care entrance. She crosses the street and turns onto Skyview Lane, a back road home. The pavement's a little less smooth, but at least it's not cobblestone.

It's wonderfully liberating, the freedom of skating, of not picking up each foot for every plodding step. She can see why Wowie still loves it. A guilt pang needles Amana Anne because she "confi-skated" them. But who'd get stuck waiting on Wowie hand and foot if – no, *when* –she crash landed? The skating's soothingly therapeutic and gives a flow to Amana Anne's thinking. It's like riding a bicycle, something in your muscle memory. Probably good for balance, too, she decides, if she doesn't crack her head open. She really should be wearing a helmet. Yes, skating gives her a feeling of childhood and freedom and fun. If only she *was* a kid again and didn't have just one week to make her life-changing decision.

Well, Lord, does this platform business mean You're trying to show me that this door is closed? Please open doors You want me to go through and close doors that aren't for me.

It feels soul-crushing to even *consider* returning to the corporate job she left years ago. Oliver, her former boss, was probably at his office when he called this morning, working on yet another gorgeous Saturday like she, too, had done for too many years after Nathan passed on.

She had left that job to pursue her dreams and now here her old job was open again, a six-figure administrative VP position in a healthcare conglomerate. If she didn't accept, there'd be hundreds of applicants happy to snatch it up. Somehow the years flew by while she was trying to figure things out, to lay a game plan, to get her moxie up to live her passion. And suddenly it was almost too late. It was time to either go back to a stultifying job where she'd forever wonder *what if...* or, to face her fears and birth the life of her dreams.

Amana Anne skates by a silver-haired grandfather shooting hoops with his grandkids, and he makes a basket from the street with a *woosh* like a pro. It reminds Amana Anne of one of the quotes she was often telling the New Life clients she had coached. *"It's never too late to be what you might have been."* Yet, *she* was always shadow-boxing a belief that this was true for everyone else, but not for *her*. Like she was a member of some exempt society where, although she could help make other people's dreams come true, *hers* were insurmountable.

She'd inspired a small army of women to achieve the lives of their dreams at any age and any stage. Like the work-at-home mom who turned her Karen's Kupcakes venture into an international business, or the great-grandmother who completed her college degree *cum laude*. Amana Anne inspired women to have great relationships, reach their peak health, and find the career of their dreams.

Clients were constantly telling Amana Anne, *You should be on TV or in convention centers giving talks.* The only teeny problem is public speaking freezes her blood. Amana Anne's the living epitome of that old joke where most people would rather be *in* the coffin than giving the eulogy at a funeral.

So why was I given this dream if I can't bring myself to actually do it? She asks God as she turns into the townhouse plan, where there's a clean scent of someone doing laundry coming out of a house vent, and relative quiet. Most of the kids are probably settled in to afternoon naps.

I'd like to go back to bed myself and start the day over, Amana Anne thinks as she turns onto Commons Drive and coasts down the hill. *I had such a feeling of hope when I awakened today... but realistically, what can happen in a week? I don't see how I can possibly become an overnight sensation. And even if by some bizarre fluke I did, I don't see how I could ever speak in public.*

As she turns into her driveway, Amana Anne mentally wrestles with herself because she's about to do exactly what she always tells her clients and everyone else *not* to do when they're depressed.

She rationalizes, *I need it and I'm tired of being good. It's been longer than I can remember since I last did it. I deserve it.*

Amana Anne tosses off the skates and heads inside for her car keys. She's not willing to wait another moment.

Twist of Fate

"This is the day." Ha!

Eliz pops open the chilled Champagne De Castellane Brut on her kitchen counter amid the dirty dishes. Droplets of condensation run down the bottle's sides and make it slippery to hold as she pours into a champagne flute.

This is one of the worst days of my life, and it's only half over.

But after a few sips, okay – *guzzles*, Eliz tells herself things might just still work out. Dwayne perhaps *would* take her back, should she hit that level of desperado. Yes, she'd rather have a root canal without Novocain on all her uppers, but maybe he *was* a distant option. On the other hand, tonight's Mr. Backup might also be a contender. A meal ticket and someone to bum rent money from.

She certainly couldn't count on her parents. They made it clear long ago that bailing her out was not an option. Her father told her when she'd graduated from college, "The bank is closed."

"Sink or doggie-paddle on your own," her mother added. "It builds character." They were happily lollygagging in their Sun City Retirement Village pool in Florida while she was sinking in the quicksand of life. She *did* get something from her parents though, Eliz reminds herself as she polishes off her glass of champagne, although they'd never admit it. As a little girl, Eliz picked up drinking by slurping leftovers of their ice-melted, watered-down drinks when her parents had a cocktail or two, three, four every night. Her earliest memory was seeing both of them bleary-eyed with liquor, cigarettes dangling from their limp hands, totally oblivious to her. Eliz loved the numbed-out "happy hour" high the booze gave her, and her parents were thrilled she was zonked so they didn't have to deal with her.

It's always happy hour *somewhere*, Eliz mentally parrots their mantra. She opens the fridge to grab what little's left of Trader Joe's cherry juice. Beyond that, all that's in the fridge is a smidgeon of salad dressing.

Eliz adds a splash of cherry juice into her second glass of champagne with a *splosh*, making a Cherry-mosa, her own concoction. The juice diffuses into pretty pink dancing tutus that pirouette happily down her throat. *Now we're getting somewhere.* Eliz's head starts to happily swirl. She loves the sensory delights of being drunk, the hyper-awareness of seeing as if everything's vivid and new. Even her kitchen counter – with the caked dishes and the book pages Amana Anne dropped off despite Eliz's disinterest – has an otherworldly cast in the afternoon sunlight.

Having the housekeeping genes of a sewer rat was oddly one of the reasons she and Jamaica became buddies. Jamaica confided to Eliz early on, over her messy desk at work, "I take care of myself but that's one person too many. At home, I put dishes in the dishwasher only when I don't have any to eat with." They'd laugh about how wet laundry would ferment in their washers until it stank. Sometimes the moldy stench was so badly imbedded into Eliz's clothes that she ended up throwing them out.

I'm surprised I can find myself *in this mess.* Eliz momentarily sobers at the realization of the truth within that thought, like a pearl within a clam: I'm *the one who's lost.*

How many lost weekends, months, years has she blown? Not only with drinking, but with men, with shopping endlessly in malls trying to chase ever-elusive worldly, conditional approval by wearing the "right" clothes? *Let's face it. It's a lost life.* Eliz downs her drink and pours another glass.

"Those are sure going down easy." She recalls the commentary from her former boyfriend, Greg, the pilot, about how she downed her drinks like a camel after a jaunt through the Sahara. Eliz immediately de-planed from the relationship because of it. You wouldn't believe how hard it is to find a man who views her own level of drinking as "fun," drinks enough so he's not a drag yet is still coherent enough to drive her home.

"Drinks going down easy" is how this whole debacle started on her thirty-third birthday at Blondie's Tavern on the border of Oakhaven and Wilksburg. Eliz initially thought of inviting Casey and Amana Anne to celebrate with her since they were all now in the twin double-digit years; Casey recently turned forty-four and Amana Anne is fifty-five. But Eliz wasn't even sure that they drank and they were about the only two people left in her life who knew her only as Eliz Wilding, rather than living up to her party nickname of Eliz "Wild Thing." So when Jamaica bailed on Eliz's birthday because of a new boyfriend, Eliz decided to fly solo.

The night of her thirty-third, Eliz sashayed into Blondie's wearing a firestorm-red sparkle top, tight jeans and five-inch red heels. The bar was lined with average Joes in jeans, and a couple wannabe Trumpsters in cheap business suits with loosened ties, slugging back bottles of Yuengling.

The clientele was at least better than the Backstreet Pub in the worst section of Wilksburg that harbored an assortment of guys you might see at a hog auction or on a chain gang. Eliz quickly canvassed her female competition but there was none to speak of, just one girl with crooked, wolfish teeth guffawing with a gal pal whose red hair and black eyebrows said her hair coloring had nothing to do with nature and everything to do with Miss Clairol.

"It's my ten-k day," Eliz announced to the barfly brigade. This was youth code for her ten thousandth day on earth, that cool, coming-of-age celebration day when you're twenty-seven years, three months and fifteen days old. She sure wasn't going to admit to being thirty-three just to get some free drinks. She only fessed up to being "nearly thirty" with people like Jamaica who pressed her, telling herself she *was* "near" thirty. She just didn't mention she was on the downhill slope side of it with her fingernails still imbedded in the top of the hill.

"Line em up for the decimal b-day gal," the Trumpster with a crook in his nose piped up, his cheap navy suit glossy in the bar light. The least attractive guy was always the first one to pony up, based on the sheer, nebulous hope he'd have first dibs on her. At least he knew what a "ten-k day" was, and flashed some cash.

The night was rapidly fogged in by a quick succession of Harvey Wallbangers, champagne toasts, and a pitcher of margaritas. A few guys offered to drive her home but even collectively they didn't add up to one serious contender. They were all BTN – Better Than Nothing – for the drinks though.

"Elizzie, you promise to call a taxi?" one of the Trumpster wannabes asked when she took a few steps and looked like she was attempting to walk on ice.

"A chariot." Eliz could hear the drunken slur to her words.

She staggered to the door past two preppies, with what she imagined was a sexy strut, flipping her hair back, tummy sucked in. Their eyes followed her, appreciatively, she guessed. Eliz slowed to hear what compliment the wire-rimmed preppie leaned in to say about her to his friend.

"Don't worry," the preppie's voice was low and assuring to his buddy. Eliz strained to hear the rest, then wished she hadn't. "The young ones come in later."

The young ones?! Eliz's pride, swollen like a bright red helium balloon, popped at the needle-sharp dart of his words. The ultimate acid rain on her ego. It terrorized her to think she was considered *old* by anyone. Who was she without the calling card of youth and looks? She blinked back tears until she was safe in the haven of her car.

No sooner had she skidded out of the parking lot, half-blind with crying, than a police siren wailed behind her. Usually she could sweet talk her way out of a ticket when she was tipsy, but tipsy wasn't even in her rearview mirror anymore. The tired officer looked like some teenager's dad used to practicing tough love. His graying, close-cropped hair emphasized a prodigious sphere of a face at her open window. "What if you had wiped out a family?" he barked at her. "This here's your wake-up call, young lady."

At least he called me young, Eliz recalled thinking. *At least he didn't call me ma'am.*

After she was handcuffed and driven to the station, she had two options: spend the night in a jail cell or call a friend to come and drive her home.

"My friends respect me," she said with drunken deliberation. "I'm not calling them to get me outta jail at two o'clock in the morning."

The truth was, the only real friends she had were Amana Anne and Casey. Eliz was too humiliated to call either of them. Jamaica was a wild-card drinking buddy who might yell at Eliz for waking her and hang up. So Eliz spent a sleepless night in jail, sitting on a filthy, blood-stained mattress.

When Jamaica came the next morning and heard the whole story, her only laughing comment was, "Heck, you coulda called at two a.m. Nobody respects you."

By the time Eliz paid the two-thousand-dollar DUI fine, she was a hundred and seventy dollars short on rent. You'd think waiting an extra week wouldn't have sent her landlord,

Mr. Yarlsbury, into a conniption. He had retired to Palm Beach and probably only rented his town home for shuffle board money, anyway.

"The first time is the last time, Elizabeth," he yelled. "If you're even a day late again, you're out."

On top of being financially busted and potentially evicted, Eliz had torn her ankle ligaments dancing in her stiletto heels at Blondie's, but was too drunk to feel it. This was the pathetic road that wound to Dr. Dwayne, who never should have asked her out in the first place if he had any professional ethics. Yet, on her own moral compass, she was so far south as to be off the map, considering it a viable option to – let's face it – possibly use him in whatever way necessary should all else fail.

Eliz pours herself another glass and thinks about her plans for wanting to put her life in order. Somehow the details keep getting lost. Not that there ever were many, really. Just vague notions of making changes. She'd come upon scraps of written goals that she'd delineated months or years earlier and they'd only serve as visual harangues that she never did what she intended, that she'd never change.

She *wants* to change. But if there's no rhyme or reason or meaning to life, why try?

Amana Anne always says, "Life without God is like an unsharpened pencil. There's no point."

Actually, Eliz intends to do the God thing and get saved some day, to have a little "fire insurance" before she bites the dust. She does worry about the possibility of hell, but hopes to get in under the wire when she's a centenarian or something. She's just not ready *today*.

Eliz holds her champagne glass up to see what's left and the bubbles fizz in the shiny glass like tiny twinkling stars, so she polishes off the little galaxy. The arrival is official at that fine line between partying paradise and the undercurrent of abject guilt that some neighbor will look in and see her stumbling about at midday in a drunken stupor, so she closes the door and pulls the draperies shut. She's quickly feeling woozy and a nap seems like just the ticket. Then she'll be fresh enough to finagle Mr. Backup into buying her a nice cocktail and dinner. Her bum ankle's starting to hurt anyway from the run.

She grabs her cell phone in case Jamaica calls with date details and climbs the steps three at a time, which she always does to keep her legs taut. Every day, every single day, she tells herself she's going to clean off the steps, the piles of clothes to be ironed, toilet tissue rolls and towels meant to be taken up or down. But the Sisyphean task of housecleaning always gets the better of her. You clean everything up, it gets dirty again. Why bother?

From years of experience, Eliz pivots around her coffee mug and gym shoes on the top steps but her foot lands on a clear popcorn bowl she doesn't see. Her weak ankle turns out from under her with a sharp, searing pain.

Suddenly she's falling backwards and the ceiling is her view, then a kaleidoscope of images: her flailing arms, miniscule dunes of dust on the wooden railing, toilet tissue rolls and beige towels flashing by as she freefalls. It seems like she'll never hit the ground and she's amazed at how many thoughts she has in seconds when everything seems slow-mo. She wonders is it too late to do that give-your-life thing, to try Jesus, and how exactly is it you're supposed to do it and what are you supposed to say and is there still time to…

THUMP! Eliz lands at the bottom of the stairs in a heap, the air knocked out of every molecule of her being.

She hears but doesn't feel a *snap!* close to her neck.

Eliz doesn't feel anything now as everything goes to an abrupt and unforgiving black, like her soul is sinking deeper into an abyss where there is no time or space or hope.

Inside the Red Door

The slightly paint-chipped red door opens with a cranky creak as Casey cautiously unlocks it. Inside, it looks to be a Sunday school classroom, since kids' drawings and paintings of Bible scenes adorn the walls. It smells of chalk and Murphy's Oil Soap as she walks through the back of the classroom into a long hallway.

There's a small office on her left, with a laptop computer on the desk. A brown leather swivel chair is turned out like someone sprang from it suddenly. In a paper tray, the return address on the church letterhead says she's in Chula Vista. On the back center of the desk is a plaque with a simple gold cross and the word "Faith."

A post-it on the laptop says, "Volunteers, feel free to use." Casey decides to take them up on their offer and type a couple of e-mails. The first is succinctly to the boys.

Arrived safely. Love, Mom

She'll be lucky if they read that much. She copies Skip at their supposedly shared e-mail address, although he always leaves it to her to actually check it for any news from relatives or friends, so it's become essentially hers. He also has his own e-mail but she doesn't even know the address. The boys will let him know she arrived. The other pithy e-mail is to Amana Anne and Eliz.

> In CA! Mission trip. Not sure when/if/how much I can be in touch. xoxo, Casey

Neither of them visits e-mail much on weekends, but they'll get a kick out of her adventure whenever they check in. Then she adds...

> P.S. Amana Anne, LOVE the book so far.

Casey only got a few chapters in before she zonked out on the plane, but she laughed out loud at the funny parables until her seatmate shot her an irritated look.

She glances across the hall into a mailroom filled with postal supplies, envelopes, large mailing boxes and a digital scale (for large packages, she supposes) similar to her own scale at home. *Oh no, a stalking scale,* she thinks with a laugh.

A piece of notepaper is taped to the door leading into a nursery. Someone's written a welcome in sprawling, curly handwriting thanking "the volunteer," saying "Make yourself at home" and "Help yourself to everything!" There's an apology that no one was able to be there to greet in person, and details about meal times in the church hall, starting with breakfast tomorrow.

The nursery's a sweet little sanctuary, with Noah's Ark wallpaper liners and draperies with pairs of ark animals. Three white cribs line the walls, with flannel baby blankets neatly folded in each crib, and an oak rocking chair sits next to the changing table. The carpet is so thick and lush compared to their thread-bare ones at home that Casey feels like she's practically bouncing on a trampoline as she walks. They must have four inches of foam underneath. Perfect to sleep on with her light sleeping bag, she decides, putting her getaway bag down against a crib.

Casey peeks in the small bathroom adjoining the nursery. Fluffy white towels and washcloths are stacked on a shelf over the commode and a thick white robe hangs from a peg on the wall, just like in a fancy hotel. Shampoo and conditioner nestle in a wire-rimmed basket, along with a box of peach soap. In fancy letters the soap box reads: Peach Botanical Fine Soap, Potter & Moore Est. England 1749, Savon Fin Luxusseife, whatever those last words mean. They could be swearing for all she knows, but the soap smells *heavenly*. The cabinet under the sink is well stocked with first aid supplies, toilet paper, garbage bags and several boxes of Epsom salts. Epsom salts for a *bath,* which would be *wonderful*. When was the last time she had a *peaceful*, leisurely bath?

But the first order of business is something she's wanted to do since she was a little girl. Her parents didn't like short hair on girls and wouldn't allow it. Then, as a teen, Skip loved her long tresses. "Don't go macho on me," he'd warn through the years, like it was her last frontier of femininity.

She's always trimmed her own hair, just a straight line around her shoulders, for her entire life. Casey always figured if she ever did get away, short hair would be like a rite of passage, a final unfettering.

Casey goes back to the office and locates the scissors. She grabs a small garbage bag from the bathroom and a large mailing envelope from the supply room and brings them outside. The light wind is spiked even stronger now with the scent of the sea and Casey wonders if it's ultramarine blue like she's seen in pictures. It's almost unbelievable that the vastness of it is near, compared with only this morning – *this morning* – when it seemed her life had been sequestered into the smallest space possible.

Without hesitation, Casey pulls her hair into a tight ponytail at the center back of her head, cuts it, and deposits it in the envelope. The ponytail is long enough to send to Toya so someone with cancer can use it in Locks of Love. She cuts large clumps of the remaining hair on her head until her hair feels a few inches long all around, then tosses the snippets in the garbage bag.

Once inside again, she locks the red door and removes her prune-juice stained clothes in the bathroom. She places the outfit, including her dingy bra and underwear in the garbage bag with her hair scraps. New underwear from Target are in her getaway bag. A clean division. Old to new.

Looking in the bathroom mirror, Casey decides she's thrilled with her pert pixie. Mostly, she loves the liberation of just not caring *what* she looks like. She already looks like a totally different person than the woman she saw in their living room mirror this morning. It was in that moment in fact, that she made the decision to leave, during the last conversation she had with her family. The one that finally pushed her over the edge...

She'd come downstairs to a sudden cacophony of the guys' screaming voices and the TV blasting to life. The shock that Skip and the twins were even up before the crack of noon this first Saturday of summer was fishy in and of itself. The boys were loafing in their La-Z-Boys and all Skip had on – sprawled on the couch – was a long green towel wrapped around his bottom half. Casey *hoped* the towel was from showering, and not some ever-lowering level of laziness, where putting on pants might have become too much trouble.

The guys' eyes were riveted to "Sports Roundup" commentators on a new, *behemoth*-screen TV, so huge that, for a moment, Casey thought strange men – beyond her own – were in her home. She instinctively clutched the top of her PJ's in modesty.

"Did it escape your notice we're not trust fund babies?" Casey asked Skip, flailing her arms at the TV like she was shooing a seagull.

"Go to Home Depot, get a ladder and get over it," Skip said, and the twins snickered. "Early Bird yard sale. A *steal*." "We don't even have enough this week for *Jumbo*," Casey slipped into the local slang for Jumbo brand baloney, their pseudo-meat staple.

"Mom, we tapped our Swiss account," Wyatt teased.

"Actually, the col-eee-gee-ate fund," Tyler couldn't wait to inform her, which meant Skip had now broken the only remaining promise he hadn't yet bailed on, that the boys would get the education she and Skip never had.

"Now, don't affixiate on us, Case," Skip meant asphyxiate. He's the living proof of what not getting an education will do.

"The moolah was just enough for like... one term at... like community college, anyway," Tyler said, stretching his hairy legs onto the wooden coffee table that Skip made in shop class a quarter century ago, the year Casey fell in love with him. Back when he was sweet.

"We're gonna be Junkman and Sons," Wyatt said.

"Oh, right, because that's the pinnacle of aspirations," she said. "For *apes*."

"Junkman and Sons and *Bonobos*." Wyatt laughed at his own joke, translating for Skip and Tyler so they got it. "Bonobos're like the closest extant relatives to humans."

Although Wyatt's brainy, he's like his dad – as languid as a koala, which Casey once taught the boys is the most slothful animal in the world. The sloth, albeit mind-numbingly slow, was at least on the ball enough to get the adjective named after him.

"The bobos are your mother's side of the family," Skip said, taking a Q-tip from the waist of his towel and cleaning his ear like he was bent on puncturing an eardrum. "Anyway, the future's in junk."

"You mean their *future's* junked because I have no say since I'm just some barely tolerated maid in my own home."

Casey reflects back on her last words to her family,

61

unconsciously running her fingers through her new hairdo, and she wonders what's going on in her own home right about *now*. Are they missing her one iota? More likely, they're having a field day, happy to be rid of her chronic nagging and glad she's gone, although they'll miss her cooking and cleaning up after them. *She* won't miss it though, she decides as she draws back the shower curtain to run a bath and relax in silence for the first time in years. A leisurely soak without the clamor of music or TV, or someone pounding on the door to ask, *When's dinner?*

Refreshingly clear water tumbles into the tub like a private waterfall, not the piddly water pressure at their house where you could take a donkey ride to Nepal and back in the time it takes to draw a bath. Casey starts to close the bathroom door and a night light blinks on, creating a dim glow that couples with misting steam to give a subterranean softness to the room.

The water's warm to her toe test and her body quickly eases into its luxurious fluidity until she's covered up to her neck. She unwraps a bar of the fruit-scented soap that's shaped in a softly curved oblong. The soap slips from her hand, adrift on the shimmering water, floating like a little canoe happily loosed from its mooring at the dock. She feels like her spirit's free now, too, in a way she's never felt before in her life, like it's finally unanchored from being landlocked on shore. Casey lingers long in the warm water until the constant knot that's tied her insides for so long has been unloosed, too.

She does a quick, cool, shower rinse and shampoo, and checks that all her stray little cut hairs are picked up from the drain. The white thirsty towels drink in the water pellets from her body, and she snuggles into her cotton night shirt. California's three hours behind Pennsylvania, and as far as she's concerned, it's the end of the day. She sets up her sleeping bag and pillow, too tired to unpack the rest until morning.

When the Noah's Ark curtains are closed in the cool nursery, there's a gentle, late-day darkness to the room, a welcome rest for all the ark animals tired from their day of play, and for Casey, too. A sweet exhaustion envelops her and a Sleeping Beauty yawn escapes like she could slumber for a hundred years as she nestles deep into the comfy sleeping bag.

Her little haven's as silent as kitten paws, a wee corner of quietude in her new world. She hadn't realized the full toll of video games, DVDs, and radio shock jocks the twins turned on that she was forever turning off. Not just the sensory bombardment, but the spiritual assault and toll. Casey sighs, ensconced in the cozy comfort of her cocoon, a different sigh than she's heard from herself in a long time. A sigh of contentment.

After a little prayer for Amana Anne and Eliz, for direction, wisdom and grace on their shared journey, Casey knows she should say more than a quick prayer for her own family, but just the thought of them and what must be decided later this week when the mission is completed, overwhelms her. There will be a time to decide, and talk to Skip and the boys. But for now all they need to know is that she's on a mission trip.

She can't try to figure out the future, worry or wonder about where she'll go from here. She doesn't even want to think about *tomorrow*. Will she even be able to do what Arnold volunteered to do? Arnold's a weight lifter and marathon biker. In fact, it dawns on her why his ticket was one-way only to California for this mission. Arnold had planned on a summer of travelling cross-country before he returned to teach high school math in September. Casey reflects that this spiritual journey of hers is like driving cross-country in the dark. You can only see a matter of yards ahead of you at a time with your lights, but you can get there trusting God that it will unfold a little bit at a time.

Well, what was that Bible passage about even the birds

don't have to worry so why should she? *Thank You, Lord, for whatever is, and is to come.* She plumps her pillow and turns her family and her cares over to God. He's always up all night anyway.

As she closes her eyes, *This is the day,* revisits her mind, like a bookend to this wonder-filled start to her adventure. Too tired to pull herself up through the surging tide of slumber that draws her like an undertow, she gratefully succumbs to the summoning sea of sleep.

Mr. Backup

Eliz comes to consciousness slowly, like emerging up through deep water and knowing you shouldn't come up too fast or you'll get the bends. Exactly what shade of hell is this murky maelstrom of pain and confusion? Is she still in the world? She opens her eyes and her vision clears through the fog of semi-consciousness. Her view is of the ceiling. At least she's still here. Although feeling half-dead on the floor at the bottom of the stairs.

Apparently there's time left on the clock, so I'm withdrawing the take-my-life offer, God, if it ever was official.

Not that she necessarily believed in God in the first place. It was just that "no atheist in a foxhole" fear-of-dying thing when it seemed her time was up.

Oh geez, what time is it? She can tell by the dimness in the room that daylight's fading fast. She lifts her cell phone, still grasped tightly in her right hand, to check the time. Pain shoots through her neck like a lightning bolt, and vertebrae in her neck pop as if in protest to her motion. *Do* not *tell me I tore ligaments in my neck on top of everything.*

Worse yet, the meeting with Mr. Backup's in three minutes.

65

She hits Jamaica on speed dial but of course gets her voicemail because Jamaica's probably still partying. She pushes Amana Anne's speed dial.

"Hello." Amana Anne's voice sounds obstreperously loud. Eliz moans both from the hangover kicking in and the searing poker in her neck as she moves the cell away from her ear.

"Bana," Eliz says weakly, the effort of getting the first word out making her momentarily nauseous.

"Eliz? What's wrong?" Amana Anne's concern makes Eliz feel a little wave of better.

"I practically decapitated myself in a fall."

There's a little gasp of alarm from Amana Anne. "Do you need to get to the ER? I'm at Community Market and I can be there in..."

"No." Eliz interrupts her. "It's not that bad. It's not like I use my head much anyway. But I have a blind date at Mulligan's in two."

"Hours?"

"Minutes."

"Minutes?!"

"Can you meet him? Please. I don't have his cell number. You're practically *there*, Bana." That was true. Amana Anne could throw a stone at Mulligan's if she had an ace pitching arm. But the last thing she wants is to meet some Casanova for Eliz.

Amana Anne tries not to sound begrudging. "I guess."

"Know it's past yo bedtime, Granny, but you never do bodiddly Saturday nights anyway."

"Hey, Miss Insulting Ingrate, maybe if I wring your little neck it'll straighten the kink out."

"Don't," Eliz begs, laughing and wincing. Eliz thinks it's funny when she drives Amana Anne into her dark humor. "That's a yes?"

Amana Anne sighs heavily into the phone to let Eliz know she's not happy but she'll do it. "How'll I know which one's your prince of the week?"

"He's a little older and he'll be the only buffo in the joint this early. Just tell Mr. Backup what happened."

"Would it be too much to hope you have an actual name for the man?"

"Hope springs eternal but in this case the spring is dry, Bana."

"All right. I'll inform Mr. Backup."

"Owe ya, Ambam."

"Just remember me in your will. At this rate I'll cash in soon."

"The streetlights are coming on, Banana. You better hurry."

Sure, the one time in – what, a year? – Amana Anne caves in to an ice cream blow-out binge, and *this* happens. The herd of Skinny Cow ice creams in her white Prius' trunk are all gonna melt like snowmen on St. Croix if she doesn't move it. *All* being the key word since she bought everything that didn't moo and gallop away.

She walks quickly to Mulligan's, daydreaming about which one she'll plow into first after briefing Mr. Backup. Maybe she'll kick off with the Strawberry Cheesecake, perfect on a sweltering summer day like this, or the Dulce de Leche "with tempting swirls of caramel."

And they're all melting in the ninety-two degree sunset heat because she has to meet this backup character. "The magic hour," as Nathan used to call twilight. The sky *does* look magical with soft, pastel pinks and apricots woven into the blue, and the white of the billowy clouds. Cumulus clouds, she thinks, but isn't positive. Nathan would have known. It would have been a magic hour with *him*.

Nothing magical ever happens to me anymore, she sighs as she opens the door to the chilled air of Mulligan's, which always strikes her as a cross between French cuisine and grandma's cooking. You can get comfort food, but their mac and cheese would have a French café twist of maybe three great cheeses like Jarlsberg, Gouda and a super sharp cheddar.

With a quick flick of her eyes around the room, she sees tables filled with families, couples, a group of senior ladies, two elderly gentlemen eating at side tables, and a few solo women reading or speaking on their cells. There's one guy alone at a table, reading an open newspaper that he's holding up. She can't see his face, but he's in neat-looking dark jeans and a white button-down shirt with the sleeves rolled up, revealing slightly tanned arms. He has a stocky build with broad shoulders. It couldn't be anyone else. Eliz is right. He's the only buffo in the joint.

He folds his paper closed and looks straight at Amana Anne like he's expecting her, and Amana Anne locks eyes with the most attractive middle-aged man she's ever seen in her life. "Mr. Backup" smiles at her with a pleasant openness, the expression of a man comfortable in his own skin. His eyes don't drift away, which she's found more and more men do as she ages, like she's past her expiration date. As he holds her gaze, time alters, and she feels like she's gliding forward. It's as though the meeting of their eyes is the key that's unlocked the entry into this other world she never knew existed, where reality has the cadence and aura of a dream.

Or perhaps I'm having a mini-stroke, she tells herself, because she's a woman whose equilibrium does not tilt easily. Until now.

Amana Anne never believed in falling in love at first sight, or in "falling" in love, period. She thought it was just an excuse for people to act loopy. Even with Nathan, she *grew* to love him. But right now, she seems to be living purely on heart and soul and spirit, with no thinking other than the awareness of the beauty and wonder of what she's feeling, as if she's finally fully alive again.

She discovers herself suddenly in front of him, trying to come back to her senses, to remember how to speak, and hopes her mouth isn't hanging open. But she was just in a world that transcended "normal," and she distantly wonders if he was there too, and feels certain she hasn't been experiencing this awakening world alone.

Or maybe it's a menopausal meltdown, Amana Anne tells herself, trying to shake it off. She extends her hand to meet him and hopes it isn't quivering.

"Hi, I'm Amana Anne," she hears a little tremor in her voice. "I know you weren't expecting me."

He rises, gentlemanly, and takes her hand firmly but tenderly, like she's precious. *I love a man who's a gentleman,* she thinks, noting that he's probably around six feet tall, and his eyes are cobalt blue. He has a strong jaw, full lips, and dark hair with the lightest peppering of gray at the temples.

"I'm Jake," he introduces himself. "You're a welcome surprise," he says in an easy-going way, still holding her hand. She thinks it just may be the best handshake she's ever experienced. His big hand is warm and strong and makes hers feel small and protected.

Hello! Back to earth, Amana Anne, remember Eliz? She chides herself, withdrawing her hand. *Did he let go reluctantly?* Then the moral voice inside her asks: *What's wrong with you? You're acting downright ditzy. Or "ditzo" as Eliz would say. His date Eliz, by the way.*

"There was a little accident," Amana Anne blurts out.

"Please sit," he says, concerned, quickly pulling out a chair for her.

I love a man who pulls out your chair, she thinks. Dreamily, she realizes, and reminds herself, she *hopes* for the last time: *It's about Eliz, remember?*

"I mean my friend Eliz had the accident." Amana Anne sits because she feels like her knees might buckle, that she really might faint. He tucks in her chair and she smells some kind of manly soap like Irish Spring. She clears her throat, although there's nothing in it, and tries to regain some composure. "She'll be okay, but she couldn't be here and I have these Skinny Cows melting in my car so I have to cut to the chase," she blathers.

"I hope you at least cracked the windows so they can breathe," Jake says, straight-faced.

"Actually, they're…" She stops because she sees the twinkle in his eyes that he's kidding, of course. She likes his little laugh line crinkles when he smiles again at her.

Who cares if those cows melt and stink up your car for the next fifteen years? When have you ever felt like this in your life?

"Would you like to order anything?" He motions to a coffee mug in front of him, and remnants of Mulligan's famous black cherry pecan pie.

Don't you dare, she warns herself, and her self complies ambiguously. "Thanks, but I really have to go." This wasn't *her* date. She was just the messenger. Supposedly.

He rises as she does.

"Here's my card." He takes a business card out of his shirt pocket and hands it to her. "If there's anything I can do for you, I'd really like to hear from you."

Maybe he says that to everyone, good for business, but her heart flutters when he looks her in the eyes with sincerity. She takes the card and glances at the black embossed ink on the rich, ivory card. It lists Sandstone Homes, Sandstone Fine Furniture and Sandstone Printing with phone numbers next to each, his e-mail, and then simply "Jake Sandstone, Oakhaven, PA." No title. Clearly none's necessary. Guess the last name says it all.

"Bye, Jake." She salutes him with his card to the side of her head. *Salutes* the man. But she fears that taking his hand again might turn her legs to rubber and she doesn't want to walk out like she's a human Slinky. He has that little spark in his eyes again as he playfully salutes her back. Amana Anne rushes out the door like she's leaving the scene of a crime. If going gaga over a guy was illegal, she'd be doing hard time.

In just the few minutes she's been inside, the sunset has turned magnificently vibrant. The sky is ribboned with deep magenta, coral and gold as if the sun is making a last hurrah before settling in for the night. It's the most gorgeous sunset she's seen in years, and she feels like running back inside to tell Jake to come out and share it with her, the way she used to do with Nathan. This is, of course, absurd, so she double-times it back to the parking lot. She still has butterflies in her stomach when she jumps into her car, and suddenly no appetite. Not even for the Chocolate Truffle Dippers, one of her favorites.

Now what am I supposed to do with all these Skinny Cows? She turns the AC up to high, as if that's gonna hit the trunk. A thank-you for Mrs. Katz and Rhodine comes to mind, so she heads up the street to the nursing home.

Sure enough, Rhodine, Mrs. Katz and a wheelchair buddy with long, straggly white hair sit gabbing like they're around a campfire pow-wow. Amana Anne pulls up in the turn-around in front of them, jumps out and hands Mrs. Katz and Rhodine the boxes of Skinny Cows.

"Here's a little thank-you. Maybe you'd like to hostess an ice cream party for your friends."

"Awww, how sweet," Rhodine says, touched.

"Oh my heavens, honey, you shouldn't have!" Mrs. Katz nearly does a wheelie in her wheelchair to show the lady next to her the truffle bars. "Agnes, look! Chocolate truffle. *To die for.*"

Agnes grabs an ice cream bar from Mrs. Katz. "What a way to go."

"Veatrice!" Mrs. Katz yells to a hunched-over woman with a walker coming out the main entrance, moving at the galloping advance of a major glacier. "Free ice cream." Veatrice revs her walker into fast clomps like she's Secretariat racing to the finish line. Mrs. Katz beckons several more residents with walkers, waving the ice cream bars.

"Enjoy," Amana Anne waves, heading for her car.

"Thanks, Skinny Minnie, but wait." Rhodine wags a French Vanilla Truffle ice cream bar at Amana Anne. "Don't even think about not partaking." Rhodine tosses a bar over the top of her car, a little high, but Amana Anne jumps up for it and snags it with the tips of her fingers. French Vanilla Truffle *is* her other favorite.

"Nice catch," Rhodine calls.

"I only jump that high for ice cream." Amana Anne scoots in the car before she gets stampeded by the charging walker brigade. Pulling out, she realizes her ice cream craving's making a come-back. Okay, the universe is returning to normal and the earth is still on its axis. She rips off the plastic wrapper and takes an indulgent bite. *Yum. Things taste so much better when shared*, Wowie always says. True. It's cow-jumped-over-the-moon delicious, another Wowie-ism that reminds Amana Anne to look up as she drives. There's already a faint moon high in the sky.

She studies the muted half moon and realizes that's how she feels about what happened with Jake. Half her emotions are light, good. She's excited, amazed that she can feel this way, that there's an experience like this at a relatively late stage of life. But the other half of her emotions are a dark, unsettling emotional mish-mash, and she can't quite put her finger on all the why's except, of course, that he was Eliz's blind date.

Amana Anne decides to have a talk with God as she pulls onto her street, and to lay it all out, even though He already knows anyway. She doesn't usually wait for some special set-apart time or place because she knows God wants a relationship all the time, so she starts right in as she parks the car.

Lord, I'm not sure I like these feelings I have for this man, for a lot of reasons. First, he's rightfully Eliz's. Second, my emotions feel out of control, an other-worldly high. Third, I don't want to ever again feel the pain I felt with Nathan so why even try love again, anyway? Okay, yes, sometimes it's a little lonely being on my own all these years but it's safe.

Amana Anne heads straight upstairs to get ready for bed, continuing her conversation in earnest.

Most of the time, You know I like just living out my life doing good. There are so many hurting people in the world who need help. Even wasting time thinking of romance seems kind of frivolous next to saving the world, don't You think?

She's talking to God now as if she has to prove her case before a judge and jury and they're not looking very convinced. Amana Anne continues as she washes her face and applies her own moisturizing mix of aloe vera gel, liquid vitamin E, and jojoba oil.

I know earlier today I said whatever You want for my life but I thought this meant primarily career-wise, not this. Don't we have enough on the table with the career decision this week? If You could just please help me squelch these thoughts about Jake, I'd appreciate it. Thank You.

She jumps into bed and pulls up her summer spread, then decides it's too warm and pulls it off again.

Well, Lord, whatever You decide, in any and all areas, just please give me a clue and direction. Ditto for Casey and Eliz. I love You and thank You for everything You've given me this day. Amen.

Before Amana Anne turns off her bedside reading light, she opens a journal with a bright gold angel on the cover. It's full of favorite handwritten quotes that she's collected throughout her life, some Bible quotes, some people quotes. She sometimes opens this journal and asks God to speak to her through them, to give her a message she needs to hear.

The first quote her eyes fall upon is by author Anais Nin, whose work she's always meant to read:

And the day came when the pain of remaining tight within the bud was greater than the risk it took to bloom.

Amana Anne turns the quote over in her mind while placing the book on her nightstand and turning off the light. It's been a long, full day and she drifts almost immediately into that twilight, pre-sleep state.

Her last thought before she releases into sleep – try as she might to resist it – is of Jake, his strong, warm hand holding her hand tenderly. Somehow as she descends into dreamland, his warmth feels like sunshine on the tight bud of her heart, unfurling it open to possibility again.

And she begins to slowly, gently bloom.

Desperado

"Help!"

Eliz's own shout of fear awakens her with a start. She was caught in one of those dreams that suddenly, sharply, turns into a nightmare where nothing is safe, especially not you.

As she surfaces into consciousness, a gnawing foreboding hits, the one that always encroaches over her when she can't sleep through a bender binge that's morphed into a hellish hangover.

She can tell by the deep darkness that it's the dead middle of the night. That means it's hours until morning, until this hangover sickness wears off. Her innards feel raw, turned inside out, but even worse is the mental. Eliz braces herself for the voices in her mind that always attack like a battering ram to harangue her:

You're such a mess.

You're a weak-willed failure. Look at your life. You're never going to change.

No matter how many times you promise yourself you won't, you get drunk.

You're hopeless.

Shaking her head to scatter the voices away causes the

pain of torn ligaments – or whatever she ripped in her neck – to scream at her with a vengeance that arrests all motion and brings a sharp sting of tears to her eyes. She can't take anything for the pain because all she has in her medicine chest is expired ibuprofen and no food to take it with. Besides, she'd throw up water on this stomach.

A hot bath and soaking her neck might help, but would she pass out from the agony of getting in the tub and reclining? It took her a half hour to get up the stairs and in bed because she kept feeling faint from the pain. What if she started to lose consciousness in the tub? Even if she *could* open the silver drain handle with her toe, the water drained so slowly she might drown in the process. She'd been meaning to clean all her hair out of that drain with some Liquid Plumber for months. Another lazy-girl procrastination. Who would have thought it could become a matter of life and death? Wasn't there some TV show about the every-day, quirky things that killed people? If only she'd been a Girl Scout, maybe that "Be Prepared" motto would have sunk in. Instead, her credo was, "Why do today what you could put off until next millennium?"

A wave of dry retching comes over her so suddenly and violently she wonders if it's alcohol poisoning from drinking so much without any food to absorb it, on top of all the alcohol from last night. Should she call 911? Can she even get up to find her cell or is she going to die here? Is there really a hell and would she go there?

Eliz feels like she's *in* hell, that there's a war being battled inside her right now, and through most of her life. She's so beyond tired of shadowboxing these unseen enemies and never winning, not knowing if there really are devils, or God. In fact, it's only at times like these that she even *thinks* about God. Her usual policy is to just try not to get on His bad side if He *does* exist and hope He doesn't notice her. To stay off His radar. Especially when it comes to men. She can only hope God takes a loooong coffee break on His night watch.

Her parents always told her there's no God, no hell, no heaven.

"The God Stuff?" her father always snortled at the absurdity of it. "A bunch of fairy tales."

"Once upon a time..." her mother would say with a laugh.

Earlier this evening, before Eliz fell asleep, she tried to read about God (through a drunken blur) from one of Amana Anne's pages:

Not once upon a time, but once before *time. When the stars held their breath and galaxies paused in their dance, God created man and woman. With a benevolent breath of creativity and love. To love and be loved. God chose to send His only Son out of love for us, and that Son chose to come out of love to show us the way.*

Eliz asks herself if this could be true. Is there really a God who came to earth out of love? Who loves her even when she's been so bad, so battered, so broken? She's always wondered, and suddenly she desperately needs to know in the core of her being. Eliz cries out with everything in her.

"Jesus, if you're real, help me! I'm sorry for everything! Please!"

With no space or time between the last word she utters, an inner voice she somehow knows to be the voice of God speaks to her:

"Elizabeth, no matter what you do, I will always love you."

An immediate, gentle peace nestles into every fiber of her heart, mind, soul, spirit, filling her with a sweet, all-encompassing love, embracing her very being. Then slumber slowly enfolds her like a blanket, drawing her into a dream of the stars holding their breath and galaxies paused in their dance, and God's love for her stretching into the arms of eternity.

~ Sunday ~

The Last Place You Want to Be

When the first slants of morning sun kiss Casey awake, she thinks it's appropriate to be in a nursery because she *feels* like she's been born again. She's had the deepest, most refreshing night's sleep of her life, albeit a couple trips were made to the bathroom during the night, compliments of the prune juice. *This is the day the Lord has made, let me rejoice and be glad*, drifts into her mind like a sweet breeze. Why hadn't she thought of the rest of the Bible quote yesterday when she heard, *This is the day?* Could it be because her first thought was usually something like, *Oh God, not another day?* Or that she normally lived like the man in Amana Anne's book who has Limburger cheese in his moustache, and thinks it's the world that stinks – not him. Casey realizes she's had her own "stinking thinking" for far too many years and recalls reading in Amana Anne's book yesterday that how you think when you start your day sets your spiritual sail – and ultimately determines your direction for the journey of your life. For the first time in ages, Casey decides to set her sail straight for today with a prayer:

Lord, I want to start each day from now on rejoicing and being glad. I'm sorry that in the past, I forgot You have to hear all my grumblings and negative thoughts that kick in the moment I blink awake. Please forgive my ingratitude for all the blessings that always were, and thanks for all that are to come.

Casey stretches long and luxuriously, noticing that for the first time in months, her chronic low-grade headache is gone. Also, she feels loads lighter, mainly on account of yesterday's prune juice and food fast. Now she's *starving.* Time to *mangia,* as her Italian grandma would say, as if Casey ever needed prompting to eat.

She throws on a T-shirt, shorts, and tennis shoes, splashes water on her face and brushes her teeth. Outside, it's a gorgeous, California-open-sky day. The air's somewhere between warm and hot, but not at all uncomfortable. It's as if the air's somehow lighter here.

Bounding down the cement steps, she follows the scent of bacon frying through the open door of the main hall and peeks her head into a kitchen where three women are fixing breakfast. The kitchen is bright with dandelion-yellow walls, and a border of suns with smiling faces. Sunlight streams in over a breakfast bar with a few stools.

A petite lady with short, gray hair, in a red gingham top and shorts, turns bacon and sausage in a skillet. Another lady, a pretty African American, loads cheese squares on scrambled eggs in a pan. She's big-boned, with ebony hair pulled into a little ponytail at the nape of her neck.

Next to them, a super-fit, young Latino woman has just blended a greenish-brown concoction in a Vita Mix on the counter. Her dark, cropped hair curls about her neck and skims the top of her multi-colored, embroidered blouse.

The scrambled eggs lady spots Casey.

"Well, hello there." She puts out her free hand and gives Casey's a squeeze. "You must be Casey. Pastor Warren called and gave us the low-down. I'm Myrna and these are my cohorts in crime." She points with her platter. "This here's Birdie…"

Birdie, the bacon lady, waves her serving fork at Casey (who notes Birdie's round tummy atop tiny sparrow legs and wonders if that's how she got her name). "Glad to make your acquaintance," Birdie chirps.

"And Zia." Myrna points her platter at the Vita Mix girl. Zia smiles, waving a muscled arm as she stuffs veggie greens in the Vita Mix with her other hand. Zia has one of those naturally fresh-looking faces, no makeup, with a dusting of light freckles. Her lower body's sinewy, like silky steel.

A wiry-looking man with graying hair and a receding hairline the size of a kiwi on both sides of his forehead strolls in. Myrna introduces him.

"This is my husband, Leroy."

"Just give me my coffee and nobody'll get hurt." Leroy laughs, and gives Casey a friendly nod. He kisses Myrna thanks on the cheek for the Styrofoam cup she's already filling with coffee.

"Nice to meet you all," Casey says.

"Reserve your judgment," Leroy says, and they all laugh.

"Hey!" Zia says, kiddingly acting offended. "That's a reference to me, Casey, because I try to limit Leroy's caffeine."

"Zia's the nutritionist for a health spa called the Organic Avocado," Birdie explains, tearing paper towels and folding them onto plates.

"Lots of celebrities, besides Leroy…" Myrna teases, "get advice from Zia."

"I'm just the best at staying incognito," Leroy says, chuckling.

"Every year Zia donates a week to help feed the mission team." Birdie spears sausages and lines them up on the paper-toweled plate.

Zia puts an arm around Casey's shoulders in a nurturing way, "I offer a variety of healthy nutritional alternatives, Casey, because your body is a temple."

"We're the unhealthy alternatives," Myrna laughs, stirring her day-glo orange, American cheese eggs and nodding to include Birdie.

"This is the heart-attack-in-a-skillet selection." Birdie takes a long, greasy strip of bacon out with her fork.

Leroy picks up a sausage with his fingers. "Was it Bill Cosby who said, 'I am what I ate and I'm frightened?'" He bites into the sausage with gusto.

"We *are* what we eat down to our every cell." Zia turns the Vita Mix back on and the greens whirl madly like a cyclone. She switches it off again. "And one brave soul's going to get to try my RCR special."

Casey doesn't mention that her *name* means "brave" because she's never been brave in her life, but is at least brave enough to ask, "RCR?"

"I'm developing what I call Red Carpet Ready, or RCR, for clients who need to be in camera-ready shape in a matter of days for, say, the Oscars," Zia explains.

"Then I better get on the program, pronto," Casey says kiddingly, prompting Myrna, Birdie and Leroy to chuckle.

"Wonderful!" Zia hugs Casey proudly like she just earned a global humanitarian award. Zia's clearly one of those touchy-feely types, who make Casey hyper-aware of her muffin-top-mounds that huggers always seem to land their hands on.

"Wait, I..." Casey protests, but Zia's already pouring her a glass of the thick, murky muck.

"This is a cleansing energy juice loaded with veggies," Zia hands it to Casey. "The kale and beets make it funky-looking."

Casey holds it up to the light, surveying it, wondering how she can get out of this.

"Do you think some of the most gorgeous women in the world care what it *looks* like?" Zia asks.

"Apparently not," Casey grimaces. Leroy hoots and Myrna and Birdie try to muffle their chuckles.

"I can assure you they do not," Zia says. "I use mega-nutrition, expunging ingredients and lots of live foods." Zia's interrupted by raucous laughter and rolling noise, like bowling balls barreling down a lane toward them.

"Speaking of what I'd like to expunge..." Leroy trails off as four laughing teens, two boys and two girls, spew into the kitchen.

The taller guy, who has pasty-white skin and dark, slicked-up hair, skids to a stop at the sight of Zia's concoction in Casey's hand. "Yo, liquid sewage."

"T!" Leroy says in a worn, warning voice. He explains to Casey, "These're the kids we're babysitting from our church's youth group."

"They're *volunteers*," Myrna says, buttering a piece of toast.

"We *hope* not vacationers again this year," Birdie eyes the kids warily.

Casey doesn't care if they're escapees from a home for the criminally insane, she's just glad they're buying her time from having to drink the slop.

"This is T," Myrna introduces the tall, skinny guy, who grabs several pieces of bacon. The other kids make a game of trying to snatch it from him. "His real name's Thomas," she explains.

Leroy mutters jokingly under his breath to Casey, "T's probably as far as he could spell it. You'll see; it really stands for trouble-maker." He tops off his coffee and heads out the door.

Zia puts her arm around a lovely African American girl with shiny, long black hair that fans around her shoulders. "This is Kanashia."

"Hi," Kanashia says, with a sweet smile.

"And Jillian." Zia puts her other arm around a plump girl whose hair's fluffed out like a show dog, as if she's trying to compete with Kanashia's beautiful tresses by sheer volume.

"*Jelly's* her nickname," T corrects Zia. "She like a lil'

85

jelly in her belly." T pretends he's going to grab Jelly's belly.

"Shut *UP*," Jelly says with a pout, but she likes T's attention. She pulls down on her tight top that bares a roll of her tummy. The boys sport those big T-shirts and shorts falling off them while the girls wear jeans and tops so tight you can see every ripple.

"And this here's Dylan." Birdie hands the short kid with reddish-brown hair the toast and egg platter. His T-shirt says, *If you can't be a good example, be a horrific warning.*

"And this is Mrs. Swanson," Myrna introduces Casey to the kids.

"It be yo swan song alrightee, yo drink dat," T warns Casey, pointing to the sludge. She's still clutching it in her hand, like maybe if she just holds it long enough it'll evaporate into the stratosphere.

"I seen that muck on *Ultimate Challenge*," Dylan laughs, "where yo got ta like pick 'tween drinkin' dat or hack offa arm and everyone finish up like dis."

Dylan pulls his left arm out of its sleeve and hides it under his T-shirt. He flaps the empty T-shirt sleeve in the girls' faces as they giggle and playfully push him away.

Myrna hands Kanashia one of the bacon and sausage plates, and Jelly a carton of OJ.

"Skedaddle!" Birdie directs the kids into the adjoining rec hall, where there are several place settings on a long white folding table.

Zia looks pointedly at Casey, who's sniffing the concoction tentatively. "Come on, girl. You can't care what it smells like."

Casey grimaces. *How did I get into this?* Myrna and Birdie chuckle, and serve themselves from the platters.

"We're getting a front row seat," Birdie says. She and Myrna sit on stools at the breakfast bar and dig into their breakfasts. They watch Casey like she's a live science experiment that might *kabang!*

Casey takes a tiny, tentative sip and rolls the fiber of the sludge around with her tongue against the roof of her mouth. Not as lethal as expected. Or maybe it's just that she's hungry enough to gnaw off one of those bar stool legs. Then a bitter aftertaste hits and Casey can't help but make a yuck face.

"Do you think my clients care what it *tastes* like?" Zia asks.

"I can assure you they do not," Casey laughs and the ladies join in.

"No matter, you're now officially in RCR Boot Camp," Zia says, pleased.

"It *does* taste like boots," Casey takes another sip to show she's kidding.

"It *will* boot your system." Zia points to the juice with her knife. "You have a dozen different veggies, liquid vitamins, protein, antioxidants, minerals. And intestinal scrubbers that'll clean you out like a Roto-Rooter."

I already got a jump start with the hot prune-ato juice, Casey thinks.

"This'll give you energy like you've never felt in your life." Zia pours more sludge into Casey's glass. "You're gonna feel like a new woman."

New woman, new life? Casey takes another sip, swishing the thickness between her teeth. "Yes, but will it make me look like you?" Casey asks, downing more. Kind of like taking your medicine. May as well get it over with fast.

"I tell clients if you want what I have, you have to do what I do," Zia says. "Minimum two hours a day of exercise."

"Never mind," Birdie says around a bite of bacon.

"Less wishbone, more backbone," Zia says. "This is where ninety-nine percent drop away."

"'Drop' being the key word." Casey drains the glass.

Zia gives her a gentle swat with a hand towel.

Leroy sticks his head in the side door and calls to the kids in the rec room.

87

"Hey! I need help with water jugs and bags *now*! The faster we load, the more people we can help."

The kids ignore him as they circle around Jelly to giggle at something on her BlackBerry. Leroy shakes his head and leaves with a hopeless sigh.

"I'm coming," Casey calls after him.

"Casey, you don't have to lift those heavy..." Myrna protests.

Already heading out, Casey assures her, "I *want* to help. Really," as she steps back into the gorgeous, sunshine-clean day.

Zia calls after her. "I'll bring you up the rest of the RCR Special for your lunch, Casey."

"Thanks for the warning," Casey calls back and hears the ladies laugh. It feels great to have people "get" her humor versus being totally ignored at home or looked at deadpan, like she's joking in Swahili.

Casey takes the stairs two at a time up to a friendly-looking, old yellow school bus with "The Lord's Bus" in black letters on the side. Dozens of donated bags filled with groceries, blankets and clothes line the sidewalk, leading up to the bus. Leroy's already bent over by the hose, filling gallon plastic water containers. Casey lifts a filled gallon in each hand from the row of full containers.

Leroy nods his thanks, "Anywhere you find space. Floor, seats, everywhere. Just leave enough room for each of us to sit. Myrna and Birdie like the front. Sit anywhere you want." He calls after her through the open bus windows as she starts to load. "And put the kids anywhere out the back door."

"Or on the roof?" Casey calls back and Leroy nods an adamant yes.

Casey goes up and down the bus steps with each load of water and bags, and feels muscles she hasn't used in years fire and burn in her arms, abs and legs. She and Leroy sink into a silent, steady rhythm of filling the containers and loading the bus until it's finally full to the gills, just as Myrna and Birdie herd the kids up. Zia follows, bounding up the steps like a graceful doe, carrying a cooler.

"Here's your chow, fluids and the mineral water you'll drink all through the day." Zia hands the cooler to Casey.

"Don't worry," Birdie chimes in. "We have a bathroom break somewhere decent around lunch."

"No sugar, no salt, no wasted calories," Zia says pointedly.

"No taste," T guffaws.

"*Real* food taste, not sugar, salt and chemicals," Zia corrects him. "Casey, I'll put the RCR dinners up in the nursery fridge so no one else eats them."

"Fat chance," Dylan laughs. "Pun intended."

Casey gives Dylan the evil eye. He best not be referring to her.

"I'm sticking with my peanut butter, jelly and banana sandwich," Kanashia says.

"We put potato chips on right before we eat them," Jelly says, licking her lips in anticipation. "And, like, the crunchy and the like, smooth banana and peanut butter and..."

"Jelly!" T tickles Jelly's belly. Dylan joins in, sending Jelly squealing.

"I like *crunchy* peanut butter," Kanashia specifies.

Casey's thinking of bartering for a schoolyard lunch trade, but she's pretty sure she'd have to throw in a new car with her lunch to get any takers.

"At the spa, clients also have high-intensity workouts all day," Zia tells Casey. "But you'll get that working the mission, trust me." Zia skips down the stairs as full of vim as the Energizer Bunny. "Enjoy," she calls back to Casey.

"She has to be kidding." Birdie laughs and follows Myrna and Casey onto the bus.

"Wow," Myrna surveys the bags, blankets and bottled water inundating the bus. Their seats are so full they all have to sit high atop blankets on the seat cushions.

Leroy admonishes the kids as they jump on the bus.

"Mrs. Swanson did more in a half hour than you kids did all week when you were here last year."

"Yeah, but Mrs. Swan-song's probably wore her ol' self *out* fo the week," T says lowly to Dylan as he passes Casey. She almost feels at home with a smart-mouthed teen being rude to her and wonders what her own kids are up to right now. Casey realizes she didn't take more than a minute to pray this morning, and, she *should* be praying for her own kids, among other things. She already needs to confess being miffed with T and ask for patience in dealing with teenagers in general.

As much as she wants to check out the scenery while Leroy drives them to Whereverville, she closes her eyes so she's not distracted while she prays, and the moving bus makes a monotonous motor drone that white-noises out the chatter.

Casey ends by thanking God for opening the door for her to come on this mystery mission, for giving direction, for His love. Then, as Amana Anne always suggests, Casey's quiet and says internally, "Please speak, Lord." She waits in quiet for whatever God may want to place upon her mind or heart. In a matter of minutes, she has a deep feeling of being in the present, and in The Presence.

Until Myrna turns around, raising her voice to bring Casey back. "We never need a passport getting *in.*"

Casey opens her eyes with a start.

Passport?!

The view out the bus window is suddenly surreal, like Casey just landed in a Frida Kahlo painting.

They're on the Mexican border!

Brown-hued men, women, and children peddle vibrant bouquets of flowers, thick Mexican blankets in pastel weaves, and bright, embroidered blouses. Their colorful carts are stacked with strung-up puppets, woven pouches and backpacks.

A huge green and black sign shouts, "Welcome to

Mexico."

"It's getting back *out* without one that's the problem these days," Birdie informs Casey as the Mexican border guard waves them through.

"The last place you want to be is in a Mexican prison," Leroy adds, as they cross the border into Mexico.

A Mexican prison?!

Nathan

The Grand Soupa Poobah. That's what Wowie had christened Amana Anne because on Sunday mornings she's the soup chef for Riverside Christian, Wowie's church. Amana Anne loves puttering around their kitchen, with its circular, stained-glass windows high up over the cutting island, which is so big it looks more like a continent. This used to be the chapel, years ago, before the burgeoning congregation outgrew it. It *is* blessedly chapel-quiet here.

When it was remodeled into a kitchen and adjoining dining hall, Sundays became Soupa Sundays, again, by Wowie's baptizing. Wowie enlisted volunteers to cook, serve and deliver soup each week to seniors, the homeless, shut-ins, the sick and handicapped. Today, the latter will include Eliz.

Softly muted morning sunlight streams in on Amana Anne's cutting board, vegetables, herbs, and on her, like a nod of divine approval. She ties on the faded "Kiss the Cook" apron, a gift from Nathan years ago, her favorite still. In fact, today's soup is Nathan's favorite, Basil Barley Vegetable with a tomato and sweet onion base. She knows it's silly, but she always wears the apron when she makes it, just like she always wore that apron for him anytime she'd make any of his favorite dishes, to remind him he owed the cook some kisses.

This memory reminds *her* that it's been years since she's *been* kissed. Except by the neighborhood's favorite dog, Fritz, a mutt that's mostly German Sheppard, who slobbers his affection on her when he sees her walking or in her garden. Kissing Jake's full lips and how they might feel come into her mind, but she smacks that thought down. Better get on with making this soup for the needy and Eliz – remember, his *date*?

Amana Anne coats the bottom of a large aluminum soup pot with a splash of olive oil and clicks on the gas stove. The blue flame bursts into being. She adds sweet Vidalia onions that sizzle softly in the golden oil, then tosses in a little barley and basil and fills the pot two-thirds full with water. She carefully washes the zucchini, cauliflower, carrots, celery, cabbage and sweet potatoes, donated by parishioners, many from their own organic gardens. Later, a sprinkling of Good Seasons Italian dry salad dressing is the last pinch to be added, the "secret" ingredient she tells everyone about when they ask her soupa cooking secrets.

"Really, *love* is the secret ingredient," she tells people, "and it's seasoned with prayer." She always blesses the food and offers prayers of love for anyone sharing her soup.

But, there's also a secret the "Keeper of Secrets" *won't* tell the church people: that she doesn't have a home church herself because she's seldom gone to church since Nathan passed on. At first she stopped going because she was angry with God. Then there were too many church memories of her and Nathan; the solid, sweet clasp of holding his hand, nudging one another during sermons when each thought the other needed to learn something, trying not to laugh when they nudged each other at the exact same time.

Another reason is that for years, church people were always asking how she was, or mentioning Nathan – his kindness, his good looks, some memory. She never knew when their well-meaning words would hit like emotional landmines and trigger an ill-timed or inappropriate crying jag, some unresolved grief or broken-hearted anger. So instead, she started "doing church" by helping with what she thought Jesus would be doing: cooking in the soup kitchen, visiting the sick, the lonely, the depressed. There was too much downtime sitting alone in church to think and remember in the wake of her loss. She needed to be active. Doing, doing, doing.

But today, as she chops the veggies, she *is* remembering. How could she not, between cooking Nathan's favorite soup *and* having had his beloved dessert of ice cream in the last twenty-four hours? Not remembering him was like trying to hold a helium balloon underwater. While she dices the zucchini and cauliflower, she stops fighting it and allows the memories to simmer to the surface.

Even the worst one: the day it happened.

It was a swelteringly hot day like today. Blistering and humid. A Saturday in August. She recalled looking at the faded, red Woody Woodpecker thermometer nailed to their oak tree in the back yard. It was noon and already ninety-three degrees. Nathan was changing to go for a run, though Amana Anne had warned him against it.

"You're going to get heat stroke," she told him. They rarely fought, but when they did, it was over things like this. The man believed he was invincible, exempt from the laws of nature and common sense.

Amana Anne decided to cool her jets with a rare treat, a double scoop of strawberry and pralines ice cream in a waffle cone. She was into her first lick when Nathan jogged back downstairs, wearing his running clothes. Amana Anne felt the little wave of love she always felt when she saw him, even when she was ticked off. He looked so cute and fit in his baggy shorts and tank shirt. His sable brown hair had a boyish bit of unruliness to it and his hazel eyes always possessed a kind of inner light.

He jogged over to peck her cheek, then grabbed her hand with the cone and stole a big, slurpy lick of her ice cream. All the way round the equator of it, contaminating everything, knowing full well how nuts this made her, and thinking it hilarious.

She angrily threw the cone in his Kashi cereal bowl from breakfast. It splattered all over the sink and her new white top. She shouldn't have been wearing the dressy top around the house anyway before she went out, so now she was mad at him *and* herself. But *he* was the underlying cause so he'd get the heat for everything. And on top of that, his cereal bowl shouldn't have still been in the sink.

"Once a *year* I have an ice cream cone and you have to slop it up." This was an exaggeration, but she threw in the once-a-year part to beef up her case.

"Why can't I have a lick? I don't have cooties." He always took it so personally, or pretended to. "You *kiss* me all the time." It was true that normally they never missed an opportunity to smooch, even if he was just taking out the garbage.

"Not anymore." She pushed him away hard as he came in for another kiss, but he just laughed.

"We're gonna test that theory when I return, little lady," he called back, talking like some cowboy from an old Western as he ran out the door.

She considered putting the ice cream in the freezer for him because she sure wasn't going to eat it, but decided against it. Too much positive reinforcement. Let him drink it warm with souring milk from his cereal bowl. It would serve him right.

Forty-five minutes later she was polishing their silverware, still miffed, thinking how she'd poke him with a silver serving fork if he even tried to kiss her when he returned. That was another of his big kicks – kissing her when he was sweaty, knowing she hated the smelly, drippy messiness of it.

95

Then she heard the wail of an ambulance, stomach-churningly close. And everything changed forever. Hours later, the melted ice cream was still in the sink. It sat there accusingly when she came home from the hospital. Nathan had a heart attack. Fast and fatal.

The Technicolor seeped out of her world that day, the colors literally bleeding into grays, then suddenly, starkly, black and white. The moment she heard the ambulance was the last moment she remembered of bright sunshine in a full-spectrum world. The colors were gradually coming back through the years, like a color photograph slowly developing. They weren't the heightened hues of their time together. Not the colors of love. Romantic love, anyway. Now her world was colored with a more permanent palette of loving others in a Godly way. *It's more important in the eternal scheme of things anyway*, she always tells herself.

Amana Anne pulls back from her memories and puts the last of the zucchini in the soup. But another memory floats to the surface, a recent one. Of yesterday. And how unusually vibrant the sunset seemed after she came out from meeting Jake, more vibrant than it had been in many years.

Don't even go there again, she warns herself as she puts the soup lid on. *You should be blessing the soupa and praying for the soupers, including Eliz, instead of coveting her date.* She disciplines herself as she flicks the last remnants of veggie peels off the cutting board and into the garbage. Time to clean up, get thinking straight, take Eliz some soup and tell her all about *her* Mr. Backup.

But an inner voice that she's come to recognize as the voice of her heart whispers, *Then why do I feel that Jake's meant for* me?

Whoops

Eliz had hoped that the whole wanting-to-booze-binge would miraculously go away since last night she asked God into her life. But the thought of cold champagne came to mind immediately upon awakening this morning when she was hit with a pitchfork of neck pain. Not to mention the bleak reality of no-job, no-money, no-man. Her wanting-men-thing was still hanging in apparently, too, since her mental image of the bubbly clearly included a really cute waiter bringing it.

At least she made it out of bed to the living room couch without her neck smarting too much. Since she can't find the remote without the pain of having to hoist thrown clothes to find it, she's reading Amana Anne's book page by page. Even if Eliz wanted to read anything else, all she can do is lift one page at a time without neck soreness. Anyway, the book is surprisingly enjoyable, full of wisdom, humorous parables, poignant stories and the Word.

Eliz hears a car door slam in her driveway and wonders if that's Amana Anne now. She twists slowly onto her side to get up, using one hand to hold her head so the weight of it won't pull on her neck, and manages to sit up at snail speed. The doorbell rings and Eliz winces as she puts weight on her ankle to walk, but it hurts far less than even earlier today.

When she opens the door, Amana Anne greets her with a sunshiny smile.

"Hey, our patient lived to see another day," Amana Anne says, a little too chipper-cheerily for Eliz's taste this morning, though she's thrilled to see her with a clear Tupperware container of soup.

"Nurse Bananza!" Eliz steps outside onto the patio with Amana Anne. No way can she let Amana Anne in. It's bad enough Amana Anne's seeing that Eliz never dead-headed the hanging flower basket of pink petunias Amana Anne gave her for the patio, complete with a dead-heading dissertation.

"It's still warm." Amana Anne hands Eliz the Tupperware.

"Thanks and I'd hug ya but it'd kill me so it's not worth it." Eliz can smell the sweet basil in the soup even through the container. It takes everything in her not to tear off the lid and suck it down on the spot.

"Did you see Casey's e-mail that our girl's in Californee?" Amana Anne asks.

"Get outta town!" Eliz says it more like a question.

"She *did*. Mission trip."

"Oh, I was about to be jealous. It's probably just a fuel stop en route to the Congo. Who knows where the God Stuff will land ya."

Amana Anne laughs but Eliz is only half kidding. She considers telling Amana Anne her own "God Stuff" that she experienced last night.

"Well, do you want to hear about Mr. Backup?" Amana Anne asks, wondering why Eliz hasn't already peppering her with questions about meeting her date.

"What're you talking about?" Eliz asks.

"Your date." Did Eliz forget about the man?

Eliz starts laughing so hard she's only getting fragments of a sentence out, and not a very coherent one at that.

"Ohhhh... noooo... you... hooo... Jam... haaaaa...

oooow." She sets the soup down on the patio because it hurts her neck to hold it and laugh.

"Are you goofy on pain killers or what?"

Eliz catches her breath to get it out, "I don't know *who* you met..." Eliz dissolves again into giggles. "But it wasn't Mr. Backup."

"What?!" Amana Anne is *not* laughing.

"Jamaica got to jammin' and forgot all about setting it up. She texted me this morn."

"Are you kidding?" Amana Anne flashes back to the conversation with Jake, trying to recall what she said.

"So who'd Miss Proper-pants hit on?" Eliz asks.

"The only buffo in the place, like you said." Amana Anne moans, rubbing her forehead like she's got an instant migraine. "I was *not* hitting on Mr. Buffo, I mean Backup, I mean Jake."

"Well, if Jake isn't too offensive-looking maybe I'll meet him anyway cause I'm a little desperate right about now," Eliz decides. Things could be looking up after all.

"Very *not* offensive-looking." Amana Anne isn't sure why she feels like she needs to sell Eliz on him. "Quite an attractive middle-aged man."

"*Middle aged?*" Eliz says, like he's prehistoric.

"You *said* Mr. Backup was a little older."

"I *meant* a little older than the guys I usually date. Not older than Adam." Eliz generally dates men several years younger because they're the most party-compatible with her.

"Heeeelllo. *I'm* middle-aged."

"And you're on your own Depend patrol, too, Nana-Bana."

"He's very fit, actually." Amana Anne finds she can't help herself from defending Jake. She also can't seem to keep her hands from dead-heading the droopily wilted petunias. "He owns a print shop and other businesses. And he's quite the gentleman."

"Sure. He grew up in Victorian times." Eliz knew it

wasn't genetically possible for Amana Anne to forego the flowers. Amana Anne's lost in pinching the dead-heads into a white tissue she's pulled out of her pocket. Eliz thinks it's a hoot that Amana Anne always has tissue to clean up whatever dirty little corner of the world she's hoping to improve.

Watching Amana Anne, Eliz again wants to tell her how she's going to try to clean up *her* world and give the God Stuff a shot. But she *isn't* ready to share what God said to her last night about His unconditional love. It seems too private to talk about. And in the interest of full disclosure, after Eliz fell asleep and woke up again this morning, she was wondering if it was a dream anyway. Still, something in her soul, her spirit, seems to keep confirming that it wasn't.

"I want to tell you something, Bana, and don't have a canary," Eliz begins tentatively.

Now what? Amana Anne wonders. Like this whole humiliation with Jake thing isn't enough? Is she going to be on some TV show because she was being "punked" and the whole thing's gonna be a national joke? Or on YouTube?

"I'm trying the God Stuff." Eliz imagines this probably is not how you say it.

"Eliz!" Amana Anne spontaneously hugs her.

"Ow!" Eliz screams in pain.

"Oh, sorry!" Amana Anne releases Eliz and air-pats her on the back.

"I'm just doing the one day – make that one min-u-eta – at a time deal," Eliz cautions.

"No one's expecting an instant Mother Teresa, trust me," Amana Anne assures her.

"*You're* gonna need to trust *me* later. I have an idea that I believe is God-inspired." Eliz turns her neck to check her range of motion and grimaces. "First, I'm gonna need a hot shower. So let's hook up later at Quentie's. Bana, my idea's gonna change your life."

"Why am I afraid?" Amana Anne asks. Some of Eliz's

big ideas in the past haven't worked out so well. Like when Eliz thought she could time an early dinner date leaving at nine o'clock out the back door, and a late movie date coming to the front door, and the guys ended up fighting in her living room.

"What's that 'Fear Blocks Blessings' chapter in this great book of yours, Banaboom? Go read it. You're gonna need it."

Eliz picks up the soup, gritting her teeth as a little spear of pain punctures her neck. "Thanks for the soup, Mana, and for pinch-hitting last night. I love that yer still boldly hitting on dudes at yer age!"

Eliz can practically see steam coming out of Amana Anne's ears, and Eliz's words actually stop Amana Anne from her maniacal dead-heading. "You do what ya have ta do when yer decrepit," Eliz says, opening the door to go in, talking like a frog-voiced old lady. "Sidle on up ta em with yer walker."

The balled-up tissue, dead-heads and all, go flying at Eliz and land on her head. She shakes off the flowers that catch in her hair, laughing.

Amana Anne kiddingly stalks down the sidewalk, calling back, "And I'm not picking them up."

Eliz calls after her, "You'll be over here in the middle of the night in your PJ's with a Shop Vac cause you couldn't sleep for worry-warting over them."

Amana Anne has a feeling Eliz's right about her being up worry-warting over *something* tonight. But only if she can't correct this mortifying misunderstanding with Jake.

Immediately, if not sooner.

101

Mexico!

I'm in a foreign country! Casey looks around in awe. Rainbows of bright colors swirl in front of her as their bus passes a canopy of piñatas: Mickey Mouse, Goofy, Nemo, dragons and dinosaurs swing in the breeze to sassy salsa music, and vendors call out, "Buy the Nemo? The Goofy? Yes?"

The scent of fresh bread baking wafts into Casey's nostrils as they pass an old woman hand-flapping tortillas and cooking them on a smoky grill. Her face is a browned roadmap of wrinkles that crinkle when she smiles up at Casey. A redheaded woman in leopard-print capris and spike-heeled sandals haggles over prices with a souvenir vendor. All the colors, smells and sounds of a culture vibrantly alive rejuvenate Casey's senses and soul with an explosion of joy.

Could it be that only twenty-four hours ago she was desperately depressed in a whole other part of the world? She feels deeply happy for the first time in more years than she can count. Okay, there *is* the gnawing undercurrent of the passport issue. She did stick her driver's license in her pocket when she dressed, not that this would cut mustard. No point in fretting about it and upsetting everyone right now. What was it that Amana Anne always said? *The present is in the present.* It's true, and there are so many gifts to enjoy everywhere Casey looks.

"Hola." A pleasant young man with caramel skin calls to them from the doorway of his leather shop as the bus drives by. The tiny, narrow space overflows outside with sandals, purses and leather coats. His sign boasts "best deals" in wobbly, hand-printed English, but the prices are in pesos.

A vendor wearing a wide sombrero and a serape holds long donuts dusted in cinnamon and sugar up to them from the street.

"Churros," Birdie informs Casey, tapping on the window to point them out. Casey had already been eyeballing them like a cat on a mouse hole. Luckily she doesn't have money or she'd be tempted to blow her "RCR" with "R 'C' for *Churros* R" and they'd have to *roll* her down the red carpet by the end of the week. *Don't even slow down, Leroy,* Casey silently begs as the cinnamon smell intoxicates her. But Leroy stops the bus at the *alto* sign next to the *churros* man.

The teens, Birdie and Myrna each hand him a dollar out the window and he hands them up donuts wrapped in white napkins that are snowy with brown sugar. Casey would bet even the napkins might taste good about now.

"Casey?" Myrna asks if she'd like any and Casey shakes her head no a little vehemently. She doesn't want to disappoint Zia and ditch the RCR in the first *hour.*

"We admire your willpower," Birdie says, sinking her teeth into a *churro* with relish.

Ha! I have as much willpower as dinero, Casey thinks. *Nada.* She chokes down some green slime-juice from the cooler to abate her hunger, glancing up at the beautiful cottony-clouded, blue sky as she tilts her head back to drink. Even the clouds remind her of fluffy mounds of mashed potatoes.

"Yo, look at this blast from the past," T yells, pointing to an old red convertible with fins and orange flames of fire painted on the sides. It sputters about five miles an hour past them in the opposite direction, with obnoxiously loud ranchero music blaring. Casey notes that even though the thoroughfare's marked as two lanes, it doesn't waylay the Mexican drivers from intermittently creating as many lanes of traffic as they want.

"I don't usually drive through yellow lights," Leroy explains to Casey as he zips through one. "But the locals'll rear-end us. They think yellow's an invitation to an impromptu drag race." He chuckles, she supposes at the thought of drag racing the Lord's Bus (with Birdie and Myrna screaming in tow) against some hot-rod Mexican *hombre*. Casey thinks she'd rather enjoy it.

Leroy turns down a dirt side road and in a matter of minutes, the vista is a panorama of sun-browned people coming and going from tiny plywood and cardboard shacks, their roofs patched like scrap quilts. At the end of the road is a large, tall, old grey stone building. It's surrounded by a matching chipped stone wall about seven feet high with a wide entrance.

"This is the orphanage," Birdie twists around in her seat to tell Casey as Leroy pulls in the stone entrance. The first orphan Casey sees is a deeply bronzed little boy of about four, wearing a too-small, faded Old Navy T-shirt and too-big shorts hanging low, exposing several inches of his skinny, ribbed stomach. On his feet are one saddle shoe and one strawberry beach thong, yet he stands atop his rock with the stature of a rajah on a bejeweled elephant surveying his kingdom.

Dozens of orphans romp in the dirt yard, several are in a circle playing dodge ball with a faded red ball. They range in age from about two to twelve. Most of the older boys wear oversized T-shirts that envelope their thin frames like tarps. The littlest orphans squat together in an old wooden sandbox absorbed at play.

An old Mexican man with a stooped back and tired smile

comes out of the lone building, ringing a school bell. Casey suspects it's mealtime as every last boy races toward him.

"Hector's the widower who takes care of the orphans," Myrna informs Casey.

"Used to be an orphan himself," Birdie adds.

Hector places a loving hand on the heads of the boys who run by him, sometimes lightly rustling their hair as they enter the building.

As soon as Leroy cuts the engine, the teens rush out of their seats, but Leroy stands up to block them from tearing off the bus. His hip lets out a loud *pop* as he straightens in a stretch. "Listen up, kids."

Dylan moans and T jumps hyperactively in place like a hot soda-pop bottle shaken and about to explode.

"Remember that we have to feed people physically as well as spiritually," Leroy says. "If people are hungry and thirsty and sick, they aren't going to care about hearing a message if we're not helping them."

"On the other hand," Myrna tells the kids, "we'd be doing them a disservice if we didn't share the Living Water and the Bread of Life so they have hope and help in their lives."

"We heard this last year," Dylan groans. T exhales noisily with testy boredom. Kanashia and Jelly compare French tips.

"Until you actually *do* it, you're gonna keep hearing it," Birdie chimes in.

"So you kids will help me unload and distribute." Leroy hands each kid a bag of groceries as they jump off the bus.

"Awwwwh," Dylan whines, the last of the kids to exit. Leroy picks up his foot and pretends to give him a kick in the rear end behind his back, then follows him off with groceries.

"Leroy," Myrna says in a wifely tone through the window at him. Birdie stifles a giggle as they grab grocery bags.

"Casey, we know a little Spanish," Myrna tells Casey, holding forefinger and thumb about an inch apart to indicate the *pequeño* amount, "so Birdie and I share the gospel."

"You're welcome in either camp," Birdie says as they walk toward the entrance to what looks like the orphan's dining hall.

The teens dump their groceries at the door and come flying out to play "pretend" hoops with the faded ball. The boys take turns bouncing the ball around the giggling girls. Jelly and Kanashia swat at it half-heartedly, intent on protecting their fake nails.

"Why do I have a hunch Leroy'll need help?" Casey says, and the ladies chuckle. Myrna gives an exasperated moan.

Inside the sparse dining hall, long old wooden tables are lined with orphans standing behind low benches, praying. It looks like a scene out of Dickens, except the orphans are happy and saying grace in Spanish. There must be forty or fifty of them, dark-haired heads bowed earnestly, and dirty, brown hands clasped. Each has a small plate in front of him with beans, rice and tiny dots of stewed tomatoes, a fork to the left and a clear plastic cup of water mid-center. As soon as they finish praying, they plop down on the benches and dig in.

Hector holds two of the smallest boys on his lap, feeding them. They take turns opening their mouths like hungry, little sparrows as he spoons in brown mush. Casey wonders if this is a late breakfast or early lunch for the orphans, then realizes it's probably their only meal of the day. Casey and the ladies set their grocery bags down on the cement floor with the other groceries for the orphans. Leroy heads past them, raising one hoping-for-help questioning eyebrow to Casey and she follows him out.

"Kids!" Leroy yells at the teens running around the yard, but getting them to help is as futile as trying to lasso bubbles and he throws his hands up in frustration.

Casey's surprised to see there's already a small gathering of Mexican men, women and children waiting patiently behind the bus in a neat line. Dozens more are coming up the hill from the nearby shacks.

A handsome, young man with shiny black hair walks toward the bus and waves his Bible in hello to Leroy. He begins to softly sing "Amazing Grace" in Spanish alongside the gathering crowd. His face is open and kind, his voice reverent. The people in line join in like backup singers, and several of them gather around him.

"This is where they hold their church service Sunday mornings." Leroy opens the fire door at the back of the bus. "They don't have a building. We're going to have what I call 'active church' today." He joins in the singing, off-key but hearty, while he hands a grocery bag and water to each person in line. Casey follows his lead and goes to the front of the bus, humming, and another line instantly forms in the front.

The young preacher holds up his Bible and begins preaching in Spanish. Hearing his words, like *La Biblia* and *Gloria a Dios,* Casey feels a grace, the presence of the Lord in a different way than she ever experienced in church. She sees Him in the very eyes of these poor but beautiful people. Casey greets them with the only salutation she knows, "*Buenos dias.*" They each smile at her, not one of them without the gift of a genuine smile, saying a simple, sincere, "*Muchas gracias.*"

Casey answers "*De nada,*" it's nothing. That's one of only a few phrases she recalls the boys saying when they were learning Spanish. Several Mexicans also touch their hearts, clasp her hand or hug her, saying something "*Dios,*" which Casey thinks may mean, or be short for, "God Bless."

She and Leroy again melt into a steady, silent rhythm of work. The lifting is surprisingly easy and fluid, her muscles warmed by the earlier light lifting of the water gallons, and the late morning sun that feels like warm maple syrup on her limbs. The hours flee as more and more of the grateful people come in a seemingly endless stream until the bus is empty and the sun is much lower in the afternoon sky.

107

It's only later, after the church service is long over and they've said their goodbyes to Hector and the orphans, that Casey feels her legs are going to collapse under her. She walks shakily onto the bus, pulling herself up the stairs with her hand, slippery with sweat, on the railing. As she falls onto the black, frying-pan-hot leather seat, there's a deep sense of fulfillment in seeing the emptiness of the bus. All that's left are the ladies' purses, the kids' backpacks, her cooler, and their lunches. Everything else was distributed to grateful recipients – perhaps hundreds. Like the loaves and fishes, Casey thinks.

Leroy stomps up the steps and plops into the driver's seat with a well-earned, senior sigh. T galumphs up the steps after him and Leroy gives T a very pointed stink eye for goofing off all day.

"What?" T asks innocently, swinging his body on the silver pole at the top of the stairs. The other kids clomp hurriedly by, wisely averting their gazes as they pass Leroy and Casey to attack their lunch bags in the back.

"P-J banana chip, come ta Daddy," Dylan says around a bite into his sandwich and a groan of enjoyment. Casey pulls out her sludge and drinks half of it without stopping.

Myrna and Birdie board the bus and sink into their seats with simultaneous *whoomps*. They each sprawl with their feet out across their seats, and sighs of relief to finally get their feet up.

"I've never seen anyone with such stamina in my life, Casey," Myrna says, pulling wax-paper-wrapped sandwiches out of her cooler and handing them to Birdie and Leroy.

"You're a little Wonder Woman." Birdie unwraps her egg salad sandwich.

"Thanks." Casey drinks up their kind words, especially "*little*." It's been decades since *that's* been used to describe her.

"Hey!" Leroy says, like he's neglected.

"Hey nothing, Leroy," Myrna says. "You didn't go up

and down those stairs with thirty pounds of food and water a hundred times. You just sat on the back of the bus and dragged things over."

"True," he laughs, taking a pleased peek inside his Dagwood sandwich. Casey brings out Zia's microscopic whole wheat burrito with tuna, sprouts, veggies and beans, and consumes it in two bites. She feels a garnish of guilt when she notes Myrna, Birdie and Leroy bow their heads in quick grace before partaking. Casey belatedly thanks God for the great nutrition she's been given as she pulls out a tiny organic banana. In the eighth of a bite she gets out of it, she savors the earthy sweetness.

Mouth full, Leroy starts the motor and pulls out as they wave to Hector, the orphans and the last cluster of people still gathered with their grocery bags and water. A man with one arm shouts "*Gracias*," and other things in Spanish Casey can't make out.

"Good journey home," Myrna translates.

With a cold chill to her spine, Casey suddenly remembers the journey home. Her stomach roils and her body parts tighten with tension at the thought of the border guard looming before her in a matter of minutes. What will happen if they get pulled over? Would she land in some hellhole of a Mexican prison? Who could she call for bail? Do they even allow phone calls?

She puts what's left of her lunch away and speed-dials God.

Please give me favor, Lord. You know I'm doing Your work, and I don't even have money for a fine. Thank You in advance for getting me through the border with no problems. Thank you. Thank you. Was it Meister Eckhart who said, "If the only prayer you ever say is thank you, that would be sufficient"? She hopes it *is* sufficient and concentrates on praising and thanking God all the way to the border, when her gut clenches again at the sight of the guards.

"We always leave before the Sunday evening rush or

we'd sit in these lanes for hours," Birdie explains to Casey as they enter a border guard lane.

"Usually the weekend traffic's so heavy from Americans going back, they can't pull a lot of people over, but you never know," Myrna adds.

Leroy slows and the guard looks at the bus suspiciously. He eyes them all through the windows, and Casey feels her heart palpitating as the guard slowly lifts his arm as though in recognition, like there's an APB out on her. He points a sharp, accusing finger.

Directly at Casey.

Lowdown on Prince Charming

A Neolithic jar of petrified, pickled pig's feet greets Amana Anne as she steps into Wowie's garage. Amana Anne still can't believe her father used to eat those things. Or that Wowie keeps them as mementos.

Next on the shelf is a murky, purple-brown wine with a rotten cork and slimy-looking, worm-like things floating in it. Wowie's vino-making attempt. *This* is why Amana Anne asks Wowie to keep her garage door shut. If some neighborhood kid wandered in, he'd be scarred for life. His folks could sue for emotional distress and life-long therapy. No doubt Wowie'll try to ply her with that would-be "wine" some unsuspecting day when Amana Anne's guard is down. Wowie always reasons that, "Vino never goes bad. It has alcohol in it."

There are flower vases with dead moths and spiders in their bases, plastic flower pots from the dollar store, and an alp of cobweb pine cones Wowie'd picked up in the woods years ago to make wreaths. Spray-painting them silver, gold and with white "snow" was as far as she got. Amana Anne estimates the number of Eisenhower-era Jell-Os, instant puddings and packaged foods Wowie has in rows as tall as corn stalks on her shelves. Worst of all, it smells like something died in here. There really could be a dead rat or two who just decided to give up the ghost rather than wade through all the boxes of mildewy gunk.

Amana Anne takes a tissue from her pocket to open the adjoining door into Wowie's hallway, powder room and kitchenette. There's been more than once when Amana Anne's hand was met with suspect sticky goo turning this doorknob. Wowie's in the kitchenette guzzling Turner's two percent milk from the carton.

"Why are you keeping one hundred and twenty-two expired Jell-Os, Momsy?" Amana Anne bunches her tissue and shoots it in the vanity garbage can in the powder room.

"There's no such thing as an expiration date, Buckaroo. It's a commie-pinko plot by the food industry to get you to toss em and keep buyin more." Wowie downs another swig of milk.

Amana Anne grabs a garbage bag from the cabinet under Wowie's sink.

"Do *not* throw them out," Wowie warns her, making a grab for the bag, but Amana Anne holds it over her head.

"The neighborhood kids and I are gonna have a finger-painting party with them," Wowie insists. "Add a little water, and we'll put some beauteous Jell-O colors on wax paper. Edible art."

"Unless you're planning on giving stomach pumps as party favors, do *not* let the kids eat the Jell-O art, Mom." Amana Anne begrudgingly returns the bag.

"You've got a point, Amana Banana. Did you see that *60 Minutes* report about that pint-sized Picasso raking in a *killing* in art sales?" Wowie puts the milk container in her top cupboard. "I should be making money off the little neighborhood buggers. I'll take a percentage."

Amana Anne grabs the milk from the cupboard and puts it in the fridge. Two of Wowie's old refrigerator magnets are so anemic in their pull that they jump ship along with the postcards they were half-heartedly holding on. One magnet says what Wowie used to always tell Amana Anne's dad, "If you want breakfast in bed, sleep in the kitchen." Amana Anne replaces the magnets, like she does every time she opens the door and they fall. Wowie calls the lame magnets her built-in, touch-your-toes exercises.

"*Tout de suite*, Momsy. Super Short Cuts closes soon." Amana Anne leads the way out.

Wowie twiddles her fingers at Amana Anne for her car keys. "I like to drive."

"Yes, but oddly people don't like your tire treads on their faces." Amana Anne closes the garage door after them. "So unless you also like rooming in the pen with Bubette for vehicular manslaughter, I'll drive." Amana Anne jumps in the driver's seat.

"I'll yell ahead for everyone to get off the sidewalks." Wowie pushes the button to roll down her window, sticking her head out like a puppy as they drive down Commons.

"Soooooooooo." When Wowie elongates her vowels at Amana Anne, it's a verbal prelude to some pontification about Amana Anne's life. It typically starts the moment they get in the car, when Wowie can hold her hostage for a drive. Amana Anne must have had temporary amnesia to even get in with her. At least this ride will be mercifully brief. Super Short Cuts (where they promise two-minute trims and ten-minute cuts) is only a few blocks away in the Blossom Brook Plaza.

"Am I the last person in the world to find out anything about my only child?" Wowie plays this card when she's learned something that's probably none of her business in the first place.

"Yes." Amana Anne finds this answer to be the quickest way to get Wowie to the point.

Wowie ignores what she calls Amana Anne's smarty-pants-ness. "My sources tell me you had a hot date last night. Your first date in fifteen years, seven months, and three days, but who's counting, and I have to hear about it secondhand?"

"Who told you *that*?"

"The usual suspects. I refuse to reveal my sources."

Wowie has senior citizen spy networks reporting in from all over Oakhaven and the surrounding communities. The coffee klatch at the senior center alone could be designated a CIA covert operations site. If they really wanted to hunt down terrorists, they could employ Wowie and her senior sleuths.

"It wasn't a *date*." This is all Amana Anne needs: The town gossip mill getting back to Jake that she thinks they're eloping and moving to Boca before sundown.

"You and an eligible man within a fifty mile radius. I call it a date."

"Mom, I spent three minutes with him."

"Leave him wanting more, good thinking, Banana," Wowie assures her. "I'm told he owns some businesses, so he'll be a good provider. We can get more of the scoop from Nikki."

"Nooooooooooooo." When Amana Anne elongates her vowels at Wowie, it means she realizes she's fighting a losing battle, but gives it a shot anyway on principle.

"Since I have more wrinkles than a three-hundred-foot Redwood has rings, clearly I wasn't born yesterday so I'll be su*b*-tle." Her mom always accentuates the silent "b" in 'subtle' whenever Amana Anne's wary that Wowie'll be anything *but*. Amana Anne braces herself for embarrassment, as if she hasn't had enough in the last twenty-four hours.

She knew it was OCD-ish of her, but she already called all three business numbers on Jake's card to set the record straight about their encounter, and only got recordings that they were closed Sundays. It was upsetting that Jake might be thinking for even another minute about this strange, desperate woman who seemingly hit on him. Not that he was necessarily thinking of her at all.

They turn into the Blossom Brook Plaza lot, and park in front of the green awning of a salon advertising twelve-dollar

114

Tuesday Specials in the window. The parking space right in front seems to be a good omen that they hit a lull in the usually busy traffic of "weekend-sprucer-uppers," as Wowie calls them.

"Watch, Sweetie." Wowie hops out of the car almost before it stops. "I'll ask one innocent question and Nikki'll be off and running with your man's life story, complete with his social security and bank account numbers."

Amana Anne double-times it after Wowie, like she's keeping up with a mischievous toddler, or in this case, an octogenarian in her second childhood. Inside, the stylists, Nikki and Jolene, wave happy hellos. Nikki's a tall, rotund woman who always reminds Amana Anne of honey because she has both perfectly styled, honey-colored hair, and skin that has a honey-like luminosity and shine. Jolene's her polar opposite, with a rough, dry face, and brittle blonde hair.

Nikki's sweeping up from her last customer and Jolene's putting color on an elderly lady's charcoal hair in the shampoo area. The lady's absorbed in a tabloid that has two women on the front – reality TV stars? – who look like they want to claw each other's faces off. The shop smells of a pungent mix of permanent solution and hairspray. Amana Anne takes a seat near the door and hopes for an occasional breeze when people come in.

"I'm here for my freebie," Wowie announces, and the girls laugh. Wowie pulls the "senior widow on limited income card" to wrangle freebie trims between cuts. Amana Anne always surreptitiously leaves a five on the counter for Nikki.

"Miss Wowie!" Nikki envelopes Wowie in a bear hug, which puts Wowie's face smack in Nikki's stomach folds.

"Hi, Pumpkin." Wowie's voice is muffled from within the hug. Amana Anne cringes at Wowie's word choice, since Nikki *is* round as a pumpkin. But Wowie calls most everyone a pet name, "...to save my gray matter from overload remembering *real* names."

115

"I'll be right with you." Nikki releases Wowie to take her broom to the back room.

"Good grief, the woman's trying to smother me to death," Wowie stage-whispers to Amana Anne. "Thank goodness there was a little air in her bellybutton or I'd be a goner." Wowie crosses her hands over her chest, hangs her tongue out of her mouth, and rolls her eyes up into her head. Amana Anne smothers a chuckle and grabs a magazine.

Nikki returns and brushes stray snippings off her chair. "Okay, Miss Wowie."

Wowie scoots onto the seat and Nikki fastens a black hair bib around Wowie's neck, asking, "So what's new?"

"Actually…" Wowie gives Amana Anne a wink. Amana Anne opens her magazine, wanting no part of this.

"We're thinking about using someone new for a bright idea we have for a little project," Wowie says. "Ever use Sandstone Printing?"

Amana Anne hates when Wowie "pink lies," as she calls them. ("I'll grant you they ain't lily-white," Wowie'll at least admit that much.) Amana Anne shoots her a look, which Wowie ignores.

"Oh my, yes, we use them for all our printing," Nikki says as she spritzes Wowie's bangs. "You cannot ask for better quality, right Jolene?" Nikki picks up and points a rattail comb at Jolene like she'll pick a fight if anyone *would* in fact ask for better quality.

"Yep." Jolene's squeezing the last of the hair dye onto the elderly lady's head and the plastic bottle makes a little suction sound like it's gasping for its final breath.

"What's this bright idea, Miss Wowie?" Nikki snips Wowie's bangs, and Wowie blows out of her bottom lip to get the hair off her nose.

"You want to explain your bright idea, Sweetheart?" Wowie calls over, but Amana Anne raises her magazine to cover her face and pretends she doesn't hear her.

"Hey, your magazine's upside down, Banana."

116

"You so fun, Miss Wowie." Nikki has a little tinkling laugh. "Reason I ask is Mr. Sandstone gives a nice price break for church printing."

"He and his wife used to go to our church," Jolene comes out of the shampoo room, takes off her plastic dye gloves with a *snap* and tosses them into the garbage can. Amana Anne's stomach churns. *Wife?*

Wowie shoots Amana Anne a look that says she'll slay the man if he got her hopes up for Amana Anne to finally find Prince Charming II and he's married.

"Cute couple." Nikki checks the cut of the bangs. "Her so petite, and him so big."

"Used to play football," Jolene places several of her brushes in a disinfectant container. "Semi-pro after college."

"Then he got some kind of injury." Nikki trims Wowie's length.

Wowie gives her daughter a look like she wants to give Jake a more current injury. Amana Anne's feeling a little wounded herself over the wife information.

"His knee," Jolene chimes in.

"I thought his back," Nikki's eyebrows come together in a facial question mark. "And Jo, what was it happened to his wife?"

"Breast cancer," Jolene answers.

"I thought cervical," Nikki says.

Jolene shakes her head no.

"Anyway, something womanly," Nikki concludes. "Maybe it had something to do with why she couldn't have kids. Who knows?"

Now Amana Anne feels a pang of empathy. She and Nathan had wanted children but she had three miscarriages. Then Nathan was gone.

"You shoulda seen the Church Casserole Brigade bringing him dinner after she passed on." Jolene says, rolling her eyes, laughing and then covering her mouth. Amana Anne's not sure if it's because of the inappropriateness of laughing or to hide a front tooth that's half chipped out. "He probably didn't have to cook for a year," Jolene concludes.

The old lady pipes up from the shampoo room, without looking up from her tabloid, "Don't forget about me with this color, Jolene, while you're out there gossiping to beat the band."

"We won't, Mrs. Abernathy," Jolene calls to her, making a dismissive wave, then whispers to Wowie. "We couldn't forget if we wanted to."

Wowie wags a playful finger at Jolene, and Jolene giggles, this time forgetting to cover her mouth.

"So Jo, how long's it been since Mrs. Sandstone passed?" Nikki asks.

"Oh, several years now," Jolene says.

"I thought just a couple." Nikki squints and looks off as if trying to see into the past to determine the time frame.

"I don't know why you keep asking me questions and then telling me I'm wrong." Jolene's miffed.

"Hey Jolene," Mrs. Abernathy yells. "You know my hair absorbs color in the time it takes to turn a hotcake."

Jolene stalks off with a huff to shampoo her.

"Jolene has no concept of time," Nikki explains in a low voice to Wowie and Amana Anne. "She'll say, 'I'll help ya in a sec,' and three months later she shows up."

Nikki offers her mirror to Wowie. "Would you like a look, Miss Wowie?"

"Naw, Wusiwug." Wowie jumps up. "What You See Is What You Get."

Nikki chuckles and takes off Wowie's plastic cape. "Now, Miss Wowie and Miss Amana Anne, I'm taking a print job in tomorrow and I'll tell Mr. Sandstone about your project, see if he can give you special treatment."

"No, no," Amana Anne jumps up like something bit her. "That really isn't necessary." She slips a five on the counter while Wowie brushes off her capris.

"But I'm happy to." Nikki nods thanks to Amana Anne.

118

"We don't even know if we'll move forward on that little bright idea, but thanks anyway, Nikki." Amana Anne shoots Wowie a look. *See what you've gotten me into this time?* Wowie has an amazing ability to shirk off all blame.

"Oh, we'll move forward on it." Wowie heads for the door with her Queen Mother wave for Nikki and Jolene, which they imitate back.

Amana Anne holds the door for Wowie but has to hold *herself* back from swatting Wowie's behind as they go out. "I just realized I *do* have a printing job, Mom. I need a sign for when I'm with you that says, *Please Adopt My Mother!*"

"If they're rich, I'm in."

"Great, because you'll have plenty of time to scout for potential adopters on your long walk home." Amana Anne hits her car keypad once for just the driver side door to unlock. She slides in and starts the car, push-buttoning the windows down a couple inches to let out the hot air.

Wowie thrusts a hitchhiking thumb out with a jaunty twist, and hitches up her capris to show a veiny leg. Wowie's found an audience for her antics in some outdoor café diners next-door and they're getting a kick out of her. Amana Anne pops open the lock on Wowie's door, trying not to laugh and give too much positive reinforcement.

"Forget the curtain call, Momsy," Amana Anne calls through the open window. "I have to meet with Eliz."

Wowie plops in and Amana Anne wonders – with a healthy dose of cautious apprehension – just what Eliz is cooking up that's supposedly going to change her life.

Gas on the Fire

The only reason Eliz even knows of Quentie's is because it's next to the liquor store. She popped in once, but upon realizing it was God Stuff, she made a hairpin turn out. You'd think Eliz would have been forewarned by the sign outside reading, "New Beginnings Bookstore," and the stenciling in pretty cursive on the window, *Specializing in Spiritual Self-Help and God Help. You do your part, God already did His.*

But today Eliz made a beeline here because she has a few zillion questions. Big questions, burning questions, like: *Who is this God who spoke to her? How do you get a new life? And can she get a miracle in a week?* If this isn't the place for her to find some answers, she doesn't know where she would.

Inside, the shop somehow feels familiar, like a second home, with friendly forest-green velour chairs to curl up in and warm sunshine slanting and shadowing onto the long stacks of books. Next to the chairs, on a little round table, is a Bible, and a glistening pitcher of complimentary lemonade with ice moons and lemon slices. Eliz noticed the refreshing scent of lemons as soon as she entered. Aromatherapy for the soul. Even though the library's just up the street, it doesn't have the small coziness of Quentie's, or refreshments. She's on her third glass of the refreshingly lemony blend. It has a nice bittersweet bite to it and puts a lid on her hunger.

When Eliz got here earlier this afternoon, she meandered down the wide aisles scanning titles. She tried to pull out a couple of books, but her neck stung like someone shot a dart into it, so instead, she sat at the little table that had *The Message* version of the Bible already on it and just flipped through the pages. On the back cover there was an endorsement quote from Bono, the U2 musician and activist. He said *The Message* has been a "great strength" to him, which encouraged her because she could sure use some spiritual muscle, pronto.

Eliz always imagined reading the Bible to be as exciting as a lifetime subscription to the *Congressional Quarterly*. Now, she saw it as a kind of treasure hunt. The more she thought about what happened last night, the more she couldn't deny it was *real*. According to Amana Anne, all the promises of God were for *her* as His daughter. So Eliz wants to find these promises, and do whatever's her part of the deal as quickly as possible.

She also has a driving need to know: *Who is this Jesus who told her of His unconditional love last night?*

One thing she *did* know: Jesus wasn't just another great teacher, like some people claimed. Logic told her He either was exactly who He said He was – God – or a madman and a liar. She intends to read *The Case for Christ* as soon as she can lift it. It was written by an atheist attorney who set out to disprove Christianity, and in light of the evidence, became a Christian.

Eliz had long *wanted* a new life. But she also wanted to circumvent the whole God being in charge thing and having to give up stuff. It dawns on her as she reads the Bible that maybe it isn't so much about giving up as *receiving* things… like this unbelievable love.

Even as a little girl, love always seemed as evasive as

trying to spell it out in her daily staple of canned alphabet soup. Now, she had it, always and forever, simply through grace. She also loved receiving that indescribable peace she felt last night, and was still basking in the afterglow of it today. And since she desperately needs direction for her life, that's another huge perk with God. Up until now, Eliz often felt like life was using her as a battering ram. But she read in Amana Anne's book this morning: *With God, things don't happen* to *you, they happen* for *you.*

Eliz has been so absorbed in her pondering and reading these last few hours that she didn't even much notice people coming and going. The few times she did look up to pour more lemonade, there'd only been a few older ladies sitting in reading chairs on the other side of the room, and once, a young couple buying a book.

One of the elderly ladies told the couple, "Oh, just leave the money and take whatever change from that basket." She pointed to a little white wicker basket of dollar bills and some change at the checkout counter.

"Quentie's not officially open for business on the Lord's Day," the other elderly lady explained. "Just open for browsers."

Eliz wasn't sure if she'd even seen Quentie. If so, she was one of the absorbed readers. *Anyone* could steal *anything*. What kind of businesswoman was this?

"Excellent taste, Eliz." Amana Anne comes up behind Eliz, tapping her finger on *The Message*. Eliz looks up from reading as Amana Anne slips down beside her. The late-day sun is peering in the window behind Amana Anne. Eliz's eyes are sore, and she plants her elbows on the table, propping her curled fists under her chin to give her aching neck a break.

"I still have excellent taste in men, too, so don't think I'll be joining the nunnery just because I'm reading a Bible, Bana."

"No worry, Sister Eliz, on that. I'm more worried about

what this big idea of yours is." Amana Anne pours herself a glass of lemonade.

"Well, Banaboo," Eliz stretches her cramped legs and gingerly rotates her head, what little she's able. "Wowie told me about your agent thing going south, so she and I have been putting our heads together to help you."

Amana Anne thinks Wowie and Eliz "putting their heads together to help" is tantamount to hearing, *We've got that gasoline for your fire, Ma'am.*

"Therefore," Eliz sighs like she's offering herself up for martyrdom, "I'm gonna be your manager-slash-agent."

Amana Anne can't help smacking her hand to her forehead. "*That* sounds like a recipe for disaster."

Eliz holds her hand up over her eyes like she's searching the table and not finding what she's looking for. "I'm not exactly seeing any other options on yo table, Banana." She lowers her hand down on the table with a *thump*, which hurts her neck. "Ooooouch."

"Ooooouch here, too, because this is very nervous-making, Eliz."

"Just be open and, as you write in your book, prayerfully consider it, Bana." Eliz uses her quoting voice, "Our fears are a potential treasure-chest of self-knowledge and growth."

"I hope I'm not going to be sorry I *gave* you my book. Or that I'm even *open* to prayerfully considering this. Out of sheer desperation, I might add."

"I'm on the desperado wagon myself, Bana-babe. *You* need a manager. *I* need a job. We had a lay-off at work."

"Oh, Eliz, I'm sorry…"

Eliz interrupts. "It's fine because I just read, God works *all* things together for our good. We either start believing and living that, or we may as well jump ship right now. This is *supposed* to be our week to *believe*. More to the point, I get fifteen percent of what you make."

"Eliz," Amana Anne says in a measured tone, trying not to hurt her feelings, "you have no leads, no contacts…"

Eliz waves her hands to stop Amana Anne from delineating. "I *know* you think this is like the blind leading the blind."

"More like the blind, deaf, mute and lame leading the blind."

"Okay, I'm the Helen Keller of managers, but as your book quotes from Joan of Arc, 'I was born to do this.'"

Amana Anne appears unconvinced.

"Believe!" Eliz shoots up her arm to imitate Amana Anne's signature move, and yelps in agony. "Okay, Bana, all this convincing is literally killing me. Let me just say I'm dreaming big for all of us. Like you wrote about in your wonderful *Don't Go to the Ocean with a Teaspoon* chapter, which you obviously need to revisit."

"I'm torn between thanking you for believing in me and wanting to put a sock in your mouth."

"There's probably a long line on the sock thing." Eliz rises and works out a kink in her back with her fist. She hadn't realized she'd been sitting for so many hours straight. Outside, the last skids of the sunset's pinks and purples skirt across the sky. "We'll regroup in the morning. I think that's enough for you to absorb tonight. I'm saving the best for tomorrow."

"I'll put out an interstate alert," Amana Anne says warily, taking their lemonade glasses to the counter and dropping a couple of bucks in the donation basket for the Women's Shelter. She expects Quentie will be in any minute to lock up. Sometimes she's just across the street at Café Coco's catching up with friends.

"Go on ahead of me, and I'll be Ms. OCD for a change." Eliz wipes the table where water droplets from their lemonade glasses have pooled. "Enjoy the only time in your life you're ever gonna beat me up that hill, Bana-boo."

"Don't dawdle." Amana Anne heads for the door. "It's getting dark."

"Dawdle? I love those eighteenth-century words you pull

124

out, Gram. Now go home and read your *own* words."

Once Amana Anne is out of sight, Eliz tosses the napkins in the trash and heads out the door. The thing is, Eliz suddenly wants – no *needs* – to at least *look* at the booze through the liquor store window. Like it's a booze binky for her to visually imbibe in the pretty champagne bottles even if she can't drink – something Amana Anne would never understand.

Eliz steps outside into the evening as the pastel sunset colors melt in the sky, sinking into the first soft shades of night. Oakhaven always gives Eliz that small-town feeling of safety. People are out walking their dogs, even late at night, and old folks sit on porches listening to the sound of crickets. Somewhere in the distance a dog barks, an off-key sound. Eliz is feeling off-key herself as she peers into the gleaming glass of the liquor store.

Booze has such a kumbaya, calming effect on her. Like everyone and everything will be alright, although a part of her knows, of course, that booze ultimately always makes things worse. Then again, didn't she just read that Jesus' first miracle was creating more wine for a wedding party? Jesus sure had His priorities straight. For that alone, He had a leg up with her.

Yes, but He didn't get a DUI.

As she peers at the champagne bottles in the window, she can almost feel the slow, happy, warming sensation that seeps into every pore of her body when the bubbly goes down sweet and easy and bright. Eliz realizes she *must* have at least enough spare change and crumpled-up dollars stuffed in jacket pockets and purses to buy *some* booze, should she get frenzied for it, which is definitely on the horizon.

She reasons with herself about why buying food and not starving to death this week would actually be the far wiser choice, heeding something inside herself like an inner warning. Was it her angel?

At least I'm aware and hearing the better *voices now,*

Eliz congratulates herself. She decides she'll probably be so famished she'll opt for groceries over gnawing her own limbs. But just for now, Eliz concentrates on the vibrantly-colored, enticing bottles of champagne, sparkling wine, tequila and rum in the polished window.

For one of the few times in her life, the "better" part of her jumps in again to reiterate that she's definitely not going to buy booze even *if* she finds enough money, and nudges her to get moving past the liquor store.

As deep twilight closes in around her like an evening cloak, another part of her, the one that seems to always get its way, still notes the time the liquor store opens in the morning.

Just in case.

The Replacement

"You the Lord Bus," the border guard pointing at Casey yells in broken English.

"He remembers us from previous years," Leroy explains, giving the guard a beep and friendly wave. Casey realizes she's sitting right above the outside stenciling of "The Lord's Bus" that the border guard was pointing at. The guard gives a brown-toothed smile and waves them through. Casey doesn't know how long she's been holding her breath, but she expels more air than the Goodyear Blimp could hold.

Thank You, thank You, thank You.

It's a relief to be safely back in the U.S., but she *has* to tell Myrna, Birdie and Leroy about the passport, so they're not unknowingly breaking international law. She waits until they're back at the church and Leroy and the ladies are off the bus with her. Casey's glad the kids stay on to finish a game on Dylan's BlackBerry.

"I have something to tell you..." Casey begins sheepishly, and they all look at her expectantly. "I didn't know we were going to Mexico," she confesses. "I didn't realize until after we crossed the border that I needed a passport."

"Oh, my," Myrna grimaces, visually checking in with

Birdie, who shrugs like *uh-oh.*

"Maybe we can get you one," Birdie suggests.

"Ahhh, that would eat a chunk of time and it's just a five-day mission," Leroy says nonchalantly, twisting his torso to crack his back. "Most of the guards know the bus from us coming all the time and hardly ever check."

"Sometimes we do get pulled over though," Myrna doesn't want to say it but feels compelled to, in total honesty. "And I don't know *what* they'd do because we've always had our passports."

"Believe me, I understand. I don't want to jeopardize the group by continuing to come," Casey says, hoping they protest, because she doesn't have the money to buy a passport and would be humiliated to borrow it from people she's known all of a day.

"The *group* wouldn't be going to jail, much as we'd want to keep you company," Leroy says with a laugh. "Just you. So it's up to you if you stay or go."

"Don't mind Mr. Sensitivity." Myrna puts her arm around Casey. "Sleep and pray on it, then decide in the morning. Either way, we sure appreciate all you did today."

"On the other hand, we're *not* appreciated on cooking and KP duty except by Zia," Birdie says, linking arms with Myrna. "Then we get to be night guards sleeping with the girls in the ladies' lodge while Leroy tames the guys in the men's lodge." Birdie drags Myrna off. "See you *mañana,* Casey."

An elderly lady built like a matchstick in a skirt comes up the stairs from the social hall and exchanges greetings with Birdie and Myrna as they head to the kitchen.

"We'll just keep this little state secret to ourselves, Casey," Leroy says in a low voice as the kids pound off the bus. "Especially from Mrs. Nettleson, the head of volunteers. Looks like she's coming to introduce herself to you."

"Mrs. Mettle-some," Dylan says at the sight of the elderly lady, and the kids guffaw.

"Scoot!" Leroy directs the kids.

"How do ya scoot?" T asks. "Is it like…?" He dashes around the bus and the other kids chase after him, screaming. Leroy waves to Mrs. Nettleson and grabs a plastic garbage bag from the bus door handle, hopping on the bus as if to avoid a dark wind.

"Hello, I'm Mrs. Nettleson," she gives Casey a curt nod.

"You must be Mrs. Swanson, the lady we'll be replacing."

"Pardon?" Casey heard but hoped she didn't.

"I'm sorry, but I didn't know your church was going to pull a switch at the last minute." Mrs. Nettleson summons a forced, apologetic laugh and a smile that pulls her lips back tight against her teeth. "The Lord's day is light lifting, but the rest of the week we need a strong man who can distribute hundred-pound food sacks. So now you can just vacation if you'd like, Mrs. Swanson."

There's a scattering of loud laughter like a sudden rainfall from the teens as they thunder toward them, chasing each other.

"Your replacement is coming in the morning, a Mr. Zagot," Mrs. Nettleson says.

On hearing her last words, T skids to a stop. Dylan plows into his back.

"Ziggy Zagot, the ex-pro wrestler?" T asks Mrs. Nettleson.

"Yes, and Mr. Zagot is still quite able-bodied," Mrs. Nettleson informs the kids proudly, like she's responsible.

"He used to like, zigzag the ropes like…" T becomes a human Ping-Pong ball against the bus, which makes the girls giggle.

He bounces into Leroy as Leroy comes off the bus with a filled garbage bag.

"Skedaddle," Leroy says to T and the kids, pointing to the social hall. "Pizza."

"Pizza!" Kanashia squeals and the kids charge like a herd of wildebeests to dinner.

"Pizza is Friday night," Mrs. Nettleson corrects Leroy like a school matron.

"Yep," he affirms. "They can be early. In fact they can stay there and wait for it all week. We'll swap all the hooligans for Casey, this Zagot, and more supplies," Leroy says. "She's better than all the kids put together."

Go Leroy! Casey thinks, cheering him on in her mind, not just because she has nowhere on earth to go and doesn't want to go home, but because she's never had someone stand up for her like this, verbalizing her worth.

"We agreed to mission mentor the children, Mr. Tucker," Mrs. Nettleson says. "We can't just leave them on the sidewalk."

"Maybe *you* can't." Leroy ties the garbage bag and tosses it fifteen feet with a *swoosh* into a garbage can outside the schoolroom door.

"Mr. Tucker, please," Mrs. Nettleson sighs like he's a bit of a hopeless incorrigible himself as he jumps back on the bus.

Mrs. Nettleson lightly touches Casey's arm in the most minimalistic gesture of compassion. "Mrs. Swanson, you understand, as good stewards, we need the best qualified people for the job, and every square inch of space for medical supplies, food and water."

"I'm actually pretty strong." Skip always had her schlepping twenty-pound bags of mulch and all kinds of handyman pick-ups he was too lazy to get himself from Best Buy Hardware and Lowe's.

"I'm sure you are, dear, at five-pound bags of sugar. Not one-hundred pounds of beans."

Mrs. Nettleson pats Casey's arm. "You go right ahead and make other plans. This *is* California. Lots to see. We can get you fantastic deals for a rental car and all the sites through a church member if you just let me know what you want."

How about a couple thousand in cash, all in twenties,

please? Casey resents when people assume everyone has discretionary vacation cash hammocking around. Mrs. Nettleson turns on her heel and walks off, putting her hand up behind her as more of a close-of-business than a wave.

Leroy steps off the bus with some scrunched-up scraps of paper in his fist that the kids were throwing at each other, which he wads into one big ball.

"Well, at least the passport's a moot point." Casey tries to laugh but feels like crying.

"We'll just pray for the Lord's will and direction," Leroy says calmly, tossing the paper ball into the garbage can. "Let's just see what God will do." Leroy gives Casey a little nod of confidence and heads for the kitchen, whistling.

She wished *she* had his confidence. Casey trudges to the nursery, her head swirling. *Was I actually just fired as a volunteer? What kind of a mess have I gotten myself into? What now?*

It's too mind-boggling to even try to decide right this minute; Casey's so physically exhausted, she doesn't have the energy to think. Something in her feels like she just *can't* go home. Nothing's been resolved. It's not like she has a ticket anyway. So… where to go? And to do what exactly with no money?

Later, stripped down to her sore, fatigued flesh, she soaks her weary bones in Epsom salts, then downs what Zia euphemistically calls dinner: veggies, herbs and a bunch of gravel or tree bark or whatever the crunchily health-prone, unidentifiable objects are in her salad.

She's tormented by worries throughout the evening, until she remembers Leroy's words: "We'll just pray for the Lord's will and direction." Here she is, once again *worrying* when she could be praying.

"Why do you think there's a 'fear not' in the Bible for every day of the year?" Amana Anne always says. Casey grabs Amana Anne's book from her bag and opens to the chapter *Stop Worrying and Start Changing Your Life.* Then

131

she reads every Bible quote she can find about believing, faith, God's love and the Holy Spirit's direction, and the Word really *is* like medicine for her soul.

Later on, as she drops off to sleep after prayers, her last image though, is of the countless Mexican workers she saw on both sides of the border waiting on the dusty street corners, their hopeful gazes on dirt-stained faces meeting every vehicle that approached, begging for work. Any work. *"Trabajo, por favor."* Just enough to feed themselves, their families, to survive for one more day.

Her very last thought before she capitulates to the strong snare of sleep is, *Save me a space, amigos. I may be there mañana.*

~ Monday ~

Jake

Morning light spills through the outstretched arms of oak trees in front of Jake's print shop like a welcoming hug of sunshine as Amana Anne pulls up. A tasteful burnt gold "Sandstone Printing" is in a sophisticated, but friendly, typeface over the top of the glass door. One vibrantly colorful poster of sea life fills an entire floor-to-ceiling window, advertising their ink specialties. On weekdays, the print shop is the first of Jake's three businesses to open, and since it's right here in Oakhaven, Amana Anne decided this was her best bet for finding him.

She really wanted to camp outside the front door and accost him before his car came to a complete stop in the parking lot when he opened at eight. But she took forever trying on seven different outfits this morning – *seven* – like she was going to the prom or something, before settling on a red v-neck with capped sleeves and white shorts.

Amana Anne walks into the shop and notes with satisfaction that everything looks clean and tidy. Stacks of paper are piled in an orderly fashion. The pens, pencils, scissors and stapler for customers at the counter look relatively sanitary. It smells like new paper, and there's the sound of multiple copies being made by the girl behind the counter. Her nametag reads "Shari-Beth" and she has cat-like, almost feral green eyes and long, wispily-thin brown hair. Shari-Beth nods hello to her while counting copies and Amana Anne smiles and nods a greeting back.

"Whoooo-a." A heavy bald man waiting for his copies says it like he's trying to rein in a horse. His rolls of fat are bulging in a tight, dingy-white T-shirt and pants that make him look like the Michelin Tire Man. "Even the big boss's pitching in today. Who died?"

At the sight of Jake down the hall, Amana Anne's heart pounds in her rib cage. She feels a tremor and thinks for one scary moment they're having an earthquake. Until she realizes it's her knees shimmying.

Amana Anne watches Jake's straight, powerful back as he retreats down the hall to a stack of boxes. She feels like she can't stop looking at him. She doesn't even want to try. The azure-blue shirt he's wearing looks crisp and fresh. He's in nicely worn jeans and walks like an athlete. Best of all, Jake has a wonderful casualness about him, like he really doesn't know how great-looking he is.

"Travis called in," Shari-Beth explains to the Michelin Man. "Claims he's so sick he's flatlining."

The Michelin Man lets out a hearty laugh. "Monday-itis."

Jake comes down the hall carrying a huge box, his muscles taut. Amana Anne's tremors subside a bit when Jake spots her and his face opens in pleasure.

"Hey, Amana Anne," he says it like they've known each other forever, and her heart flutters. *He remembers my name.* She likes the way he speaks her name, easily, fluidly, not how some people flub over it like it's a tongue twister. He puts the box on the counter.

"Hi," she says, so softly it's almost subliminal.

"Great to see you," he adds, sincerely, she thinks, as he runs a careless hand through his thick hair.

That's just good business, her practical voice puts her in her place, *he probably says that to everyone.*

Realizing she's just standing there dreamily, Amana Anne starts talking fast, like usual when she's nervous. "I just wanted to explain that the other night... I mistook you for my friend's date – who had the accident – my friend, not the date." Her voice sounds tight and escalating, even to her. "And I was supposed to tell him... the date who ended up not showing up... so I thought he was you."

The Michelin Man, who appears to be eavesdropping, looks confused.

"And I thought it was my charisma," Jake says kiddingly.

The Michelin Man chortles.

Amana Anne notes that three more customers came in the door in the space of the two minutes she's been there. "So, I can see that you're busy, but I just wanted you to know."

"I'm sorry about your friend's accident but glad I got to meet you, Amana Anne," Jake says, not seeming to notice the people who came in.

"Thank you and... that's all." Amana Anne wonders why she sounds so stiff and robotic, like she's reporting in for duty. Actually, with her voice this high, more like Porky Pig used to sign off his cartoons with "That's all, folks."

"So... goodbye." Amana Anne decides to cut her losses.

Do not *stupidly salute the man again,* she warns herself and sees that twinkle of amusement in Jake's eyes and wonders if he's remembering the same thing. Amana Anne heads for the door before she can spout any more lameness and her heart does a little jump when Jake crosses to open it for her.

"Nikki was in and mentioned you have a project for us," Jake says, and the nearness of the man and his blue eyes make Amana Anne positively swoony. "I'd love to handle it personally," he says.

"Oh, sure, great, yes," Amana Anne says, and wonders in the back of her mind exactly what "project" other than herself she's saying every affirmative word in the dictionary to Jake handling personally.

137

"Hey Jake, why do *I* always get pushed off on Travis?" The Michelin Man asks like he's in on the conversation, and apparently he is. "You never tell *me* you'd love to handle it personally."

"Because I wouldn't," Jake says kiddingly, and the Michelin Man erupts in a hearty chuckle.

"Thank you, Jake." Amana Anne can smell his clean scent, like from soap and the outdoors. She realizes she's been standing there sucking in his scent and letting out his air conditioning while he holds the door open.

"Hope to see you again soon," Jake says as she squeezes past him. A texting teenager takes advantage of the open door and slips in. Amana Anne hears two customers call Jake as the door closes, which is a saving grace because her mouth is suddenly so dry her teeth are sticking to her lips and she can't turn to get out a goodbye anyway without looking like a grinning Cheshire cat.

She welcomes the jolt of humid heat as she walks to her car, hoping it might dissipate this floaty fog she's in from him. Maybe she can get a grip on herself enough to drive home. The sound of her own cell blinging a text message brings her back to reality.

Amana Anne takes the phone out of her pocket to see the good news, that it's a text from Wowie. So her once-frozen cell still works.

The bad news is it's a three-number message.

911.

The Venture

"You realize you're putting us all on the line here," Eliz's boss – or rather *former* boss – Ed, says in his straight-shooter way.

He's on her cell's speakerphone because it still stings Eliz's neck to hold her phone up for very long. Plus, she's hands-free to pillage the purses that are piled up on the dining room table. She's not even out of her nightie yet, but booze money's a Level Five priority.

"I know I'm asking you all to bite the bullet with me, Ed, and I'm not doing it lightly." *Just desperately*, Eliz thinks, taking a sip of strong black coffee from her mug. At least she had some Columbian left in her otherwise bare kitchen cupboard to make a cup. Hopefully it won't upset her empty tummy, just get her jazzed enough to attempt water aerobics without re-spraining her neck later today.

"Plus our vendors could go out to dry," Ed adds.

"Remember when you said I had vision and brilliant ideas?" Ed was the only boss she's ever had who believed in her. "That everyone would work for me one day?" Eliz doesn't wait for an answer. "Trust me, Ed, my friend Amana Anne's gonna take off like wildfire."

Ed's uncharacteristically quiet for a long moment,

weighing the stakes. "I'm on board if Jamaica helps project-manage because I can't devote full time to this. It's up to you guys to reel in the rest of the gang, Chief," he says, and signs off.

One down and five to go, Eliz thinks as she speed-dials Jamaica while counting the dollars and change she's found in her purse. Being an unorganized slob has its perks. For one thing, the most important thing actually at present, you could always find spare change and crumpled dollar bills *somewhere*, even in odd, surprising places like the two dollars she found scrounging through some dirty jeans in the laundry.

Already she feels better, just knowing she *almost* has enough for champagne. The deep security of thinking she may soon be able to have at least a temporary shelter in the storm makes her a little lightheaded with happiness. Or maybe it's because she hasn't had anything to eat.

Which could lead to the booze turning on me again if I drink on an empty stomach, she thinks.

Don't think about it, the inner voice that allows her to always give in to booze placates her.

The newer, sensible, spiritual inner voice asks, *How's "not thinking" working for you? Isn't "not thinking" what got you into all this trouble in the first place?*

Jamaica answers her phone, unceremoniously, bringing Eliz back to her present challenge. "What, Jailbird?"

"Hey, Jami-cam, how would you like to team lead on the freelance project of a lifetime?"

Jamaica doesn't even nibble. "Sorry, Jailbird, but I'm now a NEET: Not in Employment, Education or Training. Funemployment. Ya know, a little spell of leisure when I can employ some fun. Oh, that's right," Jamaica says as if she's suddenly remembering something, "I announced this while we were waiting *all day* at my brunch for you to bring the bubbly."

"I was going to," Eliz lies. "In fact I still have the bottle here. But I was so bummed I just would have bummeranged everyone to the max."

"You bummeranged *me* to the max, I can tell you that much."

"Listen, I'll make it up to you. I'm giving everyone a cut of the profits on this project. If you and Ed help oversee, I'll give yinz the biggest percentage."

Eliz sips her coffee carefully now because the lower it gets, the more she has to tilt her head back and it pinches her neck.

"Oooouuu, I'm gonna need my calculator on that one," Jamaica says. "Let's see. A nice, hefty slice a nothing, gee-man-ezey, I'm shocked. That's *nothing*. And that's what I want to do with *yo lame ideas*. Nothing!"

"I get that you're ticked at me, Jamee-Kamee, but don't flush a good project down the toi-tee over it. I'm sorry I didn't come back to your party, okay?"

"Speaking of sorry, where's your sorry, lazy self? *We're* all here cleaning out our desks."

"I sprained my neck and can't turn my head. There's no way I can get to work unless I drive backwards."

"You've probably driven drunk backwards and in six-inch high heels, you just don't remember," Jamaica laughs. "You know I carpool and we already got five so unless we strap ya to the bumper, no can do. Have you ever heard of a bus? They're like cars, but with lotsa seats."

"All those stops and starts would hurt my neck. I'll work from home and set up a website from here. Okay, project manager?" Eliz asks pleadingly.

"You *got* a pain in yo neck and you *are* a pain in *my* neck." Jamaica says, but Eliz can tell she's softening. "So what you need marketed?"

"A friend of mine's giving a huge seminar."

"A friend of *yours*? What's a lowlife friend a yours gonna teach anyone? Dope Smuggling and Drug Running 101?" Jamaica laughs so hard she snorts.

141

Eliz understands the guilt-by-association verdict. No point arguing. "I'll e-mail you my friend's head-shot and her book in an attachment. See for yourself, Jam-o. She ain't no lame-o."

By the time Jamaica calls her back, Eliz has changed into a bright orange tankini with a ruffled skirt and sprayed on sun block. Jamaica doesn't even say hello. "A nobody giving her first seminar ain't exactly The Second Coming news, but she *looks* legit. Like one-a those lady preacher types. I skimmed the book. It's cool. This *could* have legs."

"Thank you, Ms. Jamaica, and we're going to name a country after you in your honor," Eliz teases. "Whoops, we already did."

"Just make sure you have non-bounce-ity-bounce checks for our team and the vendors by the end of the week," Jamaica warns. "I *hope* you know what you're doing for a change."

Me, too, Eliz thinks, as she closes her cell and heads for the pool.

Me, too.

Cowboy Joe

Well, at least I'll be well turned-out for the soup kitchen line or wherever I'm headed, Casey thinks, pulling her best T-shirt (with brightly colored, sparkly fish) over her head. Not only can she tuck the T-shirt in her black adjustable shorts, she's also down another waist button. Everything else is neatly packed in her getaway bag and sitting by the door in case she has to leave immediately after loading the bus.

When she mounts the bus steps to help Leroy squeeze the supplies and water containers into every spare centimeter, every muscle in her body protests. Muscles she didn't know she *had* lament. She has bigger problems though this morning, like where she'll go next, since before she knows it, they're carrying on their final gallons of water.

An ear-rupturing scream from Jelly (being tickled by T) breaks open the quiet of the morning as the teens storm up the concrete stairs en masse. Myrna and Birdie trail with Mrs. Nettleson, who shakes her head at the kids' unruliness. The teens rush onto the bus, with Jelly bringing up the rear. She tugs her tight top down over her hips, but when she clomps up the bus steps, it snaps back up like a window shade.

Even before Mrs. Nettleson reaches Leroy, she begins speaking to him, like she doesn't want to waste time. "Mr.

Zagot's en route, but he's hit a smidgeon of traffic."

Myrna and Birdie exchange "good mornings" with Casey and stand uncertainly by the bus door, like sentries awaiting orders.

"About how long of a smidgeon?" Leroy asks.

Mrs. Nettleson consults her watch. "Not more than an hour."

"Do you know how many people we can serve in an hour, or how many we'll have to cut if we *lose* an hour?" Leroy asks, taking the coolers from Myrna and Birdie and putting them on the front seat. "When Mr. Zagot gets here, please tell him he can line up the forty gallon jugs and all the supplies for tomorrow along the curb."

He motions for Myrna, Birdie and Casey to get on the bus and they quickly comply before Mrs. Nettleson can protest.

"That'll help us get a jump on things in the morning." Leroy scoots into the driver's seat.

"But, Mr…" Mrs. Nettleson starts.

"We need to be good stewards of our *time*," Leroy gives her a smile and wave as he closes the door and takes off, leaving Mrs. Nettleson with her mouth agape.

Casey sinks onto her blanketed seat with a wave of relief as the bus jerks forward.

"We're glad you're still with us, Casey," Myrna says. "And not just because we like you a lot and you're the best helper we ever had."

"Also because we were afraid Zia would have expected us to drink and eat this." Birdie hands the cooler back and Casey smiles her thanks, clinging to it like it's the verification that she's indeed granted a reprieve of another twenty-four hours. *Thank You, Lord.*

Even a sludgie sounds good right about now since Casey realizes she's starving. She downs Zia's cleansing "slime" and eats most of the veggies by the time they reach the market in Tijuana. It's a good thing she's quelled her appetite before taking in all the vendor food aromas because when the sweet scents of mangos and pineapples float into the bus on the light summer breeze, she's almost tempted to hang out the window and grab some. Piles of bright tropical fruits cascade like waterfalls on every stand; sunshine yellow and green bananas shoulder up to papayas boasting vibrant reds and oranges. Black avocados sun themselves on a flowered oilcloth while carrots, tomatoes, yellow squash and watermelons elbow each other for space.

The bus weaves through the street past mountains of herbs and spices as Casey inhales whiffs of cilantro, garlic, cloves, cinnamon and oregano. Coffee-colored sauces are flanked by red and green pastes. Nothing is sealed or wrapped. Everything's out to be touched and tasted, enjoyed. *Amana Anne would call the Department of Health,* Casey thinks with a laugh.

Leroy pulls over and parks at a stand featuring what looks like hundred-pound sacks of beans, flour and rice. Each row of burlap sacks has an open bag up in front so shoppers – mostly Mexicans and a few American tourists – can feel and eye the texture and quality. The bus engine kicks off with a sputter and a lingering hiss as they all disembark. The kids immediately zip off to explore.

"Those kids take to work like a cat to water," Birdie says, watching them vamoose.

Casey sizes up the hundred-pound sacks, wondering about the work ahead for *her* and how she can possibly fill this "Ziggie's" shoes.

"Don't worry, we're not getting those behemoths," Leroy comes up behind her. "I can't lift like I used to anyway. They have twenty-five pound bags toward the back. More per pound, but still a good price. Plus the workers'll load on this end."

"Cowboy Joe's the owner," Myrna says, motioning with her head to a short man with skin more brown than olive. "He loves old Westerns." He's in a faded, red cowboy hat and beige cowboy boots. His boot heels are so worn to slanted edges that they look like he walked from the Gulf of Mexico to Tijuana in them.

"He's a Christian, but Cowboy Joe's also one of the best hagglers here in Tijuana," Birdie informs Casey with a chuckle.

An old gentleman garbed in a voluminous, colorful serape pays Cowboy Joe from a wad of rolled-up cash. Cowboy Joe's workers haul the man's sacks to a new, pickup truck parked amid the jalopies on the dirt lot. Cowboy Joe spots Leroy and waves, giving a wide smile.

"*Hola*," Cowboy Joe greets them cheerily. Now that he's up close, Casey sees his cowboy hat is a predominant red weave of multicolored straw – purple, orange, green, blue, like a kid's birthday party hat. He wears its dark, frayed cord knotted under his chin.

Leroy and Cowboy Joe talk business in rapid Spanish while Birdie and Myrna exchange a few words with the workers. Casey surveys the sacks that are almost as tall as her. She's hit with a pang of guilt that the donated church money won't stretch as far as it would have with Ziggie being able to carry these hundred-pounders.

You have not because you ask not, comes into Casey's mind, and an idea. She sends up a quick prayer for favor, then says to Leroy, "Would you ask Cowboy Joe, if we buy in large quantities, can he give us four of the twenty-five pound bags at the hundred-pound bag price, please, because as Christians we're to grant extra favor to one another."

Leroy translates in fluid Spanish and Casey only understands the "*por favor*" at the end. Cowboy Joe's head wobbles as he listens like one of those plastic bobble-head characters people put in the back of their cars. He considers it, putting his hands in his pockets as if to finger-count his bills and see if he can afford it. He turns his dark, opaque eyes on Casey, who smiles at him in open-hearted hope.

"*Si, si*," he finally says to Casey as if giving in to an old friend, and he turns to instruct his workers.

"Why didn't we ever think of asking that before?" Leroy asks Birdie and Myrna. "Why've we men been getting hernias lugging the hundred-pounders all these years?"

"Hernia?" Cowboy Joe repeats it like he thinks the word sounds funny and his workers join in laughing.

"What was I saying about one of the best hagglers?" Birdie asks, putting her arm around Casey. "Until he's met his match in this little lady with the pretty smile who's smart enough to ask."

"I thank God for favor, and people who give multiple compliments," Casey laughs, putting her arm around Birdie and giving her a little squeeze of thanks. When was the last time anyone called her "little," "pretty," and "smart," let alone all in one sentence? More important, when was the last time *she* felt worthy of any of these compliments or thought positive things about *herself*?

Once they're loaded and on the road, Casey looks out over the dry, scruffy landscape and wonders what she *does* think of herself. Amana Anne always says no one's opinion is more important than your own opinion of yourself. So who *was* she, and who had she become? Strange as it seems, one of the multiple reasons she had to leave was to discover, or rediscover, her "self." A part of her feels if she doesn't do it before she goes home – *if* she goes home – she might feel lost for the rest of her life.

She realizes it isn't just the thought of being buried alive in her own home under all the junk that makes her want to stay away. It's more the thought of burying alive her true *self* again when she just started to excavate who she really is. Casey thinks about this all through the day as she and Leroy pour beans and rice into whatever dented, rusted pots and pans, or greasy, old paper bags the townspeople bring to them. Some of them simply, humbly present their open, cupped, age-wrinkled hands.

The teens have taken off again, nowhere in sight, which means she and Leroy need to finish dispensing before sundown because Leroy doesn't think it's safe to stay past dark with all the drug shootings on the news. By late afternoon, Casey's mouth is parched, dry as dust, but she doesn't even take a water break.

Casey can overhear Myrna talking to Birdie as they return from praying with the townspeople. "Boy, Casey sure isn't afraid to work."

It reminds Casey of when Skip said something like that about her once. "At *least* Casey isn't afraid to work." But Skip said it as though he was talking about a horse whose other qualifications might not be too readily observable. *Skip* was the one who was allergic to work. She saw statues move more than him. In fact, Skip had recently turned down a full-time computer job that his old friend Hank Stillis had offered him.

"Be on call Saturdays and evenings?" Skip had asked incredulously. "I could miss sports Saturdays and night football." If *she'd* been offered any job with full family medical benefits, even digging ditches in Haiti in one hundred twenty degree heat, she'd have taken it.

Right now, she's feeling like she *is* in one hundred plus degree heat as they finally finish and board the bus to leave. The back of her legs drip with sweat and stick like Super Glue to the searing vinyl seat, making a sucking sound as she repositions herself. The crotchety old bus has no working air conditioner, but what does it matter? This is her last trip on it.

It's time to meet her replacement.

Dream Big

Wowie's on her patio, waiting with a furrowed brow and impatiently tapping her foot when Amana Anne skids into her driveway.

"What happened?" Amana Anne jumps out and looks Wowie over to see if she's okay. She does a quick scan to see if anything's amiss around her townhouse as she rushes up Wowie's sidewalk.

"I need to file a police report," Wowie informs her. "Someone stole my skates."

Amana Anne stops in her tracks. "Are you kidding me?"

"No, I'm not kidding you. I feel so violated. Who would do that to a little old widow?"

"You almost gave me a stroke, Mom. I kept calling you and getting your voicemail. I didn't know if you were dead or alive."

"I'm very much alive and I'll make my own decisions about my own life." Wowie puts her hands on her hips. "In other words, when I want your opinion I'll give it to you. And by the way, I need to stop at Jake's because I know what project we can give him. He can make a 'Wanted' poster with your face on it. I'll play the senior-on-a-limited-budget card, so maybe he'll give me a freebie."

Amana Anne sighs, defeated. Wowie would do it, too, just to teach her a lesson. "I'll get your death-trap skates."

"I bet breaking my neck on those skates isn't looking so bad about now, huh Sweetie?" Wowie heads back inside with a wave. Amana Anne bites her tongue so she won't answer as she walks to her car.

"I had an epiphany," Eliz yells to Amana Anne from their community pool across the street. She's mostly hidden by the flocks of orange and yellow tiger lilies and shrubs that surround the pool, but Amana Anne can see the top of her shiny blonde head bobbing up and down in the water. Amana Anne heads over, hoping Eliz didn't wake any of the neighbors nearby who might be *trying* to sleep in. Well, at least it wasn't one of her Elizabethan screams.

The pure pool water ripples and shimmers in the sunlight as Eliz does underwater leg circles. It's a pretty oceanic blue pool with white trim that looks like sea foam. You can get across its width in ten strokes and length in twenty. Amana Anne can smell the chlorine – they always put too much in – and Eliz's San Tropez sun block spray.

"How's my favorite author slash client?" Eliz asks. The little ruffle on her bathing suit skirt floats around her, making her look like a human water lily.

"That depends on what my supposed manager's epiphany is," Amana Anne answers warily.

"For starters, we aren't going to sell your book to a publisher in a week because you're an unknown." Eliz motions for Amana Anne to help herself to the SPF spray.

"That's your epiphany?" Amana Anne spritzes her face. "In my book, we call that stating the obvious."

"'*In my book.*' Love the pun, Banaboo. A portentous segue to..." Eliz makes a trumpet sound. "It dawned on me that I can break down your book's chapters into little booklets in the Publisher program. We'll name them after the topic, like *Survive & Thrive in Challenging Times,* the advice of which I should have tattooed on me, since I need it so

150

much. That guy you accosted can print copies."

"And exactly what will we do with them, Ms. Manager?" Amana Anne takes off her sandals and sits on Eliz's towel to swish her feet in the cool water. It feels like it's only about seventy-five degrees, but the humidity's way up so the brisk water's refreshing.

"Sell them at your seminar."

"What seminar?" Amana Anne stops swishing.

"The all-day seminar you're giving on Saturday. Seventy-five bucks a head and they get a free T-shirt."

Amana Anne's voice shifts into high octave range. "Eliz, I can't talk in front of people long enough to fill the time it'd take to soft-boil an egg let alone give an all-day seminar."

"Bana, you can preach at us for *hours* when we walk in the woods. Does this sound familiar? 'You have a gift and you need to give it to the world. People need to drink from the Living Water that *should* be flowing *through* you to them.' You're being a stagnant pond, Banana."

"Could you please stop parroting my writing back at me, Eliz? Did you read the part yet where it says it's a lot easier to know it, and even *teach* it, than to *live* it?"

"If *you're* not living it and we can't see proof in *your* life, how do you expect anyone to believe it's true, Bana?" As she talks, Eliz moves into the five feet to submerge her shoulders because they feel like they're frying. "You're essentially saying, 'My fragile ego is more important than helping tons of people who are hurting and desperately need help.' Banana, this isn't about *you*!"

"Yes it is, and I *can't*," Amana Anne's palms are sweating so much at the mere *thought* of speaking at a seminar that she has to rinse them in the water. She wishes she could tank her whole body in because her deodorant stopped working at the word "seminar."

"Don't tell me you can't," Eliz pretends to stick her fingers in her ears. "Sleep on it. If you *can* sleep. With the guiltiest conscience of your life if you don't do this."

151

"Oh, shush up," Amana Anne kicks her feet, trying to splash Eliz. This is as close as Amana Anne has ever come to telling anyone to shut up in her entire adult life. Even as a child, her gentle father taught her to say, "Please, be quiet."

Eliz thinks it's a funny. "I'm telling God that Amana Anne said, 'Shush up' and splashed me."

"He's right here and He already knows everything." Amana Anne pulls her legs out and stomps her feet in the grass to get the water off.

"That's still kinda scary sometimes."

"Soothing actually, if you're behaving yourself." Amana Anne dries her legs off better with Eliz's towel, which normally she wouldn't do without asking, but she's miffed at her.

"Let's talk about *your* behavior, Little Ms. Shush Up. What's that quote in your book about people are like tea bags? You never get their real flavor until they're in hot water?"

"I forgot to write that I'd rather be *boiled* in water and eaten by cannibals than *speak* in front of them."

"Get out of your comfort zone and stretch yourself, as you wrote in *Jump Off the High Dive*." Eliz gets out of the pool.

"If we *had* a high dive, I'd push *you* off it just to shush you up." Amana Anne pushes Eliz back in the pool and Eliz laughs.

"Hey, send that book attachment to the printer," Eliz reminds her. "And I don't mean to freak you out, but there *may* be a little public speaking gig you need to do before the seminar to promo."

"Like what?" Amana Anne puts her hand to her stomach like she's getting sick.

"I'll fill you in on the details when I know more in the morning." Eliz dives underwater so she doesn't have to answer any more questions or see Amana Anne's anxiety-ridden face as she heads to her car.

152

Maybe it's too much to tell Amana Anne about the potential thousands she may be speaking to as early as tomorrow.

But her book *did* say to dream big.

Where Will I Be Tomorrow?

Casey can see the telltale sign that her replacement has indeed arrived as the bus sputters to a stop in front of the church. The forty-pound water bottles, bags of groceries and medical supplies are lined up in long, neat rows all along the sidewalk.

"Ziggie!" T yells as he spots a powerful-looking man built like a sledgehammer down by the kitchen entrance. Ziggie leans with an arm up against the door post like he's Samson holding it up, chatting with Mrs. Nettleson and Zia. Beyond the muscles bulging out of his tank shirt, Ziggie looks like he could be anyone's clean-cut dad or husband. Casey had half-expected some freakish-looking guy with long, dyed hair and tattoos everywhere. Although it *is* a little freakish that his neck looks bigger than her head.

She can't see from the bus, but she's sure he has those veiny arm muscles that gross her out, although that isn't the reason she won't go down to meet him up close and personal right now. It's that she's half afraid Mrs. Nettleson might kick her out this evening, citing a multitude of beautiful hotels where Casey would *only* have to pay two-hundred and ninety-five dollars with a church discount coupon instead of four hundred a night.

154

"Dude, he so big he block the sun," Dylan says, high-fiving T as they race off the bus, the girls in tow.

"I'm gonna go catch some Z's," T yells back to the girls as he runs down the steps to the kitchen. "Get it? Ziggie and Zia."

"I'm gonna go catch some *real* z's and turn in early tonight," Casey says, covering her mouth as she yawns. The ladies and Leroy chuckle and nod in agreement as she passes.

"We're right behind you," Birdie says with a contagious companion yawn.

Casey lumbers off of the bus feeling completely spent physically, and just as exhausted mentally from the constant worrisome thoughts assaulting her mind: *Where can I go tomorrow? What are all the possible options? Are there any options?*

As she locates mineral water and her grub in the fridge (multi-veggie and herbed salmon salad), Casey decides to do what Amana Anne says always helps to clear the clutter from her mind: write it out of you. "When we write about our days, we harvest our lives," Amana Anne says in her *Harvest Happiness* chapter, although harvesting happiness sounds like a luxury to Casey. She'll settle for sanity first. And that means making some life decisions. Starting now.

Almost a year ago, Casey promised herself she'd decide about Skip – should she stay or leave? – before the end of their twenty-fifth year of marriage. She made this resolution right on their twenty-fifth anniversary night, after no gifts, flowers, card or any acknowledgement whatsoever. When she insisted they at least go out to dinner, Skip took her to Hoss's. The name says it all. He even complained about having to do that much. Or that *little.*

"Doesn't our marriage mean anything to you?" she asked him over Hoss's trough of a buffet, just wanting to finally know the truth.

"Like what?" he asked, as though it was a trick question or he was expecting an open-book test and got a pop-quiz.

She took his question as his answer and that was the extent of their conversation for the night. Actually, for much of the past year unless you counted, "Where's my keys at?" or other grammar-cringing questions.

This month ends their twenty-fifth year. In this quarter of a century, Casey has had enough of Skip breaking promises. *She* was not going to break this most important promise to *herself*.

Casey grabs the laptop from the church office since Amana Anne always suggests typing your thoughts in a kind of stream of consciousness because it's faster than handwriting, then sending it to yourself in an e-mail to look at with a fresh perspective down the road. Maybe *literally* down the road. Casey opens the nursery door for fresh air and notices that someone put the rocking chair under a shady tree. A nursery lady must have taken some lucky baby outside to let the gentle breeze drift her off to sleep. Hopefully the baby, not the lady, Casey thinks with a chuckle, remembering her own rocker days with the twins.

She takes the laptop and bottle of mineral water out and hears an involuntary middle-age *umph* escape from her as she plops into the rocker. Its downy chair cushions envelope her tired flesh like loving arms. Looking up through the dappling sunlight, Casey sees she's sitting under a mimosa tree. Eliz would get a kick out of that. Casey can picture Eliz with her prettily-polished toes up in a hammock, sipping a freshly-squeezed OJ mimosa under her mimosa. Casey unscrews the lid of her water and takes a long swig. There's a sudden pang of missing Eliz and Amana Anne and wishing they were here. A brief prayer for them will have to suffice, and one for her family, too. She's been missing the twins, but as her grandma used to say, "It's a good miss. A miss you don't want to miss."

That's probably where she should start on this writing business, and figuring out her life, her future. With her family. Starting first with Skip. She does a quick check on the computer to see if Skip left any word, but of course there's none, let alone any note from the boys saying they miss her. Amana Anne's e-mail did though, with a heartwarming close of LOVE, Amana Anne. Eliz even sent one saying to have some tequila (hold the worm) for her. Casey clicks "New" to send herself an e-mail and starts with the headline: Reasons I Should Leave. She asks herself, "Does that mean leaving home for a while or leaving the marriage for good?" If she knew Skip still cared, still loved her, it would make all the difference. She could live on that, could put up with the rest of the "stuff." But if there's no love...

The late sun freckles her hands with shadows from the breeze-rustled leaves of the mimosa tree as she poises them over the keyboard. She decides delineating everything might help her answer that question later. Casey begins to write, letting it all out, to and for herself, and God.

* I don't know that there's any love left in our marriage.

He hasn't touched me in more years than I can count. He gives me no tangible love. It isn't like he's some monster. He just doesn't care. (The boys don't seem to either.) It's like that old truth that hate is even better than indifference because at least the person has some feeling for you. Sorry, Lord, but sometimes I do feel like I hate him when he belittles and undermines me. Yet I don't feel totally right about leaving him since I don't believe he's done a clear deal-breaker like cheating. He could never deal with two women since he'll barely deal with one. Shouldn't total apathy be at least considered as a deal-breaker?

* He makes stupid decisions, like the junk biz, and then I'm responsible for the outcomes.

You know, Lord, there should be a knucklehead clause regarding the men-are-head-of-the-household part of the

Bible. If the guy's a knucklehead it should revert to the wife. And you know, Lord, that might be a landslide of women.

* It may be worse for the boys if I stay.

In some sense, I feel like a horrible mother for temporarily deserting them, but the hard truth is if I stay and allow myself to be treated this way, they'll become men who disrespect women, and the pattern will just go on. How did I allow it to go on for so long already?

They need to see that a woman is her own person, that she has limits, and that if she isn't treated with love and respect, like a flower unwatered, with no sun, she will die inside. Why didn't anyone teach me this when I was young?

What message am I giving the twins about how to treat future girlfriends and wives if I allow them to continue to treat me like some second-class citizen in my own home? And speaking of the future, what if I'm there standing by impotently, watching Skip let them make bad decisions, like not going to college?

She rocks back and forth in the rocking chair for a moment, thinking of the loss it will be if the twins don't at least try college, especially Wyatt. From the earliest age, Wyatt was always the smart, inquisitive one, the one asking about everything like: "Why is the sun yellow? Why does it feel hot? Why?"

"Just cause your name's 'Wy' doesn't mean you need to wear the word out," Skip would say, dismissing his questions, but Casey would always take Wyatt to the library, where they'd search children's books until they found answers.

"I'm the brain," Wyatt sometimes said, only half kiddingly, when the twins were introduced.

"I'm the brawn," Tyler would counter, making arm muscles that looked like baby mole hills. Tyler *was* stronger, but gangly, like he hadn't yet figured out how to catch up with his limbs moving in sync with his rapidly growing height. He sometimes looked to Casey like a marionette when he walked, arms flying out, head swaying back and forth.

The twins were clueless about what they wanted to do with their lives. "Something that doesn't require work," Tyler said when she asked him. "That's all I know."

She realizes with a sudden twang that although she misses the twins, she mostly misses them as they *used* to be, when *they* still cared, too. Casey sighs heavily at the thought and looks down at her notes. It's becoming harder to read in the fading daylight, with tears beginning to well in her eyes. She pushes herself mentally back in gear and resumes her list.

* I feel like I'll go out of control with my weight.

See all of the reasons above and what's to come below as to why I stuff my emotions by stuffing myself.

She takes another sip of water and thinks about the e-mail joke Toya had sent her recently, "At least we still fit in the earrings we wore in high school." That sums it up – at least for now – because she needs to hurry and finish before the sun sets.

* I hate my home.

Since one of the many hats Skip wears as the local 'junkman' is moving man, this is the equivalent of a chocoholic working at Godiva. His motto is, "If it's free it's for me." Our home is an indoor junkyard. It's become my job to clean, fix, sew, wash, glue, mend, and sell Skip's junk at countless yard sales. My home is a pigsty where I'm sucked into an endless Catch 22; if I throw his junk out, I'm throwing out potential money. But if I fix it and sell it, he brings more home.

Casey watches a cloud drift lazily across the fading-into-sundown sky. It's all alone, like the last word of a celestial conversation. It reminds her of Amana Anne's writing room, which is painted sky blue and has lofty clouds floating across the upper sections. *Everything* speaks life all through Amana Anne's home, like her clear, scallop-edged "Fruits of the Spirit" bowl in her kitchen with the "fruits" (of patience, love and so on) in a beautiful scroll on the outside of the bowl and vibrantly healthy fruits always abundant inside the bowl.

Everything in Casey's home speaks of decay, from the turn-of-the-century food in the boys' bedrooms to smelly socks strewn everywhere, no matter how much she picks up after them. It's not that she hasn't tried to make things pretty but if anything nice is put out, it will somehow be broken, chipped, stained, soiled, or thrown by the end of the day. Not to mention Skip's general hoarding and all the second-hand junk already in her second-hand life.

Casey thinks about how Maya Angelou once said she believed that things in your home carry the energies of the people who used them. Casey always wonders if it's possible that the sadness and regrets from their used, funeral home couch are somehow present in the cells of the bedraggled thing, and how fittingly indicative it is of her life.

Which brings her back to the next confession on her list as she takes a final sip of the mineral water.

* Sometimes I hate my life.

At least before I came here. I realize that's a horrible thing to say, Lord, but You know anyway. And I'm sorry. I know life is supposed to be a gift. That You died so I would enjoy it and have it to the fullest. But I've been running on empty for as far back as I can remember. Even if the sky

160

isn't falling completely, so many times I feel like huge gray chunks of it are dropping on my head. Not that I would ever jump if I found myself on a high bridge, but I may look over the edge for a long, long time.

Casey takes a deep breath of the fresh ocean-spiked breeze, recalling Pastor Warren saying in one of his sermons, "Jesus came that we might have and *enjoy* life, and have it more abundantly. If you're miserable all the time, something's out of balance." The "something" she decides, as she continues to type, is *her*.

* I have been losing myself.

Amana Anne has a quote in her book from Amy Tan that sums it up:

I did not lose myself all at once.
I rubbed out my face over the years washing away my pain,
the same way carvings on stone are worn down by water.

Sometimes Casey feels so worn down, she thinks there's next to nothing left of her. And maybe it's this last one that turns the tide.

* If I don't do it now, I may never have the strength to do it again.

Testing God

"Where's your self-help section, please?" Eliz hears a man with a low, gravelly voice ask as he comes in the open door of Quentie's bookstore. Eliz has been sitting outside reading under Quentie's green umbrellaed café table for hours. She's chomping on the last ice cube from her herbal tea, trying to stave off hunger.

"If I tell you, won't that defeat the purpose of *self*-help?" responds a gentle female voice. Eliz hears him laugh and shuffle off to whatever direction she pointed him in.

The next moment, the lady is in front of Eliz with a pitcher of iced tea, freshening Eliz's glass. She has short-cropped gray hair and a broad, smooth face that gives the impression of calm. There are pleasant laugh lines around the corners of her bright, blue-gray eyes.

"How'd you like a sandwich to down with this?" she asks Eliz as she pours. "I'm fixing myself one up for dinner anyway. Nothing fancy."

"Sure!" Eliz says, like a lost puppy happy to scavenge a meal.

"I'm Quentie." The woman extends her free hand and shakes Eliz's.

"Grateful Eliz." Eliz pumps Quentie's hand.

Quentie gives her a wink and heads back in. She figured Eliz was starving. Once in a blue moon, there are day-old treats Oakhaven Bakery donates for readers to enjoy. Today it was gingerbread mini-muffins on Quentie's red "*You are special*" plate. She noticed that Eliz immediately scarfed down the four remaining on the plate as soon as she came by early this afternoon. In fact, Eliz was actually wetting her index finger and pressing it into the remaining plate crumbs to catch all of them. Quentie noted that Eliz had been reading for hours: *The Case for Christ*, Joyce Meyer, books by both Victoria and Joel Osteen, along with others. Eliz has books piled up around her like the Great Wall of China and Quentie maneuvers around it when she comes back with a tray a few minutes later.

"Okay if I join you?" Quentie asks, unloading two Corningware sandwich plates with chipped ham and cheese on Kaiser rolls, her own glass of iced tea, and napkins.

"Please," Eliz pulls out a chair beside her, adding, "and thank you," when she sees the generously piled sandwiches. *Gee, this woman owns the bookstore, is feeding me, and still asks politely if she can sit in her own chair!*

Quentie sits with a sharp crack from one of her knees. She folds her hands and closes her eyes, bowing her head, and Eliz follows suit.

"Thanks a lot, Lord, for blessing and providing our food," Quentie says.

"And thanks for Quentie's generosity. Amen," Eliz adds, sincerely.

Quentie nods *you're welcome* and they bite in with gusto. From the way Eliz attacks her sandwich, and since she's been here much of a work day reading, Quentie's pretty sure Eliz is one of the "suddenly poor" from a layoff.

"I'm a new Christian," Eliz says, as she finishes chewing her bite. She feels like she needs to explain why she's bummed so many of Quentie's books. In fact, one passing lady thought *Eliz* was having a book sale.

163

"Welcome to the family," Quentie says.

Eliz feels like she *is* in a family with Christians like Amana Anne, Casey, and now someone as kind as Quentie.

"So feel free to enlighten me, Quentie, cause I need a miracle ASAP," Eliz laughs, but she's serious. "I'll take the nutshell version since I know you're closing soon." To say nothing of the liquor store closing and the champagne money burning a hole in Eliz's pocket.

"Love," Quentie says succinctly, wiping a few crumbs from the crisp Kaiser roll off her mouth with a napkin.

"Well, that's a nutshell," Eliz says.

"Yep," Quentie agrees. "God first, then people." Quentie tosses a little crust of her roll to a squirrel who's been watching them from the bottom of one of the oak trees that line the sidewalk. "Next, little furry animals if you like them." The squirrel chews his bread almost as fast as Eliz. He stands on his hind legs and clasps his tiny black hands together waiting for more.

"He's not getting any of mine; I don't care how hard he prays. This is delicious." Eliz closes her eyes to relish munching another bite.

"Know what's even better?" Quentie asks.

Eliz is hoping Quentie'll say some kind of dessert that's coming next, featuring tons of chocolate, but her mouth's too full to answer so she raises her eyebrows in a question.

"A prayer sandwich." Quentie points to the top of her half of a roll that's left. "Praise on top." She points to the ham and cheese in the middle, "faith," and to the bottom roll, "gratitude."

Eliz thinks about how she *better* put the "prayer sandwich" in high gear because they have zip people signed up for the seminar, no takers on her publicity endeavors, hundreds of products underway, and only four days left until the seminar.

Quentie waves to the self-help seeking man as he strolls out the door. He's apparently not interested in what he saw of her little shop, which has been the norm with potential customers lately. Quentie hasn't had the funds to buy new books for longer than she can remember. It's been all she can do to keep the electricity on and buy groceries these past several months. In fact, she'll be starting her Going Out of Business sale later in the week. With this meager meal, she feels like the widow in the Bible who shared her last dinner with Elijah the prophet, although Quentie actually has a few days' worth of groceries left. She's in fact putting that divine principle to the acid test of giving even when you have next to nothing, which maybe should be the last thing she mentions to Eliz.

"Final enlightenment, Eliz. Plant a seed. Like if you need money, plant a money seed. God says tithe the first ten percent of what you are given. He promises to bless and multiply what you give."

Quentie and Eliz both scarf the last bites of their sandwiches and Quentie rounds up their crumbs from the table with her napkin.

"I understand sowing and reaping more than most people because my grandfather was a farmer," Quentie says. "Did you know that one seed of corn will produce seven hundred kernels in the first crop?"

"Wow," Eliz says.

"Whereas if you eat that seed you get no harvest," Quentie says.

Or drink it, thinks Eliz, *if I spend all the money I found on booze.*

"You're satisfied in the moment, but you've lost your future harvest." Quentie gathers the plates and what's left of her iced tea and stands, her knee again cracking, sounding like the snap of a dry twig breaking.

"Thanks so much for sharing food for body *and* soul. Let me help wash." Eliz jumps up, but Quentie shakes her head that she's got it.

"I enjoyed breaking bread with you," Quentie says,

heading inside.

Eliz finishes the sweet golden-brown remains of her iced tea, thinking how Quentie has no idea that her well-intended kindness makes her an "enabler." By feeding Eliz, Quentie enables Eliz to hold out another day on buying groceries so she can buy booze instead. Eliz found just enough money for the cheapest bottle of champagne in the liquor store and intends to stop for it as soon as she takes the books in.

She's been feeling a growing sense of dread – as if water's rising above her nose and she can't swim – at the things she set in motion today. Like co-workers slaving away on her big idea without guaranteed pay. Ditto the vendors. Ditto her. There was a feeling of peace and hope while she was reading all the spiritual stuff, but now that the panic thoughts are clawing at her heels again, slamming back some bubbly has a definite allure.

Eliz takes the books and her glass inside where she can hear Quentie in the back room humming. The donation basket for the Women and Children's Shelter is on the counter where she puts her empty glass down. She places her books back on the shelves, pondering giving ten percent of the booze money to plant a seed instead, to try out this reaping principle. There was something in the Bible about giving, that it's the only time God said to test Him and see if He wouldn't pour open the windows of heaven.

Seventy cents. That would be ten percent on the seven-ish dollars she has stuffed in her pocket. But that would mean she'd have to find more change in the morning to buy the champagne tomorrow. She'd find enough somewhere. It would also give her more incentive to keep housecleaning to find more money. She could finally lift light items around the house without a stabbing pain in her neck, and it was nice to see things getting orderly.

Eliz takes two quarters and two dimes out of her pocket and puts them in the basket before she can talk herself out of it.

Okay, Lord, I'm giving this ten percent to the Women and Children's Shelter and trusting in faith that I'll find another ten percent tomorrow for booze, and You know what a sacrifice this is for me. She's pretty sure this isn't the best of prayers, but she's just being real.

Eliz heads for the door, calling back to Quentie, "Thanks again."

"Come anytime," Quentie calls out.

Don't worry, I'll probably be here every night for my dinner freebie. Eliz walks back out into the cool breeze of the evening and the last peep of late June sun closing its eye on the hilled horizon. As she passes the liquor store she thinks how wonderful a champagne brunch will be in the morning. Albeit without the brunch.

She only has to hold out until ten.

LOVE

Amana Anne throws open her writing room window to get a better look at the starry constellations flowing across the night sky, like a river of diamonds on black velvet. Sweetly fragranced night air floats up, perfumed by her flower garden below. Nathan would have known the names of all the constellations, Amana Anne thinks, recognizing only the Milky Way. She may have been his Keeper of Secrets but *he* was her Walking Encyclopedia. When she'd ask him questions, mostly about nature because he was a botanist, he'd often teasingly say, "Just because my ears look like bookends doesn't mean I'm a set of encyclopedias." Except that he was.

While she *was* the Keeper of Secrets. Even with Nathan at first, when they met at a nursery, talking flowers. In time, his open-book honesty blossomed her trust and truthfulness. Not that she lied to him early on. Just the omission kind of holding back. Then it gradually got to the point where she knew the heart of the man and could tell Nathan every one of her secrets. Like all the ways she fell short from being the "Godly" woman she wanted to be. And that she couldn't wait to wash after shaking hands with someone.

There was nothing like being loved for who you really

are, warts and all, or in her case, secrets, "mild OCD" and all. The freedom of being able to tell another human being everything about yourself, to explore all the nuances, nooks and crannies of your emotions, the angles and tangles and paradoxes of your feelings, was a total unfettering of her soul.

Yet, there *was* one secret that developed after Nathan passed on that Amana Anne thought she may never share with anyone. For her, it's the kind of secret you could only share with someone you grew to deeply love and trust in a lifetime commitment, like she had with Nathan.

Not that her secret is so dark or even unusual. It just seems so intimate. In fact, it *was* a secret unknown or at least not admitted on a conscious level, even to herself, until the last few days. Until meeting Jake. Amana Anne realized she's desperately lonely, despite the people she loves in her life. She misses sharing her life with that special *someone* in a deep, romantic way, someone who cares about all the intimate details of your days. Someone to love and turn to, who has your back.

It wasn't that she hadn't dated after Nathan passed on. Granted, for the first couple of years she had no interest. But then she started testing the waters, mostly because – even though she and Nathan hadn't been able to have children – her doctors told her there was no reason she couldn't still have children if she remarried.

The problem was that her lovely city of Pittsburgh might often be rated as America's Most Livable City (and Amana Anne thinks Oakhaven is America's Most Livable Town) but it also seems to be the Least Dateable City for Middle-aged Women. She has a better chance of being hit by a train on an airport runway or lightning indoors than finding a worthwhile, eligible man her age.

In general, Amana Anne found most men her age let themselves go and were unattractive. Then there were the attractive ones who eyed up waitresses half their age. Or men who expected too much physically. She didn't even want to kiss someone until she knew them, their personal hygiene and dental habits thoroughly. Amana Anne didn't care if they misunderstood her and thought her a prude. No way was she going to be exchanging bacteria with just any old Sloppy Joe Palooka. Interestingly, Amana Anne thought she might waive the whole worried-about-germs thing when she found herself daydreaming earlier today about Jake and how it would feel to be kissed by him.

An owl hoots in the woods behind her house, drawing her out of her romantic reverie. Amana Anne wonders if Mr. Owl's hooting at her goofiness, since she's spent a grand total of about three and a half minutes with the man.

True, she admits to herself, closing the window because it's getting cool. She sits in her brown leather desk chair, propping her bare feet up on her desk as she muses. But did falling in love, or whatever this feeling was, happen only within a certain time frame? Like you had to know someone for so many months first? Had Amana Anne been asked this a week ago, she would have said "falling in love" was more like some emotional slipping on a banana peel. Let alone love at first sight when you didn't even know the person.

But there it was. How to explain what happened with Jake? Could it have been some menopausal chemical imbalance that coincidentally happened at just that very moment she first saw him? Even if so, it's some chemistry experiment she very much wants to explore in person.

If only she could figure out how to attach *herself* to this attachment she's *supposed* to be sending him. Amana Anne swings her legs down and refreshes her computer screen. She got waylaid proofing and tweaking her book and is finally satisfied with it after about eight hours of fine-tuning it to death, just in case Jake might actually read some of it.

Eliz had called earlier to say she'd spoken with Shari-Beth (to explain how she wanted the attachment formatted) and to send it directly to Shari-Beth. But Amana Anne's sending it to Jake's e-mail from his card because he said he'd *love* to handle it *personally*. Definitely one up on the Michelin Man.

So what *if he said he'd love to handle it personally?* A voice in her needles her for not sending it directly to Shari-Beth, who probably would do the actual work on it anyway. *Get a grip, Amana Anne. It wasn't a marriage proposal. Give it to the girl. Probably* every *woman tries to deal with him directly.*

No doubt a mouse in the wall could just hear Shari-Beth explaining to Jake tomorrow, "Another desperate middle-aged lady – sans the casserole – wanted to work with you personally, but I ran interference for you. Again."

Amana Anne decides not to be a pathetically obvious casserole lady and writes a pithy and business-like e-mail.

Hi Jake, here's the attachment for our project per my manager Eliz's phone call.

After proofing it and spellchecking the sentence three times, the "normal" non-OCD part of her tells her to sign off and send the stupid thing already. It isn't the State of the Union.

She's still proofing it even after she signs off and hits *Send*, then she lets out an Elizabethan scream that Casey can probably hear in Mexico. Just before her all-business e-mail blinks off the screen, Amana Anne sees she signed it in big capital letters.

LOVE, Amana Anne.

~ Tuesday ~

El Stinko

"What a gorgeous day to visit the San Diego Zoo or somewhere fun before you go home," Mrs. Nettleson says enthusiastically, intercepting Casey as she comes out of the nursery.

It *is* a fabulous California morning. Or *was,* anyway.

"I can get you twenty percent off zoo admission because it's Tuesday," Mrs. Nettleson says.

Hmmm. Casey wonders if maybe she could sneak in a zoo cage and live *there* for a bit.

Giraffes look gentle. No, she's heard they're mean and spit. And they don't live in caves. Bats do. Great. She'll sleep in a bat cave. Now she's *really* going batty over what to do and where to go.

"Just let me know in the next hour before I leave town for a conference." Mrs. Nettleson veers off onto a sidewalk heading toward the chapel.

Hopefully it's in New Zealand, Casey thinks as she enters the kitchen at the same time Ziggie enters from the social hall. His frame momentarily thwarts the early morning sunlight from streaming in behind him.

"What smells so good?" he asks chefs Zia, Birdie and Myrna as he nods "hi" to Casey.

"Me," Casey says, and everyone laughs.

"The witty lady is Casey," Myrna says, turning slices of bacon.

Casey finger-waves "hello" to Ziggie, basking in Myrna's compliment. Quite a contrast from when Skip says things like, "I'd ask you to make up your mind but ya don't have one." Meanwhile, *Casey* was the one who'd been *valedictorian* of their high school class, and Skip was the one who'd celebrate getting *C's* because he skipped so many classes, which is how he got his nickname. Back then she used to feel like she had such seeds of greatness in her. Before marrying *him*, and life in general, killed them.

"Nice to meet you, Casey," Ziggie says warmly, grabbing a plate from Birdie with one hand and serving himself Jimmy Dean sausages with the other. "I'd be formal and shake but I might have to pause from attacking this chow."

"I'm with you," Casey says as she serves herself the veggie eggs Zia said she was making special for her this morning. "Thanks to the lovely cooks and God, amen."

Zia gives Casey a smile of camaraderie as she dices tomatoes and green peppers.

"Nothing like the smell of cinnamon rolls fresh from the oven." Ziggie grabs a cinnamon roll from the pack Myrna just brought out of the oven and slathers butter on it. He sinks his teeth into a sizable bite of the roll, standing while he munches.

"Better enjoy your last *good* smells of the day, Mr. Ziggie," Birdie says, perching on a breakfast bar chair next to Casey and mopping into some over-easy eggs with a crust of toast. Casey eyes the toast half-covetously. Only *half-*covetously for a couple reasons. First, because she's down another button on her adjustable shorts, and she's feeling lighter and better than she's felt in years because of Zia's RCR special. Second, because her stomach feels twisted like one of those large doughy stadium pretzels whenever she thinks about what exactly she's supposed to do with herself today.

Frantic thoughts have been buzzing about her head like hornets all morning and much of the night. Should she call Skip? Spill her guts to Zia and see if she can offer a job or help? Ask if she can stowaway on the luggage rack with Myrna, Leroy and Birdie when they go home?

"We're taking food and supplies to people who live at 'The Dump' today," Myrna explains to Ziggie.

"Pack a clothespin for your nose," Zia kids Ziggie.

Ziggie's mouth is too full of roll to ask the question that his scrunched-up face conveys. His Adam's apple is as big as a snail when he swallows his mound of food.

"What you mean?" Ziggie asks, wary enough to momentarily pause from plowing into a sausage. His thick brown eyebrows are shaped flat across his forehead and look like two caterpillars kissing when they meet in the middle, drawn together in concern.

"The Dump, or *El Stinko* – as we sometimes call it – is the biggest garbage dump in Tijuana," Birdie explains.

Leroy enters the kitchen and waves hello to everyone, grabbing the half cup of coffee on the counter that Myrna's just poured for him. Apparently Zia's still rationing him.

"Hundreds of people live on the outskirts of this place just so they can get first dibs on finding things to sell," Zia says, dicing red peppers into tiny pieces with quick chopping strokes and throwing them in another batch of eggs.

"I can't go." Ziggie actually takes a couple steps back toward the door as if the ladies might try to wrestle him onto the bus against his will.

"I got hyperosmia," Ziggie explains.

"Hyper…?" Leroy asks and blows on his coffee.

"It's this illness triggered by my *really* strong sense of smell. I get debilitating migraines when there's intense bad smells. I may be the only husband in California who has a valid excuse not to take out the garbage when it's smelly. I'm *so* sorry, guys. I'd be of no use."

"I have the opposite problem," Leroy says. "I could probably bunk with skunks and I wouldn't know the difference."

"Smells stimulate appetite," Zia waggles an eggy spatula at them as if to emphasize her warning. Ziggie points to himself with his fork, his cheeks bulging like a chipmunk, the living testimony of this truth.

"Maybe that's why Leroy's so skinny," Myrna says, looking at Leroy enviously, unconsciously rubbing her own ample tummy as though weighing the difference.

Maybe that's why I'm so *not*, Casey thinks, because her sense of smell has always been acute. In fact, Skip usually took diaper patrol when the twins were babies. Back when he actually *did* something.

"I prefer to think of myself as a lean, mean machine," Leroy says, chuckling, downing his coffee.

"You sound like a George Foreman grill," Zia laughs.

T bursts in from the social hall, balancing all the kid's plates one on top of another, like a Leaning Tower of Pisa. "Don't try dis at home, folks."

Myrna comes to the rescue and takes some off the top.

"Casey, are you game for *El Stinko*?" Leroy tosses his drained coffee cup in the garbage. "Or is running for the hills home looking better to you right about now?"

"I'm in!" Casey's so relieved to be given another day she feels like her body's in melt mode.

"Yo *in* fo, alrighty," T says to Casey, laughing like he's in on a big secret.

Birdie waves him back into the social hall, "Scadoodle."

"Ziggie, if you'd get us set up again for tomorrow, that'd be a huge help," Leroy says and Ziggie nods.

"That whole storage room needs organizing." Ziggie dips a cinnamon roll in his coffee. "I'll keep outta trouble."

"This is the only day we go to The Dump," Birdie assures Ziggie.

"And we better *get* going," Leroy says, calling to the kids in the social hall, "Load em up."

"Don't forget your coolers," Zia says, lining them up on the counter.

"Sadly, I have never forgotten to eat in my life," Myrna says with a chuckle.

"Me either," Jelly says as the kids stampede through to grab their lunches and run off to the bus.

Zia hands Casey her cooler. "I had a feeling we'd get another day out of you," Zia winks and Casey gives her a thankful bear hug.

Leroy bows to the ladies and motions with a swirling wave of his hand toward the door, like a subject heralding royalty out, "Ladies…"

Birdie's arm links with Casey's as they troop out into the glistening sunlight. "Last warning, my dear. Myrna and I are down about a half *mile* from The Dump praying with people, and when the wind sends a drift, I about pass out. I kid you not. I think it must be what hell smells like."

"I can't stomach it either," Myrna agrees. "Casey, you really don't have to come."

Oh, yes I do, Casey thinks, jumping on the bus, *or I'm heading for the bat cave.*

"I don't think you realize what tour of duty you just signed up for," Birdie stomps up the stairs and plops onto her seat.

"I've been choking down green sludge and eating tree bark all week." Casey roosts atop a hill of blankets piled on her seat. "How bad can it be?"

Birdie and Myrna exchange a look and leave the question hanging in the air. Leroy starts the motor and the bus sputters into gear with a kickback that makes the ladies all grab onto the seat in front of them.

"Well, brave one," Birdie says, looking back at Casey with a look of concern, "you're about to find out."

Unexpected Visitor

"Hi, Flower Lady!" Amana Anne's five-year-old neighbor Brianna calls to her from the street. She's cute as a button with strawberry blonde hair half in and half out of a pony tail. "Flower Lady" is the neighborhood nickname for Amana Anne because she's always giving posies to everyone who passes.

"Hi, Daisy Girl," Amana Anne calls back from her side yard, using Brianna's nickname since the daisy is Brianna's favorite flower.

Amana Anne is under her wooden arbor with the climbing crimson roses. She's tilling around her elegant new favorite fuchsia, Shadow Dancer Ginger, as its tiny coral-pink sepals dance delicately in the gentle morning breeze.

Yes, of course, Amana Anne nods for Brianna to help herself to the multi-colored gerbera daisies from her front yard. Brianna chooses her usual trio of pink for her mom, red for her gram and yellow for herself. Brianna's probably up this end of the street doing her daily search for Lumberjack, their orange tabby. Lumberjack earned his name by often being a lick of an orange flame high up in one of the neighborhood trees.

Brianna blows Amana Anne a dramatic kiss of thanks as

she skips happily off. Amana Anne blows a return kiss and stretches her back. She isn't exactly feeling "fresh as a daisy" after tossing and turning half the night over her "LOVE" faux pas to Jake. She moans inwardly every time she thinks about it.

Well, stop thinking about it and get moving, she tells herself because the sky's clouding quickly, and "popcorn" showers are predicted, the kind that pop in and out all day. It'll be one of those days where it's raining one minute and sunny enough to sunbathe the next. It's been a few days since she last gardened, and she's missed the smell and feel of the earth. Amana Anne picks up the dark, moist humus and raises it to her nose to breathe in its rich earthiness. It's not yet eleven o'clock, but it's stiflingly hot. She wipes the beads of sweat she can feel forming on her forehead with the back of her hand, thinking her face is probably a dirty mess.

"Beautiful."

Amana Anne looks up with a start, squinting to see who it is as her eyes angle into the rising sun. Jake smiles at her from the stone sidewalk that leads from the front yard to the garden. He surely couldn't be referring to *her* in her flopsy white sunhat and denim gardening get-up. He's dressed like he's just played a round of golf, sporty and preppie-like. She tries to quell the unexpected happiness his handsome face brings to her heart.

What is he doing here?

"Oh, gee, thanks," Amana Anne's going for breezy, but she's pretty certain she's not pulling it off because her voice has jumped into the Minnie Mouse range. "I love flowers," she says lamely, working to bring her voice down a few octaves.

"I think *they're* beautiful, too." He takes in her lush garden of corydalis and marigolds, ruby zinnias and the tiny but abundant "Fireland" yarrow with hot pink petals and yellow-flower hearts.

A hopeful thought races through her mind: *Does he mean*

I'm *beautiful and so are the flowers? Or just the other flowers?*

The keep-yourself-in-check part of her chimes in, *Hey, Ms. Prideful Ego, just get through the conversation at hand like a normal human being who can speak in a pitch that doesn't break glass and don't get all ga-ga wondering if he thinks you're cute.*

Jake opens the Sandstone Printing white plastic bag he's holding and pulls out a thin booklet with a gorgeous salmon-colored cover. "I left you a message that I was passing and would drop this prototype outside your door."

Why did she always forget to check her messages when she went in?

"But I couldn't resist checking things out back here when I saw you." He seems to be waiting for some response, but she doesn't know what to say. *"Oh, that's nice?"* Nothing but inanities keep coming to her mind. Like that she wrote "LOVE" to him in her e-mail.

"Oh, I see you got my attachment…" Amana Anne starts, then suddenly, "got my attachment" seems to have double meaning and it flusters her, like he "got" that she wanted to be "attached" to him. "I mean e-mail and I wanted to explain that I'm… ah, so used to… uh, signing off to loved ones…"

"Hey, no apology necessary. Made my day," Jake says easily, like he's got a handle on talking down nervous women.

Is it so blatant that I'm just another casserole lady?

"Soooooo," he says in a drawn-out way, as though to fill the awkward silence when a joke klunkers. "I'm on my way to a meeting. I'll let you get back to work."

Jake steps forward to hand her the Sandstone bag but thinks better of it when he notices her dirt-filled hands and Amana Anne realizes she's been pretty much frozen in mid-motion since he arrived. He places the prototype on the garden bench between them.

"Nice seeing you, Amana Anne," Jake says with a wave.

Amana Anne waves back and the dirt she was holding plops to the ground, which activates that laughing twinkle in his eyes.

Amana Anne could swear she hears a low chuckle as he walks to his black Lexus on the street. She's so focused on trying to hear if he's laughing that she doesn't notice Eliz walking through the back yards until she's almost in her garden. Jake waves as he drives by and Eliz waves back enthusiastically.

"*That's* the printer?" Eliz spots the Sandstone Printing bag on the bench. "Or should I say my Mr. Backup? Ooooouuuu la la."

What? Amana Anne jumps to her feet. *Her* what?

"Hooo, my, my, my. I'll handle this from here." Eliz takes the prototype booklet out of the bag and fans herself like her temperature's rising from the attractiveness of the man. "This could be a Godsend. Banana..." Eliz says like a brilliant idea just struck her. "Maybe God was trying to set me up with him."

Or *me*, Amana Anne wants to say.

"Bana, you always say there are no coincidences, just divine opportunities."

"Yeeeeees," Amana Anne admits slowly and wants to add, but this one's a divine opportunity for *me*. She's not sure exactly what to say to Eliz, but she'd like to get some kind of dibs on the record. *I liked him first?* She never felt that was fair, even in grade school, because it really came down to who the guy liked back anyway.

"As soon as I can lift my hands enough to wash my locks without killing my neck, I'm definitely gonna pop in on Mr. Sandstone. I'll probably be good to go in the a.m. Look, Bana." Eliz lifts both arms shoulder-high to demonstrate.

"I can almost do your signature "Believe" move, Banana, and I *believe* maybe God wants me to be with a solid, mature kind of guy."

Not to mention someone who has some bucks that could

come in handy, say for rent, Eliz decides. Or groceries. Who probably has a nice liquor cabinet.

"Financially secure, too," Eliz says wistfully.

"Why does the term 'gold digger' come to mind?" Amana Anne wipes the dirt from her hands with her gardening towel a little too fiercely.

"Oh, please, he's a printer not a sultan." Eliz glances at the booklet. "This looks good. *He* looks better." She puts on a snooty voice like she's introducing him at some future swank event, "I'd like you to meet my first husband, Jake Sandstone."

"What do you mean your *first husband*?" Amana Anne hears her voice sliding again up to the moon, then chides herself mentally: *Why are you being so territorial about a man you just met, and yes, supposedly* did *meet for Eliz, anyway?*

"Well, I *would* probably outlive him," Eliz clarifies. "But enough about the distant future. I've got everything set up so *tomorrow* you're gonna be L-I-V-E on Christian radio to promo your seminar. They said tomorrow or Thursday at the latest. Target audience, Banaboo. Thousands of listeners."

"Uuuugggg," Amana Anne moans like she's been sucker-punched in the gut. "Who're all going to hear me be sick. L-I-V-E." Amana Anne reclines on the garden bench like she's already nauseous at the thought, her floppy hat falling off.

"Listen, Bana, I'll go to the radio station with you." Eliz fans Amana Anne with the booklet and the stray, sweaty tendrils sticking to Amana Anne's face are liberated in the fan's breeze. "My neck'll be good enough for me to drive and I want to swing by the office anyway. I'll meet you at the station and if you can't spit it out, *I'll* talk. I'll say I'm your manager and blah, blah, blah. Toot your horn. We can't lose."

"We'll need a bag handy in case I get sick," Amana Anne says weakly. "I mean it."

"There's a lady looking suspiciously like you who wrote

about doing things through faith even if you're afraid."

"Okay! I'll do it afraid of *wetting myself*!"

"You just open your mouth and talk. How hard can that be? I always loved when I got to present at work. Everyone paid attention to me. What's not to like?"

Eliz replaces the booklet back in the Sandstone bag. "Speaking of what's not to like, I'm gonna go call my future husband about our little order." Eliz waggles the booklet bag in a goodbye wave.

Amana Anne's heart sinks like a dropped anchor. Of course, Eliz would be attracted to Jake. And, let's be real, most men would be attracted to her, too. But maybe Jake isn't the kind of man who'd be attracted to a woman like Eliz.

So, exactly what kind of man would *not* be attracted to a beautiful, fun, young blonde? A comatose man?

Eliz calls back to Amana Anne as she heads across the grass, "You'll see, Banana, I'll have a date with him by the end of the week."

Amana Anne watches Eliz's cute young figure retreat across the backyards.

And she'll have him down the aisle by the end of the month.

No Holds Barred

The stench hits like a wave. No, a tsunami. When they dropped Myrna and Birdie off to minister to the needy in the community half a mile back, Casey could already smell a potent hint of what was to come from *El Stinko*. Leroy left everyone but Casey off at the last homes in the area, some decrepit house trailers on wheels, their yards cluttered with rusted cars on concrete blocks and dented coffee cans with flowers. One trailer had a brownish tub with algae sitting in the front yard and Casey hoped people weren't bathing in it. On the outskirts of the trailers were more make-shift homes of battered wooden planks, plywood and black plastic bags.

The teens, of course, insisted on disembarking with Birdie and Myrna. T screamed at a pitch even higher than the girls at the stink, and the kids all ran off the bus, collectively holding their noses and gagging, wildly waving their hands in the air as if that would dissipate the smell.

"I got that hyper-whatever-too-much-smell disease, like Ziggie," T explained when Leroy tried to talk him and Dylan into helping at The Dump. T faked a swoon like he just might faint dead away.

"He's got a hyper-whatever disease alright," Leroy muttered to Casey when T ran off after the girls with a

186

sudden charge of energy.

T may have had the right idea, Casey thinks as they draw closer to *El Stinko*, where a blackish, moving haze hovers over it. She realizes it's a massive swarm of *flies*. Ziggie may have his hyper-whatever but Casey has a terrible fear of bugs and hopes to heaven they can unload at the base of The Dump away from them. Smaller swarms surround patches of litter that line the sides of the dirt road from overfilled garbage trucks dropping debris along the way, a warning of what's to come.

The landscape's increasingly brown and scruffy-looking, as if the sun's been especially harsh here, scorching the bristling land, a dust bin of dryness. Everything has a dirt-powdered cast to it, kicked up from the garbage trucks going up and down the hill, creating a habu. Even the sunshine has a dusty filter, seeming both stronger and yet veiled.

Leroy pulls over at the base of *El Stinko* and cranks the bus to a stop. "Casey, breathe through your mouth as much as possible after this dust storm settles if you want to survive the day," he tells her.

Casey feels like retching and even Leroy's looking a tad pallid himself at the stench, despite his sense of smell being weak. She's trying to get the hang of this mouth-breathing because every time she forgets and breathes through her nose, the stench hits her with a wallop. Before them is a literal mountain of garbage, and it reeks of rotting food and excrement and what must be animal corpses, (or worse) and it's being baked in the heat like some recipe from hell.

Scavengers, some cadaverously skinny, dot The Dump in all sizes and species. Bedraggled humans, mangy cats and dogs, and cawing crows all compete to sift through the rubble. Several floppy-eared, red-eye-infected mongrels with large scabs and patches of missing hair lay at the base, spent in the heat. Two hawks circle and badger each other, then swoop down from the sky when they spy rodent treasures.

As she and Leroy get off the bus, Casey notes that none

of the people have gloves on as they pick through the broken glass and rusty metal parts of cars. She worries for the children in particular, that they won't have access to tetanus or any medical care and hopes the medical supplies they brought will be enough. Still, it feels like their efforts amount to putting a Band-Aid on a situation needing open-heart surgery. She reminds herself that Amana Anne always says to just help the people God has put in front of you. *You can't save the world, but you can help change* their *world for the better today. Leave the echoes of your kindness up to God.*

Some scavengers spot Casey and Leroy and wave excitedly as they run for the bus. Casey smiles and waves back, forgetting to breathe through her mouth and it's everything she can do to keep from dry heaving.

"You're a living angel to them, Casey," Leroy says.

Casey's thoughts aren't very angelic at the moment. She's thinking about how they could be done in a quarter of the time if those lazy teens pitched in, but thank God one of the local pastors and men from his congregation pull up in an old pick-up truck to help handle distribution. Casey starts to work in tandem with one of the churchmen, a darkly-sunned Mexican whose low voice carries traces of tobacco in it every time he says "*gracias*" to her, which is often.

While she unloads, Casey recalls some statistics Pastor Warren shared recently in one of his sermons: "If you have a roof over your head, you're better off than seventy-five percent of the people in the world. If you have fifteen dollars in your pocket, you're in the top eight per cent of the world's wealthiest people." Could this be true? Not that she's ever known Pastor Warren to lie, but it seems unbelievable. She always feels like she has so little.

Just this morning Casey was reading a quote by Gunilla Norris from Amanda Anne's book: *"Guard me against the arrogance of privilege, against the indulgence of feeling that I don't have enough, and the poverty of spirit that refuses to acknowledge what is daily given to me."* And then something like, *"Instruct me in gratitude with no holds barred."* When was the last time she spent her day in gratitude instead of mentally complaining about all she *didn't* have? Yet this humble, Mexican man working with her, who had next to nothing, must have said *"gracias"* to her a dozen times in a matter of an hour.

Casey *did* say "thank You" when she prayerfully made it through the border each day so far, and was *starting* to be more grateful. But beyond these past few days of reconverting her life to God, she doubted she had said "thank You" to God a dozen times in the last year.

When they leave The Dump at the end of the day, Casey receives countless hugs from the people who still call out thanks as the bus winds down the dirt road. As Casey and Leroy drive the dusty roads to pick up the gang, she thinks about how wonderful it feels to be appreciated for what she's done and given. It dawns on her that God appreciates gratitude, too, for all He's done for her. But she's been largely blinded by her spirit of selfish ingratitude, looking not only at what she doesn't have, but what people don't do for her. She closes her eyes and asks God for forgiveness, promising she'll cultivate an attitude of gratitude more and more each day.

Casey starts in the present moment by thanking God that she's able to breathe decent air again when they stop to pick up the gang, because even though there's a trace of stench, it's like roses after The Dump. Myrna and Birdie wait patiently in front of a little wooden shack that has two six-foot tall sticks at either end of the small dirt yard. There's a run of string tied to the top of each stick and little strands of white toilet tissue hang down.

"These are the decorations for their teenage daughter's coming out party," Myrna explains when Casey and Leroy alight from the bus.

There's only one shabbily-dressed man in the yard, the father, Casey presumes and she wonders if everyone else is taking a siesta or out. The Mexican stirs what looks like watery soup in a huge black kettle over a wood fire. He says something in Spanish to Casey and motions with a welcoming gesture for her to look inside his shack. Casey steps forward to see a bloody pig's head surrounded by flies on a small wooden table. The dark blood seeps off the table and onto the dirt floor.

"He's offering to share it with us," Birdie explains. "The poor here only get meat like this maybe once a year, for a special occasion." The man proudly lifts the pig's tail out of the water with his ladle.

Leroy takes the man's hand in sincere thanks and says *muchas gracias*, and more in Spanish. Casey supposes Leroy's thanking him for his generosity or wishing him and his daughter well. The man's smile broadens and he says *muchas gracias* in return; with a nod to the ladies, he retreats inside. Casey notes again how generous and thankful these indigent Mexicans are with almost nothing, and thinks about how wasteful and ungrateful some of the privileged people of the world often are with almost everything.

Kanashia, Jelly, T and Dylan come running up from behind one of the trailer homes, and Leroy gives the ladies a wink that makes Casey wonder what he's up to as he turns to the teens.

"Kids, this family's got a pig's head they want to share with us," Leroy says with all sincerity, pointing it out in the shack, and the kids stop in their tracks.

"We don't want to be rude to these good people," Leroy continues, "so I'd like to ask each of you to try a little piece of the pig's head, even if it's just an ear, or an eye, or the snout." The ladies are trying hard not to laugh as Leroy includes everyone in his directive with a sweep of his arm.

The kids are speechless, their eyes widening in fear. Casey can see Leroy's own eyes dancing with humor, but he keeps his face serious. "T, you've got that smell problem and maybe a little snout would somehow help. You never know."

Leroy turns to the ladies. "Ladies, *please* leave the snout for T." Casey, Myrna, and Birdie nod, trying not to crack up.

"Ohhhh, ohhhh, I don't need *more* snout," T puts his hands out in protest like the pig's going to jump up and bodily attack him. "I got too *much* smell like Ziggie."

"Then maybe you could try..." Leroy starts to suggest, but he's interrupted by Dylan.

"Yo, don't even talk eyeballs, man," Dylan holds his stomach and the girls put their hands over their mouths like they might be sick.

"Gross!" Jelly says through her hand and Kanashia gives a muffled agreement.

"An ear, then," Leroy suggests. "They're pretty thin. A *delicacy* in some countries."

The girls stifle screams and the kids all stomp hurriedly onto the bus.

"I hope you're going to confess all this tonight," Myrna says with a grin to Leroy as they get on the bus.

"I could still grab that tail if you and Birdie want to split it," Leroy says to Myrna as they plop in their seats.

"What about Casey?" Birdie says teasingly. "Misery loves company."

"I think Casey's already doing her penance in the food department." Leroy glances in his rear view mirror to see Casey thirstily swigging the brownish-green juice from Zia.

"I was going to say we'll trade you the pig's tail for that, Casey, but it's a toss-up," Birdie says, watching Casey swish the slime around to break up the dark pulp, and they all laugh.

As the bus pulls out, Casey looks out the dusty window over the poverty-riddled landscape. *El Stinko* was beyond her worst nightmare and she lived through it, albeit, her clothes reek and she may have to bury them. She can't wait to take a shower... but she's thankful that she even *has* a change of clothes and *can* take a shower as she closes her eyes to pray.

Lord, all my life I've asked You for things and

191

complained that I didn't have enough. I'm sorry and I intend to live a life of gratitude. Instead of always looking to receive, I'm going to look for ways to give. Just show me where to give, what to give, and most importantly, how to give Your love and how to love You. Let me put aside all my self-pity and selfishness to see all the blessings that already are. I praise You and thank You. Amen.

As the Border guard waves them through and Casey gives another prayer of thanks, she reflects on the Bible saying "give thanks in all things," and that God promises He'll work all things together for our good. Casey acknowledges to herself that she doesn't know where she'll be or what she'll be doing tomorrow. But she decides that to truly have a new life, today and for the rest of her life, whatever the day brings, she will greet it with the prayer:

Please Lord, instruct me in gratitude with no holds barred.

The Big Kiss

"Tilt back," Amana Anne instructs Wowie, demonstrating on her swing by pumping her legs, tilting her head back and looking up at the sky. "It's good to reverse your circulation." They're taking in the cool evening air on the swing set at their community's playground, since the kids are still at supper, at least for the moment. Wowie leans back in her swing until her upturned hair skims the dirt.

"Geez, Mom, I didn't say it's good to graze your head on the ground til you snap your neck." Amana Anne pulls herself up to monitor Wowie.

"Speaking of breaking necks, Banana, I love Eliz like a great niece but if she competes for the only man you've dated this millennium, I'll snap her like a twig." Wowie pulls herself up to nod her head definitively at Amana Anne as if to put an exclamation mark to the statement.

"How could you possibly know about Eliz liking... ?" Amana Anne stops herself. She's aware that her next-door neighbor, Mrs. Merkin, likes to keep her windows open and eavesdrop on Amana Anne's life, or lack of one, so she's probably the culprit.

"A couple of points, Momsy: I'm *not* dating the man, and have you seen Eliz's biceps? *You'd* be the snapped Twiggy."

193

"You underestimate the strength of a mother – whose daughter is on her last minute of youth – in flattening the competition." Wowie pumps her legs to go higher and her swing jumps as the swing chains jerk because she's going too high. Amana Anne hates when Wowie pulls her "tootsie-touch the sky" swinging, but she's certainly not going to say anything and earn another lecture after the stolen skates fiasco. Wowie might well try to do a full circle swing over the iron bar to prove some kind of point.

"Mom, Jake might just like *Eliz.*" *Hope not, hope not*, Amana Anne thinks, then admonishes herself. Of course she wants Eliz to be happy, just not with Jake.

"My future son-in-law likes *you*, Amana Anne." Wowie uses Amana Anne's full name when she's getting peevish. "He could have had any number of his flunky underlings drop something off. You think a man who owns three businesses runs them by being a coolie for every print job?"

"Don't jump to conclusions, Momsy. He was passing by. And maybe God wants a good, solid Christian man in Eliz's life to help her get closer to Him. Who are we to judge?"

"*I'm* the mother of a woman who may never get a date again if she doesn't snag this one, *that's* who I am to judge."

The truth is, Amana Anne can't judge the situation clearly for herself. She doesn't know if she should say something to Eliz about having feelings for Jake and fight for the opportunity to explore her feelings, or just let Jake decide. Or God. *I personally see Jake as more mentor-age for her, Lord, as you already know.* Let's hope *Jake* sees it that way.

"I'm going to Punxsy with your Aunt Fran tomorrow to visit the old folk and if you haven't told Eliz to bug out by the time I get home, *I* will."

"*I'll* do it." Amana Anne better figure out *something* to say to Eliz or who knows what kind of damage control she'd have to do if Wowie does it.

"Hey, Flower Lady and Miss Wowie!" The Daisy Girl,

Brianna, pulls up on her cotton-candy pink bike and jumps off it, letting it fall on the grass. Wowie uses her once-white Keds to skid her swing to a stop and speed-walks to the slide, pretending to try to beat Brianna as Brianna makes a run for it. It's a game they play often.

Brianna hoists herself up the slide and Wowie's hot on her heels. "I'm gonna get you," Wowie teases her, grabbing for her with fingers crimped like crab claws. Brianna laughs with delight as she slides down, waving to Amana Anne in triumph, blowing her a kiss. Brianna hops off the bottom and claps as Wowie slides down behind her.

"Let's blow the stink off!" Wowie yells as she slides down. "Weeeee!"

"Miss Wowie, when I get old, I wanna be just like you," Brianna says.

"When *I* get old I want to be just like me, too," Wowie says. Brianna erupts in a belly laugh and takes Wowie's hand.

"When *I* was a kid, back when dinosaurs walked the earth..." Wowie's voice trails off, along with Brianna's giggles, as they head for the see-saws.

Amana Anne enjoys a moment to herself as she swings a little higher, inhaling the sweet, floral scent from the wildflowers around the play yard. The evening breeze feels like a gentle caress on her face as she takes a moment to touch base with God, tilting her head back and closing her eyes.

Thank You for this beautiful day, Lord, for my health and for good people to love throughout my life. Amana Anne thinks about how sweet it is when Brianna always blows her kisses and how blessed she's been all her life to love and be loved by relatives, friends, co-workers, neighbors and so many others.

In the midst of thinking this, Amana Anne hears the inner voice of God suddenly say to her:

If you took all the people you've ever loved,
and all the people who've ever loved you,
it would be infinitesimal compared with My love for you.

Amana Anne stops pumping her feet, stops moving, as she takes in this awesome moment of grace and love, and the full realization of the gift of God's love. Amana Anne always felt she had so much love from so many people. *But it's "infinitesimal" compared with His love for me!*

It's been several years since she heard the voice of God, but she thinks about how this one message alone is enough for her to live on for the rest of her life. With her eyes still closed as her swing slows to a stop, she blows kisses up to God and says to Him on the inside, "Thank You for loving me. I love You so much." She opens her eyes to look at the sky as if to check that her kisses are floating up to heaven "special delivery" and she's awestruck to see a majestically huge white "X" from skywriting against the bright blue sky, like the biggest kiss in the world back from God.

She wants to tell Wowie and Brianna to look, but it's a sacred moment and it's fading fast. As the God-sized kiss melts into the sky, Amana Anne feels a surge of energy from the deep realization of how much He loves her and wants good in her life. Then a powerful thought comes into her mind and a knowing that she should act on it immediately. She jumps off the swing and waves to Wowie and Brianna as she passes.

Amana Anne answers the question on Wowie's face about where she's going.

"I have a battle I need to go fight," Amana Anne calls over. "Starting right *now!*"

I Need a Drink

"I hope yer buying that for me, Jailbird." Jamaica comes from seemingly out of nowhere down the liquor store aisle. But then Eliz has been so engrossed in deciding between the cheapest champagne or a mini-wine 4-pack that a grenade could have gone off unnoticed. Eliz stops mid-motion from pulling the Great Western Brut off the shelf. There's no way she's gonna buy this only to fork it over to Jam.

"Actually I was just going to read the ingredients," Eliz fibs.

"It says b-o-o-z-e, boozie." Jamaica points to the label and spells slowly for Eliz like she's an idiot. "What more do ya need ta know, Jailbird? You *do* owe me one."

"I told you, your champagne's at my place." At least Eliz is consistent in remembering her earlier lies.

"Booze still in your house un-drunk?" Jamaica makes a scoffing raspberry. "And I just saw a flying orangutan. Hey, speaking of unbelievable, no one at work believes you're gonna pull this seminar gig off anymore. Only Amana Anne's *mother* and a few of her cronies signed up and they all may not even *live* til Saturday."

Eliz and Jamaica squeeze together to let a man pass with

a cart full of bottles. If Jam wasn't rattling on at her, Eliz would ask the man where the party is and get herself invited.

"Just about everyone in the office jumped ship today," Jamaica jammers unrelentingly, although Eliz is trying to edge herself to the door by pretending to look at champagne bottles up the aisle. "Which is why I'm here in the first place, cause I'm bummeranged," Jamaica continues. "Only ones left are me and Ed cause we're in this so deep already, we may as well drown."

"Listen, Jam, Amana Anne's going to be promoting the seminar on Christian radio in the next forty-eight hours. Guaranteed. And I'm gonna get her a promo shot on one of the local TV morning shows if any of the scheduled guests cancel."

"Those shows have a list of standby people as long as your nose, Pinocchio," Jamaica says.

Eliz decides she's gonna have to break open a fifth and guzzle it dry right here if she stays one minute longer listening to Jamaica.

"Jami, I have a prep meeting with Amana Anne and the talk show host of the radio station so I gotta run." Eliz lies, backing out the door with a wave. "I'll buzz you tomorrow with the on-air time." She doesn't wait for Jamaica to reply since her rolling eyes shout a reply Eliz doesn't have the stomach to hear anyway.

Outside, into the soft blackness of early night, Eliz heads down Blossom Brook Boulevard in the opposite direction from the way Jam will go home. Halfway down the block, she leans against the glass window of Stephanie's Classic Clothes to wait. As soon as Jamaica leaves the liquor store, Eliz is going back in to buy a four-pack of those little screw-off wine bottles, some of the already cold ones in the cooler.

She's going to drink every one of them on her long walk home.

~ Wednesday ~

Are You Loco?

Casey crashed like a freight train hitting a steel wall when her head hit the pillow last night. She doesn't even remember her head actually touching the pillow before she went out. The sound of the Lord's Bus being loaded this morning awakened her. She missed breakfast, never even heard the seven o'clock church bell. She rushed getting dressed so she can at least help finish loading. Not that she'll actually be able to lift much of anything, with her sore and screaming muscles. It's everything she can do to drag her packed getaway bag down the hall toward the school room door when she hears Ziggie's booming voice though the open windows.

"So what's up for today, Leroy?" Ziggie asks. From the hall, Casey can see Leroy and Ziggie's torsos through the low, kid's-eye-view school room windows as they stand across from the bus.

"How'd you like to shampoo a few hundred people after we drop the supplies off?" Leroy asks with a chuckle.

Casey's made it to the classroom with her bag and can see Ziggie's face now.

"Shampooing?" he asks, like he's trying the idea on for size. His expression says he doesn't think it's a great fit.

Ziggie and Leroy are too tall to see through the low windows, or are so absorbed in their conversation they don't notice her unintentional eavesdropping. Casey's arm muscles are already so achy from dragging the bag that she's resorting to kicking it forward a few inches at a time across the classroom floor.

"Once a year the municipality lets us use their water at a public works building and we shampoo people who don't have access to water," Leroy explains.

"Sounds great," Ziggie says. "But frankly, if you didn't need me to unload those hundred pound sacks I'd finish cleaning the storage here and maybe hit the road home tomorrow."

"To tell the truth, we aren't getting the hundred pounders," Leroy confesses. "Casey got Cowboy Joe to give us the same price for twenty-five pounders so we *can* manage them ourselves."

"Then why doesn't Casey go with you?" Ziggie asks. "You're a work-team now anyway."

Through the window, Casey sees the teens run past like wild ponies, chasing each other, almost knocking into Leroy and Ziggie.

"Well, half of you work anyway," Ziggie laughs.

Casey comes out, not wanting to miss her cue, and sets her bag down by the door, realizing maybe she won't need it after all.

"You up for another day, Morning Glory?" Leroy asks her with a smile.

"Abso-toot-ly," Casey says, borrowing one of Wowie's favorite words, and relieved *beyond* words that she's being given one more day.

"It makes more sense anyway," Ziggie says, taking Casey's bag from her and setting it back inside the school room for her. "Casey's just a little peanut. I'd take up at least three of her in supply space."

Casey's never been called a little peanut in her life and

hopes her head doesn't swell to the size of a watermelon over it and kill the whole peanut analogy.

"I'm sure Casey's probably better at shampooing, anyways," Ziggie says.

The teens come to a petered-out halt in front of them and lounge on the remaining supply boxes setting in front of the bus. Dylan wipes sweat from his forehead with his T-shirt that says, *Save energy. Don't talk to me.*

"I'll bet the kids are all going to be great shampooers, too," Casey says, ignoring the T-shirt dictum and hoping positivity will help convince them to do their share for a change.

Ziggie and Leroy give Casey a "nice try but fat chance" look and load more boxes onto the bus.

"Yo, you *loco*, lady?" T asks Casey incredulously. Jelly and Kanashia shake their heads affirmatively.

"Now why would it be so 'loco' to think you kids are here to work?" Casey asks, eyeing each of them.

"Ahhhh," Dylan says sarcastically, just like Tyler and Wyatt always did as a precursor to pointing out something to Casey that they felt should be obvious. "Cause *we* ain't shampooing like five hundred peoples with lice."

Casey wonders if Dylan could possibly be kidding.
Lice?

Not Again

Rotten Food Facials. That's what Wowie calls Amana Anne's "beauty secret." People are always asking Amana Anne how she has such satiny, luminous skin, especially for her age. She credits it to her own concoction of whatever healthy but overly ripe fruit or veggies she has on hand thrown in a blender and smeared on her face. Today's facial is just going to be papaya that's so over-ripe the orange fruit has turned juicy red and mushy, and Amana Anne's adding a couple splashes of some low-sodium V-8.

Amana Anne turns her blender on, whirling the papaya-tomato mix into a frothy foam while she thinks about what God said to her yesterday. God's love is so amazing! People just *have* to know how much God loves them. It's been a growing realization since yesterday that *she* needs to step up to the plate and be one of the people who tells them.

God did not give me a spirit of fear but of confidence, that's one of many truths she must have told herself a few dozen times last night before falling asleep. She let it all gel a good eight hours and when she awakened felt like she could take on the world. Good thing, too, because Eliz called and confirmed that Amana Anne'll be on Christian radio KJOY first thing tomorrow, and Amana Anne feels almost ready for it. She'd been doing spiritual warfare all night and again this morning, battling her fear of public speaking. She intended to do more of it as soon as she got this facial on, by reading the Word of God.

Amana Anne takes the blender lid off and the fruity, refreshing scent of the facial wafts into her nostrils. She pours the bright, red mixture into a shallow bowl and takes it into her powder room. Her hair's already up in a Pebbles Flintstone ponytail so it doesn't get in the way. Since her mouth and chin are where she's holding tension at the thought of public speaking tomorrow, she concentrates on that area, massaging the facial in, starting around and over her mouth and chin in slow circles. This is where a lot of women miss it – putting natural moisture-rich facials only on their skin and skipping their lips. She always puts part of the facial right on her kisser and she still doesn't have even the lightest traces of lip lines.

The cool, smooth texture and massage soothes her into a kind of hypnotic peace until Amana Anne hears what sounds like Wowie's roller skates coming up the street. It's probably best to unlock the screen door before Wowie tries to skate through it again. Or better yet, maybe Amana Anne should *close* the door and keep her God time uninterrupted.

As Amana Anne walks into the hall to close the door, she's paralyzed in place. Jake's coming around the corner off her driveway onto the sidewalk, heading straight for her. Should she jump behind something? *That's stupid,* she tells herself. *He's already seen you.*

He's carrying a printer bag, looking at her with barely reigned-in amusement. The fastest way to get the muck off her face is to wipe it on the back of her arm, since her hands are both still laced with the fruity mix. Oh, *this* is dainty, she thinks as she wipes what she hopes is the bulk of it off with her arm, but can still feel much of its stickiness on her face.

"Hey, Amana Anne," Jake says casually. *Teasingly,* she thinks. "I don't suppose you got my message again that I'd just leave these booklets at your door?"

My memory got left on menopause's *door again and I didn't check my messages,* she wants to tell him.

"Ahhh, no..." Why was she always in such a mind-muddle that she couldn't even process her thoughts, let alone *speak* coherently to the man? Not to mention how to explain why she has rotten food on her face.

"Your manager said these were needed ASAP." He brings the colorful mock-ups out of the bag to show her. "Last drop-off. I promise."

Amana Anne realizes she can't even open the locked screen door to get the booklets. She shows him, holding her muckily slathered hands upright like a surgeon going into surgery.

"Sorry to have interrupted your lunch," Jake surveys her hands and hangs the bag on her doorknob.

What?! Does the man think I'm some Neanderthal who globs up food with my hands?

"Jake, the reason I have all this tomatoey stuff on my face and hands is..."

Jake waves her explanation off like it doesn't matter. "My nephew, Sam, looks like that when he eats spaghetti, too."

Amana Anne's too flabbergasted to speak. *What kind of slob does he think I am? Like I just throw spaghetti in the vicinity of my face and hope some goes in?*

"Sam doesn't believe in using forks or napkins either." Jake's eyes glisten with held-back laughter. "He says we have perfectly good hands and arms just hanging there doing nothing and we may as well use them. But *he's* five."

Jake gives her a smiling wink to let her know he's kidding and starts back down the sidewalk. Amana Anne can see his broad shoulders ripple with a laugh he tries to cover with a fake cough.

"Travis is dropping the rest of the thousand at the library," he calls back with a wave, then turns the corner and hops in his car.

The rest of the *thousand*? Amana Anne stands in shock and horror, looking after him as he drives off. There must be some mistake. She regains her senses and grabs her cell from the counter to speed-dial Eliz. Maybe he's pulling her leg. He *has* to be, but she's not getting Eliz on her cell to confirm. *There's only one way to find out.*

When Amana Anne arrives at the library, sure enough, a golden-tan van with "Sandstone Printing" stenciled in chocolate-brown on the side is pulled up in the unloading dock. A young man in a Steelers T-shirt unloads boxes of the booklets.

"Hi," Amana Anne calls to him as she parks behind him and hops out. "I'm Amana Anne, the booklet lady." By default, she wants to add. De-fault of Eliz. "I was just wondering if you had the order correct?"

He checks the bill on top of the boxes and shows it to her. "Here's the bill with your manager's signature." Sure enough, there was Eliz's bold, curly-q signature, big as day on the ASAP order for a thousand. "In fact, she said to give the bill to you," Travis says as he hands it to Amana Anne, wiping back a thick strand of dark hair falling on his forehead and scrutinizing Amana Anne. He turns his head from side to side like he's trying to take in different angles.

"You don't look like him."

"Who?" Amana Anne asks.

"Jake," Travis answers like she should know.

"Why would I?" she asks, confused.

"Jake gave you the 'at cost' discount. He only does that for family. Aren't you related?"

"No." Amana Anne sure hopes not.

"Ahhhhh," Travis smiles, like something's dawning on him. "That's a first." He picks up a box and double-raises his eyebrows at her like he's onto something. *You don't know Eliz,* she wants to tell him as she opens the library door for him and he nods his thanks. *In fact, right about now, I wish I didn't know Eliz.* She hops back in her car and fast-tracks it to Eliz's townhouse, wondering, *How do you fire someone you never really meant to hire in the first place?*

Hot Date

"I was wondering if you could please chill a bottle of Brut Champagne in your cold case for me to pick up later?" Eliz speaks into her cell on speaker phone so she can turn onto her tummy to tan evenly. She's wearing a hot pink bikini, sprawled out on a lawn chair in her front yard.

The liquor store employee assures her he will and Eliz feels better already, knowing the champagne will be ready to splash down soon. Last night, Jamaica was yammering so long with the booze-party cart guy that the store manager had to practically kick her out at closing time. Eliz drew the line at beating down the "closed" door to get some wine, but barely. *Just as well,* she thinks, as she spots Amana Anne traipsing across the lawn, *or I'd be too hung over to deal with Ms. OCD.*

Amana Anne foregoes the normal niceties like saying hello and starts right in. "Who exactly's buying these one thousand booklets besides me, Miss Manager-who-doesn't-consult-with-me-first?"

Eliz props herself up on an elbow to turn on her front.

"Bana Babe, the people who come to your seminar. Who do you think?" Eliz has a little white plastic table set up next to her with ice water, Hawaiian Tropic suntan lotion and her cell phone. She takes a sip of water and the sweat beads glisten on the glass in the sun as she drinks.

"And if, say, the four people signed up don't want two hundred and fifty each, to wallpaper their homes?" Amana Anne asks.

Eliz shakes the lotion bottle. "Hey, Banana, you're the one who wrote, *Don't Go to the Ocean with a Teaspoon.*"

"Apparently I should have also written, *Don't Go to the Ocean Thinking Someone Else is Going to Foot the Bill.*"

"Look, tomorrow you'll be on KJOY with thousands of our target audience members listening." Eliz rubs suntan lotion on her arms and the coconut scent fills the air. "They're gonna come in droves to your seminar." Amana Anne's stomach churns at the thought. She was so confident all morning. Now, at the mention of it, she envisions herself falling in a dead faint into the radio microphone.

"Remember the story in your book about the ship captains?" Eliz smoothes lotion on her legs. "How in ancient times they used to burn their ships so there was no retreat and they *had* to have victory? This is kind of like that. We *have* to sell these things." Eliz reclines again.

Amana Anne closes her eyes and counts to ten slowly, like she's often told clients to do. She breathes in deeply and out three times and feels calmer. Saner. She knows Eliz means well. She's just a little overzealous. At Amana Anne's expense. Literally. Well, Amana Anne tells herself, the booklets are a done deal. But it reminds Amana Anne that the Jake situation isn't.

"Speaking of the booklets," Amana Anne begins, trying to figure out how best to broach the whole topic of Jake. Amana Anne's sure that once Eliz knows she has feelings for Jake, she'll gracefully bow out. "I want to talk to you about Jake," Amana Anne starts.

"Oh geez," Eliz says, sitting up on her lawn chair enthusiastically, "I've been meaning to tell you about a hot date with him this weekend."

Amana Anne blanches as Eliz's cell rings and Eliz checks the caller's number.

"Bana, this is the KJOY station manager finalizing details. I'll call you." Eliz answers the phone and shifts into a measured, professional tone, "This is Amana Anne Moore's manager."

Too bad I don't have someone to manage my emotions *right now*, Amana Anne thinks as she walks numbly down the sidewalk to her car. *Because for the first time in years, I feel like I want to go have a good, long, self-pitying whale of a cry.*

Something Great Could Happen

"Casey, so help me," her father hissed at her in the dark, "if I hear another whine out of you I'm getting the belt."

When she was a little girl, Casey's family once stayed at a flea-bag hotel, the Tropical Flamingo in Kissimmee, Florida, en route to her grandfather's funeral. There were two saggy, creaking double beds; her parents took one, her two brothers the other. The hotel manager found a rusty, old cot for her that stank to high heaven. Throughout the night Casey kept telling her parents she was getting bitten by bugs, but since they couldn't see them when they turned the lights on and did a perfunctory glance, to her parents, they didn't exist. Under threat of being beaten "within an inch" of her life from her father, Casey was the silent supper to multitudes of bedbugs for eight torturous hours.

The next morning, she was covered with tiny, red welts over every square inch of her body. Her face was so swollen from bites and crying she could barely see out of the razor-thin slits from her puffy eyes. To this day, the smaller the bug, the more Casey fears it.

The only thing worse than a crawling critter was the double whammy of having to get, say, a spider in a ceiling corner because she had to climb up on a chair. That was as high as she'd venture since her fear of heights was about parallel to her fear of bugs.

Could be worse, she tries to tell herself as she and the mission team are jostled along the bumpy road to the lice shampoo site and her trepidation grows. At least I'm not being pushed from a plane at thirty thousand feet with a parachute full of fire ants dropping on my head when it opens. Skip had a saying for times like this: "Worse things will happen." As if that was comforting. She preferred Amana Anne's, "The bigger the challenge, the bigger the blessing and spiritual growth, especially if it's done out of love for others."

Nonetheless, Casey feels like a mini-panic attack is coming on as Leroy pulls up to a squat municipal building the color of dried mud, set on a couple acres of dead-flat, barren land. There's a large dirt parking lot and hundreds of people already patiently lined up in a twisted snake-line that elongates down the unpaved road. It again strikes Casey how the people seem so good-natured, patient and jovial, in an almost party-like atmosphere, even with critter-filled heads of lice.

A half dozen Mexican workers wait on the corner in front of the municipal building, hoping for work, and one of them runs to the shampoo line when he sees their bus, dust rising from every step he takes. The Mexicans in line wave and smile, already calling out their thanks as the Lord's Bus gang disembarks and waves back "hello."

Birdie motions with her head to a small group of Mexican women who cluster by the entrance of the building. "Myrna and I meet with the local ladies' ministries that we mentor," Birdie tells Casey. A woman at the head of the group has her black hair in a thick, braided coil on top of her head and wears a full apron over her dress. She puts her hand up like a Native American chief's greeting and Birdie does the same in return.

"Leroy meets with the local officials about logistics, like

having access to the water again next year," Myrna explains.

"And the officials take credit for what we do, and get their faces on the local Mexican news." Leroy points to a Mexican camera operator taping a rotund official who sweats profusely in a cheap, beige suit that's too big for him. The official stands in front of the gallon containers of lice shampoo, holding a hose over some pitchers and talking in Spanish to the camera.

Birdie explains, "We don't care who tries to take the credit here. As long as people are helped, we know the glory goes to God."

"None of us really want to be on TV, but we let them cover us," Myrna adds.

T and Dylan spot the camera and showboat by trying to get into the shot behind the local official, waving their hands wildly.

"Okay, maybe none of *us* want to be on TV," Leroy says. "None of us they actually *want* to interview."

"Hola, amigos!" Dylan says, jumping into the camera's view beside the ruffled official.

"See what zee gringos are up to south of zee border!" T says, jumping on the other side of the official. Jelly and Kanashia giggle in the background. Leroy shoos the kids out of the shot, and Casey tries not to laugh as she hears him add, "You little putzes" under his breath, giving an apologetic nod to the peeved official.

"You kids get over here and help Mrs. Swanson shampoo," Leroy calls to the teens.

T runs away, arms akimbo, screaming, and the other kids race after him. There's a small slant of shade along the ground at the base of the municipal building, against the far wall, where the kids hunker down. T sits with his knees up, his back braced against the wall. Dylan and Jelly sit-slouch against it as Dylan's cell phone "blings" with a text message they read together. Kanashia hugs her knees and bends her head, her arms and hair creating a cave for her head.

Leroy chuckles, "Kanashia looks like an ostrich sensing danger and hiding her head in the sand." Actually, Casey thinks, it's a myth that ostriches do this; they do what any other animal does when in danger – runs. But there's really nowhere for the kids to run and find shade from the pounding sun.

"Maybe the kids could help at least get things organized," Casey suggests, surveying the shampoo gallons, pitchers and hoses.

"Ha," Birdie says, "those kids couldn't organize a two-car funeral."

"Just do what you can," Myrna says, giving Casey a little back pat of encouragement.

"We've never even gotten half the line finished when it's all done by one volunteer, Casey," Leroy says.

"We're lucky some years to get a quarter done," Myrna adds.

"You mean whoever doesn't get shampooed has to wait a whole *year* with lice before they have another shot at this?" Casey asks incredulously.

"Whoever gets done by the last rays of sun," Leroy adds. "No electricity." Leroy waves to the official who's finished his TV interview and the official flags Leroy over. "Good luck, Angel Girl," Leroy says to Casey as he heads for the official.

"It's horrible that it's all left to you, Casey but…" Myrna motions to the lounging kids.

"We've tried everything with them," Birdie says, "positive reinforcement, praying for them, having compassion, encouraging them…"

The thought that these poor people never get to shampoo and bathe, that they only have access to water once a year, and that many of them waited in line year after year to no avail because of lazy kids fills Casey with righteous anger. Not to mention that she wants some "misery loves company" in having to shampoo the lice out of them.

215

"Excuse me, ladies, I'm going to go give these kids a little 'doing unto others,'" Casey says, stomping over to the teens.

"You kids are going to help me shampoo these people so everyone gets done today," Casey says, and T and Dylan laugh.

"I'm not messing with *lice*," Kanashia says, shaking her mane.

"They nasty," Jelly says, surveying her fingernails with concern. "They for sure get in my French Tips."

"I'll give you all a tip and it's not gonna be in French," Casey says, her voice rising, which gets their attention. "It'll be in plain English so there's no way any of you are going to misinterpret it. If you think these people are going to go another *year* with lice because you won't help, you can forget it. You're going to do unto others what you would have done for you or I'm going to do unto you what others have to live with because of you."

"*What?*" Dylan asks, like he's trying to figure out something that's unfathomable.

"If all of you don't help, I will hire these men to hold you down," Casey points to the workers waiting on the corner to be hired. "And I will get lice from these people and put lice in your hair. So help me, I will do it."

Casey can't believe what just spewed out of her mouth, but it's working. T and Dylan exchange worried, questioning glances and the girls look scared.

"They can't hold us down," Dylan says, but uncertainly. "She's bluffing."

"Or," Casey says, determined, "I can always collect a bag of lice from the heads of these poor souls and when you're sleeping…"

"*Okay,*" Kanashia jumps up and drags Jelly up with her. Jelly drags Dylan, who drags T up.

"But look at that *line*," T grumbles as they begrudgingly follow Casey to the waiting Mexicans.

"No, don't look at the line," Casey says, smiling down at the sweet, sun-kissed face of the little boy at the front of the line. "Look at the *person* in front of you and help them. Do that. Then look into the eyes of the next person and help them."

Dear Lord, help me take my own advice, Casey prays as she screws the cap off the lice shampoo and pours a blob into her hands. The gray-blue shampoo mixture smells like pungent chemicals and feels harsh and abrasive against her palm. Why didn't someone think of gloves so she wouldn't actually have to touch the little vermin? Amana Anne would have thought of full body armor with a hazmat suit.

"Guys, you fill the pitchers with more water," Casey instructs the boys. "Girls, you wet their heads and translate to each person that they should cover their eyes and tilt their heads back. I'll shampoo. You guys rinse the shampoo out with the hose."

Jelly instructs the little boy in Spanish and he clamps his small, dirty hands like cups over his eyes. Casey motions for Kanashia to pour water over his dark brown-black head and Casey lathers in the shampoo. His hair is oily and stiff from lack of shampooing and teeming with the tiny, dark little critters the size of sesame seeds, and Casey recalls reading that some lice take on the color of the host's hair. There are also translucent clumps of little lice eggs that freak her out but Casey keeps her mind stayed on how she can do *all* things with God.

It's amazing how quickly Casey can give a good shampoo while simultaneously keeping a sharp eye out for lice that might jump ship onto her arm hairs. When the little boy goes to T for a hose-off, Casey lets Dylan hose off her hands and arms just in case. Both T and Dylan hold their hoses with arms extended to keep maximum distance. The little boy seems to enjoy trying to shampoo himself as he's hosed, which gives Casey an idea.

"Girls, please tell all adults and kids who can shampoo

themselves that they'll get lathered up by me, then they can stand off to the side and shampoo themselves and get hosed off," Casey says, realizing there's no reason they can't shampoo themselves and move the line.

As she instructs the girls, Casey lathers up an old woman who has so many lice that not a strand on her head is without a solid layer of them. Although Casey keeps her elbows locked straight out so she has the most distance between the lice and herself, she finds that with every beautiful, smiling Mexican her fear of the little buggers diminishes until they are literally under her thumb. With each shampoo, the bugaboo gets easier. Casey remembers Amana Anne talking about a kind of therapy where you just jumped in and did the thing you were afraid of over and over until you realized that the stupid little thing, next to the bigness of God's help, can't stop you. Or in this case, those millions of little things collectively.

By the end of the day, Casey's hands feel like they've been soaking in Ajax, and her arms quiver like she was Moses trying to hold up the rod all day. Every single person in line has been shampooed as the sun sets a brilliant farewell over the horizon with a last golden blink. The final remaining friends and relatives waiting for their just-shampooed loved ones get up from their hunkered down positions to applaud Casey enthusiastically in appreciation.

It reminds Casey of Skip always saying, "What do you want, a standing ovation?" whenever she pointed out that she accomplished something, even if it was "just" a perfectly clean house. Yes, she thought now, every wife or mom should get a standing ovation at least once in her life and this was certainly indescribably touching and meaningful and sweet.

Casey can see that the teens are moved, too, when the Mexicans turn to include them in their applause as the kids load onto the bus, deservedly exhausted for the first time on the trip. Leroy, Myrna and Birdie say good-bye to their groups and join them, plopping into their seats. They notice the teens' smiles and looks of satisfaction, the pride in themselves.

"Tell us your secret weapon so we can use it on the kids ourselves," Birdie says as Casey sinks into her seat, not caring that it feels like a heating pad on "high."

"Just put a little fear of God – and critters – in the little buggers," Casey laughs and checks her hands and forearms for lice, but it looks like she dodged the bullets. Just in case, she brought the last remnants of the shampoo from one of the jugs with her. She'd have a good hair and full body shampoo before she gets in bed. *If* she can lift her hands.

Her mouth is dry with thirst and her head's pounding from her day in the sun, but she has to admit she feels pretty great herself. As Leroy starts the bus and they pull out, she closes her eyes and rests her head against the back of the seat, spending a moment in gratitude.

Thank You, Lord, that even if I do nothing else with my life, You allowed me to help hundreds of people today. And conquer one of the biggest fears of my life to boot.

Though physically exhausted, she has a feeling of invincibility with God, that all things really *are* possible, and that something truly great could happen with the rest of her life.

Getting Out of Shittim

"We're down to baloney," Quentie says to Eliz as she comes out of her bookstore balancing two generously-piled sandwiches on plates, along with a pitcher of sun tea. "Is that okay?"

"*Wonderful*, thanks." Eliz sees that the sandwiches are made with the fabulous, huge Portuguese rolls from Oakhaven Bakery and her mouth is watering already. She gets up from Quentie's umbrella table to help with the sandwiches. "And since my life *is* baloney..." Eliz really wants to say another word for what her life is but she doesn't want her mouth washed out with soap, "...a baloney sandwich fits right in."

They share a chuckle and Quentie does a quick blessing over the sandwiches.

"Where are you in your Bible reading?" Quentie asks, nodding in reference to The Message Bible Eliz has open beside her.

"I'm right before the ingrates cross over into the Promised Land," Eliz says, pausing for a sip of sun tea. "I'm not meaning to swear here cause I'm not sure how to pronounce this, but I thought it was extremely apropos of God to call the place they were in before crossing over

Shittim."

Quentie laughs mid-bite and tries to grab the baloney falling out of her mouth with her teeth because she's got both hands on her sandwich, which causes them both to laugh.

"Well, I feel like I'm *in* Shittim!" Eliz takes a bite but Quentie's again laughing so hard, trying to keep the food in her mouth that Eliz starts laughing and trying to keep her bite from spilling out of *her* mouth. After a minute they wind down to chuckle-sputters but start up again when people passing keep gawking and smiling at them, and some start laughing themselves at how Eliz and Quentie are carrying on. Eliz and Quentie both sit back and catch their breath, afraid to chance a bite for a moment.

"I needed a good laugh," Eliz finally trusts herself to take a small bite, closing her eyes and enjoying the most delicious baloney sandwich of her life, peaked by near-starvation.

"We all do. It's medicine." Quentie takes a nibble. "In fact, the guy at the meat counter told me a baloney joke when I bought this. Wanna hear it?"

Eliz stops midway to taking another bite. "I hope it's not *too* funny. I want to eat."

"It's not like a ha-ha joke. It's more of a short parable," Quentie assures her.

"This is the first time I've ever hoped a joke wouldn't be too funny," Eliz says, sinking her teeth into a bigger bite.

"Okay," Quentie stuffs the baloney better into her sandwich, "so this guy was taking his lunch break at work. He opens his sandwich and complains to his coworker, 'Every stinking day I get a baloney sandwich. It's never anything but baloney sandwiches. I've had it!' And his co-worker says, 'Well, why don't you just make your own sandwiches?' and Mr. Baloney says, 'What are you talking about? I do!'"

Eliz chuckles. "So in other words, we make our own baloney in life? And then complain about it?"

"You're a quick-study," Quentie says.

"Studying's easy; living it's hard."

"Yep, though we're the ones who usually make the baloney, the hard part is we also need to be the ones to change the menu," Quentie adds. "But don't take that literally because if you come tomorrow, baloney *is* all you'll get."

A potential customer enters the store and Quentie wraps the rest of her sandwich in her napkin and goes to help him.

Eliz finishes her lunch and thinks about what she's been reading in the "Book of Joshua." It was surprising to read that once God's chosen people were in the Promised Land they actually had to *fight* battles to win more and more territory. She thought the Jewish people would just waltz in and be given the land and all the gifts. God said everything was theirs, and He did His part; but *they* had to do battle and do *their* part.

It strikes Eliz that this booze thing is a battle both spiritual and physical, and that Jesus already did His part for her by dying on the cross. Maybe her first step out of her own personal "Shittim" was to do *her* part, since the Bible says, "Submit yourself to God, resist the devil and he will flee." In truth she wasn't doing a lot of submitting or resisting, and maybe that was *her* part of the battle to get a new life.

What if, she wonders, *just for today, I decide not to buy that bottle the liquor store has chilling? Wouldn't that be a first step into my Promised Land, the first little battle won?*

Amana Anne's always saying: *Your decisions determine your destiny.*

Eliz closes the Bible and takes it back inside. She places it on the shelf, deposits her trash and sets her plate on the counter for Quentie who says, "You're leaving early today. Where you headed?"

"To my Promised Land." Eliz laughs, but she means what she says as she walks with purpose out the door. "Because I'm getting out of Shittim!"

~ Thursday ~

When It Rains

When Amana Anne awakened, she noticed the sky was darkening, turning a sullen, pregnant gray. By the time she showered, a ceiling of steel-colored clouds closed in, the kind Wowie could always predict because of her arthritis. Portentous clouds? Certainly ominous-looking. She opens the front door and can hear the low rumbles of thunder. Beyond that, no birds chirping. No dogs barking. It's unusually quiet.

Amana Anne wonders if maybe she shouldn't wear the sleeveless, white linen suit she chose for her radio interview, but it's too late to change now. She wants to allow extra time for getting there. It's a good thing because it's suddenly raining in earnest, like the wind opened the ashen sky with hands of lightning and thunder.

The air smells moist and sweet as Amana Anne runs to her car in the driveway, jumping around puddles already formed. Rain pelts her umbrella like it's trying to puncture through and goosebumps rise on her bare arms from the cool pellets that hit her like needles. There would certainly be a Babushka Alert today for the wind, a Pittsburgh joke for days when you need a scarf to hold your hair in place. Leaving the car out in the rain to rinse off the dust that had layered it in recent days seemed like a better idea before this torrential downpour began.

She escapes into the cocoon of her car and listens for a moment to the pounding pitter-patter on her roof. If raindrops are angel tears, as Amana Anne's father used to kiddingly tell her, a few legions were having a very bad morning.

A sharp clap of thunder causes her to flinch as she drives slowly up Commons Drive. Amana Anne hadn't caught the news or weather and had no idea they were in for anything like this. Some points south of them were getting hit hard in the aftermath of Hurricane Julian, which just missed Florida's coast, but the hope was that Pittsburgh was to largely miss it. She's thankful she's leaving early and will have time to pray en route.

Most of yesterday and this morning was spent in prayer and speaking affirmations based on reading the Word. She didn't have a cry fest yesterday after all. On the way home from Eliz's, Amana Anne realized she had much more important things to focus on than self-pity over Jake. Like building her faith for this radio show. Eliz was counting on her, to say nothing of her co-workers and the vendors. Plus, there would be radio listeners Amana Anne knew she could help. This was her one and only shot at promotion for the seminar and she didn't intend to blow it. For the first time in her life, she felt not only ready to do public speaking, but eager to banish her fear forever, so she could give people a first hand account of victory in a new life with God.

Granted, the idea of only talking to the morning radio show host and taking caller questions helped a lot, too. She was great one-on-one. Why hadn't she thought of radio sooner? Eliz had done a brilliant sales job of talking *Change Your Life* host Bill Winston into giving the whole hour of his weekly talk show over to helping people get a new life, and promised at least four mentions of the seminar. Bill usually devoted the hour to callers wanting to talk about what was going on locally or globally, life or relationship issues, the full spectrum.

Eliz promised to be there with her and Amana Anne wonders if Eliz has even left yet. Eliz always teases her about "having to be a century early for everything." Hopefully, Eliz's neck will feel okay her first day back at driving and she can make it. After the radio show, Eliz was heading to her office to rally the troops for what she hoped would be an inundating influx of seminar reservations.

Amana Anne eases slowly onto Blossom Brook Boulevard in case the road is slick. There aren't many vehicles on the road. She turns on the radio to find a weather report around the static and lands on news station KQV giving current conditions.

"Heavy rain is predicted through the morning. Watch for possible flash flooding. Power lines down..." Static breaks up what the announcer says next.

Another strike of lightning cleaves the sky, followed by a loud crack of thunder. As Amana Anne passes the library, the wind causes the shutters that frame the windows to bang against the bricks and churns the trees on the side of the road into a frenetic dance. It's suddenly impossible to see more than a foot in front of her through a wall of torrential rain. She pulls off the road into a Sunoco station as rain assaults her windshield like it has a vendetta against her.

Amana Anne presses the arrow on the radio search until one announcer comes in clearly: "A funnel cloud was apparently just spotted on Mount Washington. We're awaiting official confirmation. We have reports of flooding along the rivers and creeks, and again, a potential tornado watch. All residents of Allegheny County should stay home if at all possible and seek shelter. We will continue to have our team of meteorologists following..." She hits the button for KJOY, the Christian station, and gets nothing but static.

Her cell signals an incoming text with a *bling*. It's one word from Eliz: *Cancelled.*

A clap of thunder sounds and sharp spikes of lightning spark the heavens like golden zigzag scribbles. It's as if God is writing on His sheet of gun-metal gray sky, giving her a message she may not want to receive.

She listens for a long time to the pellets of rain accumulating to a dull roar on the roof of her car. And wonders if this is the final washing away of her dreams.

Killer-man

"Don't you dare ask Casey to go up Killer-man on our last mission day," Myrna says, pausing to give Leroy a warning look as she brings a bite of blueberry pancake to her mouth.

The whole gang's sitting at the long wooden table out on the social hall's back patio, the adults at one end, kids at the other. Zia brings out the last of the breakfast platters on a tray (whole-grain waffles and sausages) and sets them on the table, plopping down beside Casey.

"Killer-man?" Casey asks, digging into her veggie eggs. Casey can't think of any situation she wouldn't try versus having to figure out where to go and what to do today.

"The locals call it Killer-man because they feel it's like climbing Kilimanjaro for them to get up there with basic supplies like food and water for their families," Birdie says.

"Leroy's been trying to go up this goat path for years," Myrna says with exasperation. "I won't say he's *been* as stubborn as a goat."

"You better confess that, Sweetie," Leroy kids Myrna. They seem to have a running "confession" joke.

"It's Killer-man cause, like, twisted vee-hic-les..." Dylan says.

Kanashia jumps in, "Trucks and *buses* are deep-sixed at

the bottom."

"From people loco-coco enough to go up it," Jelly adds, living up to her nickname by slathering mounds of grape jelly on her toast.

"Widow-maker, fo sure," T says, reaching over Jelly to spear a waffle.

"Even if I'd survive, my wife would kill me for trying it cause she'd be stuck with the kids," Ziggie says kiddingly.

"I only have two grown teenagers and a husband who probably wouldn't notice if I didn't come home," Casey says. They all laugh and she doesn't tell them she's not kidding.

Ziggie rises and picks up the empty egg platter and his plate, bowing to Zia.

"Compliments to the chef, Zia," Ziggie says. "I'm going to go lick the pans before I start KP. Please excuse me, but I want to hit the road early." Zia nods her thanks to Ziggie as he heads for the kitchen.

"Here's the thing." Zia points with her fork, getting back on topic. "I lived a few miles from Killer-man when I was a little girl. That used to be a gargantuan garbage dump, before *El Stinko*. So of course, a lot of really poor people scavenged off it and lived up there." Her eyes look off as she goes to the place of her memories. "But the trucks couldn't make it up there anymore as the years eroded the road. Men with families went to get work where they could. That left a community of old widows, women and kids who still live up there."

"Those people have to walk for miles to get water and groceries, then trudge it back up that hill," Birdie says.

"Half the time it isn't even clean water and the same old containers keep getting contaminated from dirty water," Myrna says.

"People are *dying* up there," Leroy adds. He's working to keep himself in check emotionally, but a little blue vein pulses on his temple. "They don't even have clean water to wash with when they get infections. And no medical

230

supplies. We *have* the water and medical donations. I'd go up myself, but I need someone to walk beside the bus and tell me how to get around the rocks or move them..."

"I'll go," Casey says as spontaneously as she had the day she volunteered for the mission trip.

What?! The sane part of her asks. *A woman who won't climb a step ladder without wanting a Valium?*

Yes, another part of her answers, *and a woman who has nowhere else to go today.*

"Listen, Casey," Zia puts her arm around Casey. "You better at least *see* Killer-man first."

"*Really,*" adds Myrna emphatically.

"God said if we have just a little faith, we can move mountains." Casey's talking herself into this more than anyone. "So I guess I can have at least enough faith to go *up* one."

"Amen!" Leroy says gleefully.

Myrna casts Leroy a sidelong glance. "No truck has even made it up there in years, let alone–." Myrna's cut off by Leroy.

"If worse comes to worst, Jesus said there's nothing better than laying down your life for someone else," Leroy says, teasingly.

"Sure, *you're* old and don't have a lot of time left on the clock, buddy," Myrna points out. Birdie and Zia can't help but chuckle. The kids hoot at this. They'd been engrossed in chowing down and texting. "Casey's young and has a family," Myrna concludes.

Highly questionable on both counts, Casey thinks.

"Yo like a type T personality, Mrs. Swanson," Jelly says.

"That means thrill-seeking," Kanashia informs Casey.

"Not T like me, no worry," T assures Casey.

"Yo have a death wish, Mrs. Swan-song," Dylan says, coming up to their half of the table to fork a sausage since the teen's meat platter is empty.

It was a horrible thing to admit, but sometimes Casey *did*

just want to get to Heaven, to have the pain and uncertainty of the world behind her. Sometimes she wishes she could just go be with God. Casey comes upon a fleeting thought that feels far too comfortable: *What better way could there be to leave than on a mission trip?* She wouldn't have to worry about where she was going or how she'd survive. No one would ever know she took leave of her family. It actually seemed like a viable solution. *Just what shade of crazy was that?*

"Killer-man gonna be *yo* swan song, Mrs. Swan-song," T says.

The kids hoot, and Leroy gives them all a pointed, warning look. Birdie and Myrna exchange a glance of concern.

Casey's stomach lurches at the thought of what's ahead as they all rise to get going.

I guess it's time to find out.

Champagne-o

"Going out of business?" Eliz asks Quentie, not because she can't read the three-foot-tall GOING OUT OF BUSINESS SALE sign on the counter that Quentie's finishing in thick, black magic marker. She just doesn't want to believe it.

"Saturday," Quentie says quietly. She caps the marker with a *click* and the chemical scent lingers for a moment in the damp air between them. "Unless God sends me a very avid – no – downright omnivorous reader who'll buy, say, a few hundred books this week."

"Oh geez," Eliz says, letting out a sound like a punctured balloon, "like I wasn't bummeranged enough." As if their radio interview being rained out, no *tornadoed* out, earlier today wasn't enough.

Quentie chuckles at Eliz's colorful word choice. It makes Eliz laugh because the self-pity comes out of her mouth before she can even censor herself.

"Isn't it interesting how I somehow twisted this into being all about me when *you're* the one going out of business?" *I'm just the one who'll be out on the streets*, Eliz thinks, but doesn't say because Quentie's already on the edge of an emotional cliff. If waterworks start, Eliz is going to want to chug a whole bottle of chilled champagne the minute the liquor store opens.

"Oh no," Eliz says in an overly dramatic stage voice to get Quentie to laugh again, "*Your* world is caving in but *I* need a foot massage." Eliz flounces onto the couch like an over-the-top actress, lifting her feet to Quentie as if she better get right on it. She's rewarded by a laugh from Quentie, but Eliz can see she's still on the verge of crying.

"Tell you what," Eliz says, suddenly realizing she's been nothing but a freeloading borrower all week, and it *has* been about her doing nothing but taking and Quentie doing nothing but giving. "Will work for baloney."

"Will accept gracious offer," Quentie says, and Eliz can see that both the laugh and the offer broke Quentie's spell of being near tears.

"Ever hear the saying, 'No act of kindness goes unpunished'?" Quentie asks.

"Uh-oh," Eliz says, jumping up from the couch and pretending she's about to sprint to the door as Quentie points to piles of books stacked on the reading table.

"You better have a lot of baloney, lady," Eliz says.

After a few hours of organizing, stacking and arranging hundreds of books, Eliz sees the truth of Quentie's saying. They break briefly for their baloney sandwiches (Quentie piled Eliz's with baloney like a mini Eiffel Tower) and apple juice; the patter of rain is their only company. Not a single customer has come in all day. For that matter, Eliz hasn't even gotten one call back from the dozens of "Plan B" seminar promotional possibilities she's contacted.

Vacillating between worry and prayers of faith, Eliz goes back to arranging books for a few more hours, until Quentie notices Eliz rubbing her neck in pain.

"Hey, you're getting promoted for all your great work," Quentie calls over and Eliz's face brightens. She's hoping the promotion involves more food in plenteous quantities.

"Promoted out of here," Quentie comes over to give Eliz a hug of thanks and a gentle push towards the door.

234

"Notice I'm not arguing with you," Eliz says as she kiddingly double-times it to the door, glad to see it's at least stopped raining.

"That's because you're a smart cookie."

Eliz wishes Quentie hadn't said 'cookie' because it only serves as a reminder that she's still starving, which only serves as a reminder that she doesn't have money beyond the booze money. She's about at the end of her rope, all of which suddenly depresses her fiercely again.

"Tomorrow," Eliz says with a wave as she goes out the door, and the sight of Quentie trying to smile back amid her GOING OUT OF BUSINESS signs *really* bummeranges Eliz, so much that before she knows it, she's robotically gone in the liquor store, bought the champagne, and is sprinting home.

She's only three-quarters of the way when her neck throbs with pain from carrying the champagne; she has no choice but to set the stupid bottle down on the pavement, and plop herself right next to it. A soccer-mom type in a black SUV passes and glares at Eliz and her bottle pointedly, like Eliz is single-handedly bringing down the real estate value of Oakhaven. Eliz wishes she had thought to bring sunglasses and a hat so she could be incognito, and hopes the lady doesn't live in their townhouse plan.

Have I really sunk this low? Eliz asks herself as she buries her head in her hands, to hide her face from shame.

Sitting on the side of the road with a bottle of booze in a brown paper bag like a wino?

Okay, a champagne-o.

Still.

Eliz bites the bullet on her pain and gets up from the curb, wiping the back of her jean shorts, wet from the rain on the curb. Now she's a wino who looks like she's wet herself and the property value for the tri-state is officially tanked. Luckily, she's almost to her townhouse. Only a few more minutes.

Her orange tank top has perspiration rings under the armpits from the humidity, but at least the rain hasn't started again. The champagne *was* cold when she left the store. Now it's hot and sweating through the brown paper bag, ready to fall through the bottom and crash on the sidewalk if she doesn't carry it from underneath. If she has to roll it the rest of the way, that's what she'll do.

Eliz trudges up the last leg of the hill, asking herself how she could have been so full of faith less than twenty-four hours ago, praying her heart out, optimistic, feeling she was overcoming her battle with booze, about to have a great victory, and now zip.

How did it come to this again?

She walks in her front door, thankful for the relative coolness. The air-conditioning isn't on but the closed drapes kept the sun from overheating the room.

Here's how it came to this, she answers herself, taking the bottle out of the soggy bag and throwing the paper on the counter. *We had one sure thing with this Christian radio station and what some people call an "act of God" blew it out of the water. Lord, I'm sorry. But it seems like we weren't on the same team on that one. I'm just being real with You. Why the storm, Lord?*

She has no calls on her home phone from any of the potential promotional venues and no messages at all except for a warning call from her shuffle-boarding Floridian landlord that she better have her rent in by tomorrow.

Lord, if You don't give me some kind of sign that things are gonna work out, and darn fast, I can't hold on. Throw me a bone here, please God.

She prays as she paradoxically puts the champagne in the freezer. She knows from years of fast-tracking booze experience to by-pass the fridge.

It'll be chilled within the hour.

Park Your Enthusiasm

Amana Anne's taking her second cold shower of the day because the humidity's making her clammy, and the water feels bracing and refreshing. Relaxing, too, until someone suddenly reaches in and gooses her. She erupts in an Elizabethan scream that could startle her *chica* Casey *en Tijuana*.

"How many times have I told you to lock your screen door?" Wowie demands from the other side of the shower curtain.

"Mom, you gave me a heart attack!" Amana Anne turns the shower off and Wowie's hand appears inside the curtain to give her a seashell-embroidered towel, which matches Amana Anne's shower curtain.

"Amana Banana, I'd rather you die fast and safe of a heart attack in my arms than a slow, torturous death by some serial killer."

"These are my two options?"

"Unless you lock your door."

Amana Anne sighs at Wowie's "logic" and dries off in the shower stall. "So, how was Punxsy, Mom?"

"Remember the Civil War? That times two with your Aunt Flo and Uncle Ketch battling over him dousing everything she cooks in ketchup. *Hello!* How do you think the man got his nickname, 'Ketch'? After seventy-five years he's not gonna give up the red. He even squirted it on his birthday cake, just to tick her off."

"Ketchup is actually good on scrambled eggs," Amana Anne concedes, although Uncle Ketch grossed her out when she was a little girl and he squirted it on her eggs for her to try.

Wowie wipes the steam off the mirror as Amana Anne wraps herself in the towel and steps gingerly out of the shower, giving her mom a little derriere-tap in thanks and to get her out of the way.

"*Danke*, Momsy." Amana Anne's father used to always sing a Wayne Newton imitation of Danke Schoen that made them laugh, so they said that a lot.

"Don't call your mother a donkey to her face, dear. I don't care *what* language you disguise it in." Wowie perches on the closed toilet seat. She has on hot pink capri pants and a bright yellow tank shirt. Wowie always maintains that colors don't have to match, they just have to be "happy" colors.

"So anyway, Banana, then I ask your Aunt Flo what's new and she interprets this as I want to hear about every last Punxsy relative's edema, hangnail, or disease of the month down to the flea count on her daughter's boyfriend's chihuahua."

Amana Anne chuckles and moves aside a dish filled with starfish soaps to get a pretty bottle of her homemade moisturizer.

"Speaking of boyfriends, did you talk to Eliz?" Wowie asks.

Yes, and I hope you've picked out your dress for the wedding because Eliz is moving like a hot poker through ice with this guy, Amana Anne thinks as she opens the cabinet under the sink for her Calendula Blossom Natural deodorant.

"We talked enough." Amana Anne leaves it at that as she

applies her deodorant. After the radio interview cancellation, she's in no mood to be hauled over the coals by Wowie about the whole Jake and Eliz dating business. Wowie would hear about it soon enough from her senior spy network.

Wowie takes the Calendula Blossom from Amana Anne and applies it liberally to her neck because she likes the scent, even though Amana Anne has explained countless times that it's deodorant.

"I'm going to Jake's tomorrow morning," Amana Anne says as she runs a pick through her hair. She was actually only going to pay her bill. She knows it's OCD of her, but she wants closure on both her dream of being a public speaker and everything to do with it, as well as on Jake. She figures he probably won't be there now that Travis is back. She'll go around noon so even if Jake is at the shop, he'll be out to lunch and she won't run into him.

"Something exciting's coming down the pike," Wowie squirts great globs of moisturizer on her face and neck under the theory that tons once in a blue moon equals a normal amount daily.

Curb your enthusiasm, Amana Anne wants to tell Wowie but doesn't have the heart. *Better yet, put it in park. Because tomorrow I'll close the chapters on the biggest dreams of my life.*

Anywhere in the World

"The last thing we need is to hear one of T's girlie screams when we go up," Leroy says, laughing, as he and Casey approach Killer-man. He dropped the kids off with Myrna and Birdie a couple miles back to "help" the ladies give donated New Testaments *en espanol*. By the time Leroy and Casey unloaded the gang and bought supplies, it was already turning into *siesta* time and they were only passing a few walkers and cars along the dusty road.

"I'm almost disappointed in Killer-man," Casey says kiddingly to Leroy as she catches sight of the half mile of dirt road on a gradually building hill. Steep, but not roller-coaster steep as she imagined it. "I had Killer-man built up in my mind to go into the clouds or something from the way everyone was talking."

"Casey, do you really think I'd have let you come up here with me if I thought I'd be killing you over it? The only cars that have gone over are from kids who're drunk and come here joyriding at night. Or people who try to make it two lanes and neither will back up." Leroy revs the motor and picks up speed as they head for the base of Killer-man.

"We have to get a running start to make it up," he explains, and Casey's stomach tightens as they start the

240

ascent, because it didn't seem scary until now that she's actually on it.

"You'll just need to hop off a few times and move some rocks." Leroy notes Casey's growing anxiety, how she's tensely looking straight ahead, still as a possum playing possum.

"Just keep your eye on Jesus and know that He's with us here, now, helping these people through you," Leroy says.

"I appreciate you talking me down, or up, as the case might be," Casey says, digging her fingernails into the leather seat, hoping she doesn't tear it.

Leroy points ahead to a rock and stops to open the bus door for her to hop out. She thanks God that the hill is next to the passenger side of the bus so the door opens into the slope of the hill rather than the Great Beyond. Her peripheral vision picks up the drop below of several hundred feet.

"Just put it on the hill side, out of the way, Casey," Leroy calls from the bus. "You don't need to take it to the edge."

Thank heaven, Casey thinks, because she had a vision of trying to throw the large, golden-brown rock over the hill and going with it. Instead, she deposits it against the hill slope and jumps back on the bus.

"Great job, Angel Girl," Leroy says and Casey feels a small victory. She didn't realize when she dedicated her life to God that she'd seemingly have to face all of her biggest fears in a matter of days. Otherwise, she might have renegotiated.

"People are always magnifying their fears instead of magnifying God," Leroy continues as they ascend to the half-way point, and Casey is seriously wondering if they could just back down. "Fear is faith in reverse, in the enemy, instead of faith in the goodness of God," Leroy continues.

"I know," Casey agrees, and hears a little tremor in her voice. "God says we can't please Him without faith, so this is my opportunity to make God really, *really* happy."

Leroy laughs and points at another rock and Casey hops

out. It's a smaller rock and easier to maneuver, just a little over half the size and weight of the last one. She hoists it out of the way and jumps back on.

"You just have to trust the Lord," Leroy continues. Casey's thankful he must know how much she needs to hear this. It reminds her of when she and Skip used to donate blood and Skip would always talk her through it so she wouldn't think about the needle going in. Back when he still talked to her that much. Back when he still cared.

"This might be the last one," Leroy says, pointing to a grayish rock in the left tire path, at about three-quarters up the hill. Casey grits her teeth when she goes out because the drop is so high now, she feels light-headed enough to faint. Thankfully, the rock is relatively small, albeit sharp-edged.

As they take the last quarter of the hill, women and children at the top come running at the sound of the bus, cheering when they see it's the Lord's Bus. The Mexicans pour down the path, and when Casey and Leroy reach the top and stop, the locals don't even wait for the two of them to descend before they come on board to hug them or kiss their hands in thanks.

Casey and Leroy spend the afternoon unloading amid a growing ocean of love and gratitude. The hours once more seem to pass like minutes on a wave of grace, with the people laughing, loving and working together like the true brothers and sisters that they all are in this beautiful family of God. Casey realizes that these moments, these days, are among the most deeply meaningful and joyful of her life. It comes too soon when they are finished and garnering last, lingering hugs, hand clasps and heart-felt gratitude.

The people stand at the edge of the dirt road and wave as Leroy and Casey descend the hill, and although the bus is empty, Casey feels full and fulfilled. And *brave*. As the bus edges down, she summons the courage to look over the drop and sees a big, sprawling world, a view from the top like she's never seen before, and although it's frightening, it's exhilarating, too. It's a panorama of people and land and buildings and cars, of lives being lived and changed in the great wideness of the world.

Why am I even considering going back home, being miserable, making my family miserable, when I could be touching lives for the better out in the world?

Maybe for the first time in her life, Casey's aware that she has, in Christ, tremendous power like no other in the universe: The power of love. These last few days, it's been unharnessed in her life in a way she's never experienced. And she wants to give more of it. Somewhere, anywhere it's needed, where it will be most fruitful and appreciated.

Casey thinks about where she should go tomorrow, if she should return home... or trust that God will again lead her wherever she should go.

She closes her eyes to give thanks and pray as the bus lurches to the bottom of this "Killer-man" she's conquered. *Lord, I'm trusting You to lead me tomorrow where You most need me to give my love, just like You led me here, on this mission. Please send me where I can make a difference.*

Anywhere in the world.

Double for Your Trouble

Eliz is reclining on a lawn chair in her bikini on the back patio, catching the last rays of the sun, when she hears the flip-flops of thongs rapidly approaching.

"Hey, we still have zip, except a few geriatrics for yo seminar, Miss Cabana Girl," Jamaica says, flicking a piece of lint off her red swim suit cover at Eliz.

"When I invited you to be my guest at our pool to cool your jets, I didn't mean stop by here first to douse my fire, Jami." Eliz sits up, shielding her eyes from the low-sky sun.

"Our vendors're all putting a lot of skin in the game for this seminar and their return on investment best pay off," Jamaica says, riffling through her beach bag for a comb.

"No worry, Jam, I have a brilliant new angle that the local news is *loving*."

"The *news* is all about where the tornado smacked down, in case you failed to notice," Jamaica says as she twists her hair into an up-do.

"Za-zactly my point, Jam. I told our local news contacts that all funds from the I Want a New Life 4 U Charity Walk we're having before the seminar will go to helping the tornado victims. So they practically promised to give it a mention." They actually promised no such thing unless you consider "highly unlikely" hopeful, which Eliz did because at this point she was going to hitch her wagon to any star, no matter if it was as dim as a nightlight.

"Go relax before the pool closes," Eliz says. "I already swam. Just sign in under my name."

"Okay, I'll sign in under M-U-D cause that's what yo name's gonna be by tomorrow if this gig doesn't pan out." Jamaica flip-flops her way back across the yard. Eliz reclines again, letting out her breath. Eliz came *this* close to almost having to share her champagne with Jamaica because she was about to get it when she heard Jamaica coming.

Eliz *almost* thanks God that she didn't have to share the champagne but she realizes how silly that is and closes her eyes to instead apologize for what she's about to do.

Lord, You said our only work is to believe, so I've been trying to only believe, which means I have no back-up ideas if this gig goes south. God, I know in your Word it says You will give us double for our trouble.

I'm asking you to please give me some kind of sign that you will. Not just for me but for Amana Anne and Casey and Quentie. I know this is ironic since I'm about to resort to champagne, but You know our paths to victory aren't always straight. All I can say is I'm trying. I'm hanging on by my fingernails. I am sorry for what I'm about to do. I just can't hold out any longer.

Eliz opens her eyes and starts to rise, but what she sees in the sky stops her in mid-motion, sending chills up her spine. Above her is the biggest, widest, most colorful rainbow she's ever seen, and *another* beautiful rainbow is materializing as she watches, right above the other one. A thought comes into her mind like an answer to her previously questioning God about why they had to go through that storm this week: *You're never going to have the beautiful rainbows without the storms.*

Eliz doesn't even blink because the bottom rainbow is fading already and in a matter of seconds, it's completely

245

faded from the sky, with the higher rainbow quickly following. The scriptures she's been reading come to mind, that the rainbow is a forever symbol that God keeps His promises. No exceptions. And she's standing in faith that this double rainbow means God is going to honor His promise to give them all double for their trouble.

Thank You, Lord, Eliz prays with renewed fervor and excitement and passion that she's never felt over a job, over men, over anything. *I knew you were going to do something big for us. I can't wait until tomorrow to see what it is!*

~ Friday ~

The Invitation

Before Amana Anne enters Jake's shop, she turns the car's rearview mirror to check her face for the third time. *Clear,* she assures herself, her eyes scanning the full scope of her face as she turns her head to every possible angle. *I probably have toilet paper stuck to my shoe or something,* she decides as she gets out of her car.

The sun's already fry-an-egg-on-your-head hot as she walks to the door, eyeing the parking lot for his Lexus. There's only one other black car near the print shop, and on closer inspection, she sees it's a Honda, probably someone from Spot-off Dry Cleaning next door.

"Good morning," Shari-Beth greets Amana Anne from behind the counter, as she comes in the otherwise empty shop. "Or is it afternoon?" Shari-Beth asks, turning to look at the wall clock that reads five to noon.

"I think I can talk the Accuracy Police out of arresting you," Amana Anne assures her.

Shari-Beth laughs good-naturedly, "What can I do for you?"

"Nothing, thanks," Amana Anne starts, and Shari-Beth jumps in.

"Those are my two favorite words in the English

language when I ask that question," Shari-Beth says.

Amana Anne chuckles and hands her check to Shari-Beth. "I was just passing and thought I'd pay for my order." Amana Anne's heart beats faster in anticipation as she scopes the storage areas and back offices for Jake, just in case.

"That was quick," Shari-Beth says, appreciatively. "Half the time we have to stalk people for eons. Thanks!"

"Sure," Amana Anne waves good-bye to Shari-Beth, still eagle-eyeing for Jake in the back while she heads for the door – and plows into him as he's entering the shop.

"Whoa," Jake says with a laugh. "I've been meaning to put a traffic light over this door."

"Whoops! Sorry, Jake." She's flustered at the sudden nearness of him, his clean, manly scent.

"Was the order alright?" he asks.

She had noted the perfection of the samples he left, how the staples were at the exact fold in each, perfectly spaced apart, no bends or even little imperfections in the paper.

"Thanks, they look beautiful," she says, and notes he's pleased that she's pleased. *I love a man of excellence.*

"And you're very kind," Amana Anne adds. "I don't know how to thank you for the discount."

"Let me take you to lunch," Jake smiles at her and she has to remind herself to breathe.

"*I* thank you by letting *you* take *me* to lunch?" Amana Anne stalls to answer because she's so disconcerted.

"Okay, if you insist," he says. "We'll go somewhere nice so they have napkins."

"Ha, ha," Amana Anne says without laughing, though she does think he's witty, even if it *is* at her expense by recalling the facial fiasco.

"How about Sunday brunch at Hoffstatts?" Jake asks.

"Ahhhhh," she hesitates. *What's the man trying to pull? He's going out with Eliz. Or did Eliz corner him into something she just wishfully thinks is a date?*

"It's okay either way." He quickly tries to put her out of

her indecisive misery. "I go to the eleven o'clock service at Covenant Church. You know where it is, right?"

"Sure. Down from Hoffstatts."

An elderly woman with a cane comes up the walk outside and Jake opens the door for her. She nods her thanks at Jake, and Amana Anne steps out of the way, closer to Jake, as the lady stops to catch her breath.

"If you want to go to brunch, Amana Anne," Jake continues, "meet me outside afterwards and we'll walk over. You're welcome to join me for church, too. If you don't show for brunch, I'll just arm wrestle some church buddies to go."

Oh sure, Amana Anne thinks, *like a few dozen casserole ladies.* "Okay, bye." She squeezes past him, out the door, and resists an almost irresistible urge to kiss his handsome face.

Amana Anne can't help but note as she walks past the glass window outside that Jake has gone to help the elderly lady. Her order isn't in a big box, but Jake carries it for her anyway. *I love a man who helps old ladies.* The romantic in Amana Anne sighs a little dreamily.

Yes, but how about a middle-aged *man who dates* young *ladies? And at the same time wants to date* you?

By the time she's almost home, she's pretty much convinced herself that of course she's not going to go out with him if he's going out with Eliz. Doesn't matter what her feelings say. Doesn't matter if she's never felt this way before in her life. She's going to do The Right Thing.

Then again, Amana Anne knows Eliz well enough and has heard all the wily ways Eliz uses to get a man to take her out. Maybe Eliz asked *him* out under some pretense. Maybe he's too nice to say *no*, which also could be viewed as a spineless push-over, which is not Amana Anne's type. She doesn't think Jake is a push-over, though. Far from it. And since *she's* far from figuring all this out, there's no point in really trying.

As she passes Eliz's street, she remembers Eliz said to

remind her to tell about a "hot date" with Jake. *Maybe it's time to get the story,* Amana Anne decides, and turns down New London Lane.

Eliz is closing her mailbox, coming out empty-handed when Amana Anne pulls up to the mailboxes across from Eliz's townhouse. Before Amana Anne can even get a greeting out, Eliz starts rapid-fire talking.

"I only have a sec, Bana, cause they're gonna mention our charity walk on both the noon and evening news. FYI, I told them the charity walk's gonna be before the seminar. You know, it'll be on that trail that loops around the library. We'll donate proceeds to help tornado victims."

"Great idea, Eliz," Amana Anne says with a resurgence of both hope and fear about the seminar, and a healthy dose of questioning if it's really going to happen. Amana Anne puts her car in park. She normally hates when people gab here at the mail boxes, spewing car toxins in the air, but a one-time exception won't make a carbon footprint the size of King Kong.

"At least that's what I *think* the message I got from God means," Eliz back peddles. "I saw a double rainbow yesterday. Could mean we'll be on TV twice."

"Eliz, it's powerful to have faith in God's blessings and possible signs, but leave the specifics up to Him." Amana Anne doesn't want to dampen Eliz's enthusiasm, but it's best to leave the "how" up to God.

"I know, Banaboo, but the local news is our last shot. The Christian station has all national programs today so this is our only hope." Eliz gives the top of Amana Anne's car a couple of thumps in goodbye. "Gotta run, Bana, in case they lead with it."

"But, I wanted to talk to you just for a sec about..." Amana Anne's cut off by Eliz.

"Tomorrow, okay? We'll meet in the woods and go from there to the charity walk. It's walk-casual dress for the seminar."

The seminar with six people? Half of whom are going to do a "wheelchair" walk? Then again, if they really *do* get promos on the news, she'll have a much hotter front-burner challenge of public speaking than worrying over Jake today.

Eliz thrusts her hand in the air, pointing to the sky, in Amana Anne's signature move as she heads for her door, "Believe!"

Believe me, I'm trying, Amana Anne thinks as she circles the mailboxes to head for home. *With everything I have in me.*

Surprise!

"I'm ready for my red carpet, darlings," Casey announces in a mock movie star voice to Zia, Myrna and Birdie as she sashays into the kitchen where they're munching down at the breakfast bar. "I lost *ten* pounds!"

The ladies whoop with delight and swarm Casey to embrace her in congratulation hugs.

"Look how tiny you are," Myrna says, patting Casey's waist with her hand.

For the first time since high school, Casey *does* feel little. Or more important, healthy, and good about her body. Proud of herself. She even fit into the smallest shorts she packed, the one with the matching sunflower T-shirt. Although she cut out the shorts size long ago, it was definitely down a size or more from a week ago.

"You look like a new woman," Zia says. Casey *had* also noted in the mirror that even the puffs under her eyes were deflated and she had a tannish glow about her.

"In the interest of telling the whole truth though, I fell asleep without eating because I was too exhausted, and I weighed in this morning on the mailroom scale before eating my dinner from last night," Casey confesses. "Then I ate like a wild animal, sticking my head in it, because my arms were too sore to lift a fork."

"And look how good God is – cause you didn't have to spend a week at one of those fancy-pants fat farms to get in shape," Birdie says, then remembers Zia works at one and covers her mouth. "Oops, sorry, Zia," Birdie says sheepishly.

"You're right, Birdie," Zia laughs. "I always tell clients to do something useful to help others with their time instead of pedaling endless miles on an exercise bike that goes nowhere."

"You may have lost ten pounds, Casey, but it looks like you suddenly gained a few hundred," Myrna says, smiling and looking over Casey's head behind her.

Casey turns around puzzled, then stunned, to see Wyatt, Tyler and Skip cramming through the doorway toward her. Her heart jumps with love at seeing the twins, but it's all too much to take in – this mix of feelings rushing through her heart and mind.

What are they doing here?!

"Whoa, Mom," Wyatt says, stopping in shock as he sees Casey. "Where'd your hair go?" Wyatt embraces her with a speedy but tight hug, then stands shyly to her side.

"Where'd *you* go?" Tyler asks, putting his arms around her back and waist as much to feel her and see where she went as to give her a hug. He gives her a little pat on her back like kudos for a touchdown and smiles at her like he's impressed. She's too flabbergasted at the unexpected sight of them to answer.

Skip gives her a quick, searching look in the eyes before he hugs her; although it's so fast she can't read everything in his eyes, she sees uncertainty, questions unasked.

"I got your long e-mail and had a wake-up call," Skip says quietly in her ear as he hugs her. "I don't want to lose you."

Casey realizes with a jolt that Skip went into their "shared" e-mail (that had essentially become hers, to check for news from relatives or friends) and read her *Reasons I*

255

Should Leave journaling draft letter to herself. When he releases her, she notes he has his hair slicked back like he normally only does for weddings and funerals. Only for the most important occasions. Like he used to do on their first dates.

"We've already met your lovely family," Myrna tells Casey.

At the description "lovely" Skip comically uses the tips of his index finger and pinkie to smooth his eyebrows like he's daintily debonair, which makes the ladies hoot with delight.

Birdie comes up with what she thinks is a more accurate word choice, "Your *fun* family came while you were sleeping."

"I've never slept into the afternoon before in my life," Casey says. The week of work caught up with her, and she still feels out-of-it from so many hours of sleep. On top of that, the surprise of Skip and the boys suddenly *here* is fuzzily surreal. It's taking time for her to wrap her head around it. What *should* she do now?

"Yeah, right, Case," Skip says teasingly, looking at Casey like he used to early in their marriage when they would kid each other and he would smile to let her know a zinger was coming but he would softball it. "We have to roll the mattress over near every day to get her out of bed by sundown," he says to the ladies and they laugh.

"We'd never believe that," Birdie replies. "She's the best worker we've ever had and we're gonna miss her."

"Dad said we better come 'escort' Mom home or she might not come," Wyatt says, laughing, like he's trying to live up to this new rep of being a fun family, and the ladies think this is hilarious. A joke.

Casey glances at Skip to get a read on him and he looks back at her, then drops his eyes. He's suddenly shy with her, like he doesn't know her. Like he was when they were first getting to know each other, when they were falling in love. A

256

week wasn't that long, but so much had changed. Especially in her. She *is* a different person. Is it possible Skip's changed, too? That her absence *there* was as important as her presence *here*?

"We had to sell the big screen to buy the plane tickets, Mom," Wyatt says.

"I was kinda on the fence," Tyler says. "Big screen..." He pretends he's weighing the big screen in one hand, "...or Mom..." versus her in the other hand, moving them in an up and down motion like he can't decide. Tyler's clearly enjoying the audience of Zia, Birdie and Myrna, who're being entertained as if they have front-row seats at improv night.

"I'm just messing with ya, Mom." Tyler puts a loose arm around Casey's shoulder like they're a "Happy Days" rerun. Casey hasn't had the boys touch her or speak this much directly to her in years. She doesn't want to break the spell, even if it means she's just the vehicle they address on the road to impressing Zia, which is what Casey now realizes the boys are trying to do.

"We got to see the ocean for the first time, but we can't make it a beach vacation cause Dad's job starts tomorrow," Wyatt says, like he's letting Zia know he's really a beach dude at heart, and cool.

"The computer gig," Tyler explains at the look of surprise on Casey's face.

"Congrats on the new job, Skip," Birdie says around a bite of salad and Myrna and Zia add their kudos, lifting their milk at him in a toast.

"Thanks," Skip says. "I think Casey will be thrilled with anything after my last 'gig'."

"Mom, like, your bus pulled away and, like, Winifred says to Dad, 'So Junkman,'" Tyler imitates Winifred's foghorn voice to get Zia to chuckle, "'when's the fundraiser sale?' and Dad goes to Pastor, 'Like, how's this week?'"

"I've never said 'like' how's anything in my life," Skip

says and the ladies laugh.

"Winifred's dentures like almost fell out from shock," Tyler takes the stage back.

"We got rid of *a ton*," Wyatt chimes in as though competing for stage. "Not *everything*," he clarifies, lest Casey would imagine coming home to a clean house or some other such fantasy.

A scream erupts from the social hall and T, Dylan, Jelly and Kanashia come dashing into the kitchen, followed by Leroy sauntering in with a cryptic smile.

"We just got a call about a little surprise for your wife," Leroy says to Skip as he closes his cell and puts it into his pocket.

"Yeah, if yo idea of 'lil' is like a few million people," T says, giving a laugh like some evil villain who's just escaped an institution for the criminally insane.

Casey looks questioningly to Skip, but he's clueless, his face as blank as a rock.

What!?

I Believe in Miracles

"You have a special call on your life."

Amana Anne's curled up on her cozy, off-white living room couch. She pauses from reading in her Bible about Queen Esther's calling to save the Jewish people, remembering her father telling her these words when she was a teenager. It was after God had spoken to Amana Anne for the first time, and she later talked about it with her dad.

Her father had heard from God, too, in his youth, and prayed about being a minister. Instead, he ultimately felt called to be a Theology professor at Geneva College, where he met Wowie.

Throughout her life, Amana Anne and her father had countless deeply spiritual discussions, and she wished she could talk to him now. Wowie had faith, but she didn't discuss it much. She'd always mime like she was trying to keep her head above water when Amana Anne and her dad got "too deep," and she'd make some excuse to escape.

"I believe you're going to help the multitudes," Amana Anne's father often told her. "You're going to give a lot of people faith. That's why we named you Amana, because it means faith, or believe." His words reinforced what Amana Anne always felt but never voiced, not even to her father, that she would someday preach around the world.

Maybe that's why it's so difficult to relinquish this dream, she thinks, as she places her Bible on the white oak end table next to her couch. Because she always felt it in her heart, and believed it was from God. Could she have interpreted it wrong? That would answer why she somehow got sidetracked for most of her life into the security of a regular paycheck and a corporate job, in staying with what was comfortable and safe. Now there's only one more day before she needs to call her former boss, Oliver, about her decision. Although maybe it'll be decided *for* her since it doesn't appear that any doors are opening to this new life of her dreams.

She hasn't had the TV on at all today since Eliz would have called her if anything about the charity walk or the seminar had made the noon news. Amana Anne glances at the white oak wall clock. The gold hands say it's almost six-thirty, which means the charity walk and seminar weren't mentioned on the evening news either, so nothing short of a miracle could pull it off at this point anyway.

Well, Lord, she talks to God as she mindlessly picks at her cuticles, a girlhood habit she never did break herself of completely, *guess this is the end of the line.*

It dawns on Amana Anne, and she believes it's an insight from the Holy Spirit, that she's done everything she knows to do to manifest her vision this week – read and speak the Word, pray, go into silence, agree with others – everything that is, except totally surrender her *specific dream.* Amana Anne knows in her heart of hearts that she's never completely given the dream to God. Like somehow she could surrender her life but still hold onto enough of it to be the life of *her* dreams.

She closes her eyes to pray.

Lord, You know I always thought I was supposed to be an inspirational writer and speaker for You, but maybe I missed it. I guess that was just what I wanted, and perhaps for the wrong reasons. I give my dream to You now, Lord.

Father, I know You have a great and marvelous plan for me wherever You choose to use me. If it's back in the corporate world, although it isn't my dream, Your will be done. I know there are many hurting people everywhere and I only want to know, love and serve You more deeply.

Amana Anne closes her eyes, lifts her hands heavenward and sings with all of her off-key voice but sincere heart, "I surrender all, Lord, I surrender all…"

The back screen door suddenly flies open, stopping Amana Anne mid-note. Wowie's sleepy-eyed and has lounge chair slat indents on her right cheek from napping on them. She's in green shorts and a red tank top and looks like an angry Christmas elf.

"Hey, Celine Dion." Wowie's tone says Amana Anne sounds *nothing* like the songstress. "When I need someone to pierce my eardrums during naptime with a lullaby serenade, I'll know who to call."

"*Calling* before you come, Momsy! What a novel idea. *What* are you doing hiding in my backyard anyway?" Amana Anne had no idea Wowie was even out there because her lawn chair is in a blind spot, hidden by her flower garden.

"I'm getting my twenty minutes of natural vitamin D from the sun here because that pervert McGillicutty is always gawking out the window at my legs when I do it at home." McGillicutty's her ninety-year-old next door neighbor who's blind in one eye and can't see out of the other.

"Mom, visit reality. You have varicose veins as big as rattlers."

"I *told* you he's a pervert." Wowie closes the door with a slam and returns to her lawn chair. The one thing that cranks Wowie's chain is being awakened from naps, which now can be anytime up to five minutes before she goes to sleep for the night.

Not my fault, Amana Anne decides as she starts to feel guilty about waking her mom. *The little bugger was hiding.*

Amana Anne sings more softly, "*I surrender Mom, Lord, I surrender Mom...*"

"I can still hear you, Miss-remember-the-Honor-thy-Madre-commandment," Wowie calls in.

Amana Anne sighs. It sure is easy to feel all spiritual until some *person* comes around. She closes her eyes to silently finish her prayer.

I accept your will, Lord. Either way, I'm excited and thankful for whatever tomorrow will bring. Amen.

She rises from the couch and tip-toes to the kitchen to see what's left in the frig to fix for dinner, though Wowie may have already raided it when Amana Anne was at Jake's. Wowie always maintains, "Hey, I fed you the first twentyish years of your life. It's payback. I only hope I live another twenty so we're even or you'll owe me in Heaven."

If Wowie didn't eat yet, she'll be hungry as a bear later, but hopefully not still acting like one, too. Amana Anne decides salmon patties might be a nice change. As she gets out her wooden cutting board and serrated knife to chop an onion, she also decides to add a postscript to her prayer.

P.S. Lord, I'm coming boldly to Your throne to let You know: I still believe in miracles.

Last Call

"Are you aware there's a bounty out on yo head, girl?" Jamaica's practically screaming.

There's no way Eliz will pick up her landline to get eaten alive. And anyway, there are more pressing matters at hand. Eliz is in the process of putting a champagne flute in the freezer to chill. It's her best champagne glass, the flowered one that always makes her happy.

Well, at least until now.

"We'll *profit* share?" Jamaica continues her rant, echoing Eliz's former prediction. Eliz is pretty sure Jamaica knows she's standing there. From the kitchen, Eliz is watching as the local evening news team signs off over Jam's blathering. Eliz has been frantically flipping between the local stations since the four o'clock afternoon news started, and nothing about the walk or seminar was ever mentioned.

"You best not come in to the office to get yo things," Jamaica continues. "Let's just say I'm accepting applications for a firing squad."

Eliz hears the slam of Jam's hang-up as she takes the already-chilled champagne out of the refrig and sets it on the counter. She never even made it to Quentie's today for her sandwich because she spent the entire day making calls to every and any media contact to no avail. Although drinking on an empty stomach will end badly, the pain of now and the fears of tomorrow are too piercing to wait.

Look, Lord, she prays as she wipes the sweating bottle with a towel to keep it from slipping out of her hands when she pops the cork, *You have to admit I've come a long way in a week, since I've had no men or booze this many days. I know what I'm about to do is wrong, but why did You have to make it feel so good and why do I have to need it so bad? Sorry, Lord, didn't mean to blame You. Really, I've held out as long as I can.*

The phone rings and Eliz thinks seriously about throwing it in the toilet but lets the answering machine pick up again.

"Hey, Buddy." It's her boss, Ed, who put himself, his reputation, staff and biz on the line for her.

And she blew it.

He's waiting for her to pick up, which she's not about to do. "Well…" he says it slowly, as if to postpone the inevitable. "We only have a few people signed up, so I guess we'll cancel everything, Kiddo. We're going to have to square with the vendors and… everyone. I'll be leaving here in a few if you want to let me know what we should do."

Ed clicks off softly. The sadness and lack of blame in his voice make her feel far worse than Jamaica's brow-beating. Eliz *will* call him back. She owes him that. But not without first getting one sweet, looooong sip of the bubbly in her. A half-flute's worth, for sure; the other half while she dials him. At *least* the other half. Enough so she can speak to him, but not too much – yet – where she's incoherent. She's saving the amount that will numb her into oblivion for after the call.

She turns up the sound of the TV with the remote, as if to drown out the defeatist voices that are clambering to flood into her head. For just a few minutes, she'll zone-out with booze as she watches the national news, so she's transported (momentarily at least) to anywhere but here.

Eliz grabs the champagne flute from the freezer, touching

its circumference and deciding it's optimally chilled. But the first words she hears from news anchor Brian Williams make her drop the flowered flute in shock, and it shatters into a dozen tiny pieces as it hits the tile floor.

Making a Difference

"And coming up next on Making a Difference," Brian Williams announces and Casey suddenly sees herself big as life on the "monster" five-by-eight-foot flat screen in the church's social hall, "one stay-at-home mom makes a spontaneous, unselfish decision that brings hope, help and healing to hundreds south of the border."

Casey lets out an Elizabethan scream and everyone on the mission team laughs. Skip and the twins look almost as shell-shocked as she is. *Now* she understands why the mission team wouldn't allow her to watch the news that everyone else on the team had been trooping in and out of the social hall to see. They wanted to catch the earlier Making a Difference promos for her segment. That would also explain why T, Dylan, Jelly and Kanashia were even watching news, and their sudden *whoops*.

The adults had been keeping Casey sequestered in the kitchen with a pizza party, featuring Zia's whole wheat pizza with ricotta cheese, roasted eggplant, red peppers and sweet onions. The ploy was successful, so Casey was largely unsuspecting of anything, dismissing T's earlier warning as just another joke.

Now, everything seems surreal again as one of those

prescription drug ads comes on that shows happy people skipping while the voice-over announcer says side effects may include limbs falling off and losing all your senses. Casey feels like *she's* got side effects because her legs are trembling and she falls into a folding chair at the end of the long metal table beside her. Zia fans Casey with some napkins to help revive her.

"Mom, what's going on?" Wyatt asks as Skip and the boys plop into chairs on either side of Casey. She can't move her mouth to form words, not that she has any semblance of an idea what's going on.

"Yo, Mrs. Swan-song," T hollers while Dylan hoots, followed by Jelly and Kanashia screaming.

"Take two," Leroy points out to the patio for the mission kids to go carry-on out there and they Mexican-jumping-bean off each other in excitement on their way outside.

Birdie hunkers down on a chair across from Casey and speaks to her gently like one might to a little sparrow who just fell out of its nest. "Remember that Mexican cameraman from the local news in Tijuana?" Birdie asks Casey, who nods numbly.

"He met up with an NBC crew there, shooting something about the drug wars," Leroy tells Casey, pulling a chair out from the table and straddling to sit on it. "They asked if there was anything positive going on, because people are getting sick of all the negative stuff. So, they picked up our story and footage from the local station."

"When you and Leroy were on Killer-man, we told the NBC guys your story and they thought you were perfect for their Making a Difference segment," Myrna adds.

"MOM!" Tyler yells like he's coming out of his stupor, getting the full impact, and wants to snap Casey out of it. Everyone laughs at his sudden outburst and Skip pats him on the back to calm down. Casey becomes aware that her mouth is hanging open and clamps it shut.

"We didn't even let your family know because we

wanted to surprise you," Zia says.

"It worked," Casey finally finds the voice to say, and they laugh.

"It's on," Leroy yells as Brian Williams comes back on the screen. The mission kids charge in as he turns up the volume with the remote.

"And finally tonight," Brian Williams says, "our Making a Difference segment asks the question: Can you change your life and the lives of countless others in a week? We'll let Casey Swanson's story answer that question."

A close-up of Casey's suntanned face appears on the screen and the miniscule part of Casey that's still able to think wishes she'd plucked what's becoming a uni-eyebrow. Besides that, she decides she looks rather spunky. Her hair's spiked up, like one of those cool hairdos she's always admired on middle-aged, with-it women, even though hers is spiked from sweat and pushing it off her forehead. If Casey didn't know it was herself, she'd say the woman she sees on TV seems to have some kind of inner peace and quiet confidence as she looks out over the Mexican landscape.

"One week ago," Brian continues over the shot, "Casey Swanson was a working-from-home mom helping with her husband's estate liquidation business in Oakhaven, Pennsylvania." That was what Casey euphemistically called it when the ladies asked what Skip did, thank heaven. "Then, last weekend, she made a spontaneous decision at her church to step in for an injured mission volunteer," Brian continues.

"On a moment's notice, she left the comforts of home to serve the poorest of the poor on the outskirts of Tijuana, Mexico, with the Lord's Bus mission team." Over Brian speaking, there's a series of shots with Casey in front of the bus handing out blankets, hugging kids and unloading supplies.

"Because of Casey, countless people received water, food, medical supplies, and blankets to keep them warm for years to come. And hundreds of locals who would normally have no access to water even got a shampoo."

Brian Williams is interrupted by screams from Jelly and Kanashia, who're in the background shot of Casey shampooing the little Mexican boy with lice. The camera pans out to include the long line of people waiting their turn.

"One moment of compassion and action can make a difference and create a memory of kindness that will last a lifetime," Brian says over a visual of a toothless old Mexican lady smiling at Casey and taking her hand in thanks.

"We're told that Casey literally gave part of *herself* away. She lost ten pounds during this super-strenuous mission week..." There's a shot of Casey unloading one of the twenty-five pound sacks off the bus. "...and got quite a workout distributing a ton of supplies, goodwill and love."

There's a group shot of children from *El Stinko* hugging Casey, and she realizes that she was always so caught up in what was going on that she didn't even know the cameraman was there most of the time. T and Dylan let out *yips*, interrupting Brian's closing words, because they're in the background of another shot on the happy, shampooed people.

"...and hundreds of lives changed south of the border," Brian's face is back on camera, Casey's smiling face is in a box to the side of the screen. "Casey Swanson, making a difference."

"Mom!" Wyatt yells, hugging her.

"My mom's a celebrity!" Tyler extends his arms out to display her like she's a circus act.

"Proud of you, Case," Skip whispers in her ear as he hugs her. "Love you."

Casey fights tears welling in her eyes in a rush of emotions, and she's not sure if it's that her family loves her and is proud of her, or that they came for her even before they knew she was a "celebrity." Or maybe it's that she finally validated *herself.* Casey's lifted to her feet in a rush of everyone on the mission team hugging and congratulating her.

"It was a *team* effort," Casey protests, and she realizes she's hugging them goodbye, too, as she sees Skip check his watch and pick up her getaway bag that she set by the door earlier.

"Don't worry," Birdie assures her. "The rest of us will be on Persons of the Week next Friday. Which we *prefer*."

They all share a laugh and Casey realizes that it's their last laugh together, too, and she'll miss these wonderful new friends she's grown to care for so deeply in only one short week.

"Here's our info to keep in touch," Zia says, handing Casey a piece of paper with e-mails and phone numbers. Casey gives her a final tight, lingering hug that says thanks more than words.

Leroy shakes Skip's and the boys' hands goodbye. "It was a pleasure to meet our little angel's family," Leroy says to the guys.

"Her wings are gonna come in handy if we miss our flight," Skip says, putting his hands on the shoulders of the twins to steer Wyatt and Tyler toward the door.

Casey and her guys shoot into the blue Ford Focus rental parked out front of the social hall, and the mission gang waves goodbye as they pull out. Casey's heart is filled to overflowing with gratitude, though there is a twinge of sadness when they pass the Lord's Bus. She wonders if maybe she'll be on it again some day and blows the rusted yellow, old friend a kiss.

Thank You, thank You, Lord, for all these good people and for this great week. I guess when I asked You to open the door to where I'm most needed next, at least for now, it opens to home.

She waves until the mission gang is a little speck and realizes that maybe her new life is seeing her old life with new vision. Through the eyes of God. Maybe she and Skip and the boys could have a new life *together*. As a family. Not a perfect life, but a better life.

270

Then again, maybe sometime soon, she'll be off on another exciting adventure. Perhaps there's a stand-by list for other mission opportunities around the world. But for tonight, sleeping in her own bed sounds wonderful, and nothing seems so inviting as getting to her own little place in the world.

~ Saturday ~

Suddenly?

Amana Anne pulls back her lace sheers and looks out the kitchen window to check the morning sky. It's turned a deeper shade of blue since earlier, with a few cottony-white clouds drifting across it. *All and all a gorgeous Saturday*, she decides, rinsing out her "Hope" tea mug, even though she's feeling without much hope for the new life of her dreams.

At least today will be a day of closure, Amana Anne thinks. Closure about her career *and* about Jake.

With a resigned sigh, she opens the top kitchen drawer for her address book to call Oliver, her old boss, and soon-to-be current boss again. She actually likes Oliver and enjoyed working with him. That was never the problem. He always thought the best of her, even once telling her she wasn't OCD but *kaizen*, a Japanese business philosophy of continuous improvement of work practices and personal efficiency. He was sorry when Amana Anne left. *She's* sorry she's returning.

Amana Anne taps her finger lightly upon the page with Oliver's number. Thinking. Postponing, actually. Does she really have to cement this thing just yet? Oliver *did* say she had a week and that's not officially up until later today. *You never know what God might do*, she tells herself, shutting the address book back in the drawer. She can always do it later.

Right now, it's almost time to meet the girls, and she has the longest trek out of all three of them. She grabs her house key from the gold heart container on the counter and tucks it securely in the side pocket of her shorts. Eliz left a lovely peach T-shirt with *I Want a New Life* in pretty, cursive black lettering (inside a plastic bag on her doorknob), and it's a perfect fit so she's wearing it. *A consolation prize?*

Her thoughts are broken by the sound of Wowie's roller skates rapidly approaching – too rapidly – and Amana Anne hurries outside to prevent Wowie from plowing into her screen door again. Instead, Wowie plows into Amana Anne and pushes *her* into the screen door as a human blockade. Amana Anne holds Wowie for a second by the arms to make sure she's stable, then releases her with a pointed look.

"Don't look at me in that tone of voice," Wowie says, adjusting her helmet. She has on a sunshine-yellow *I Want a New Life* shirt and red capris. Clearly Eliz is trying to unload these in the neighborhood. Amana Anne spots a flick of Lumberjack's orange tail as he vaults up the oak tree across the street and wonders if he has one on, too. Apparently, Amana Anne isn't getting the new life she's advertising on her chest; she seems to be exactly where she was a week ago with a roller-skating mama and lumberjack *gato*. She locks her door and starts down the sidewalk, with Wowie grabbing at the back of her shirt.

"Not so fast, Banana," Wowie tails her. "My sources tell me you have a brunch date tomorrow with my future son-in-law."

"*Un*believable." Amana Anne stops in her tracks and Wowie plows into her back. "Mom," Amana Anne walks onto the street and motions for Wowie to come up beside her. "I'd prefer not to *wear* you all day."

Amana Anne tries not to think that she should have tripped that sweet little old lady who came to the print shop while she and Jake were talking. "I hope you're not paying your snitches, Momsy, because they're feeding you false information."

"They're right," Wowie says, skating smoothly beside Amana Anne. "You just don't know it yet. And when you *are* out to eat with Jake, if you prissily clean the silverware with your napkin, I'm going to come in and saw your fingers off with a butter knife."

"So you're thinking if I ever do have a bite to eat with Jake, you'll be standing outside the restaurant watching us?"

"Heavens, no. I'd pull the widow-on-a-limited-income card and I'm pretty sure he'd invite me to join you."

"I'd be worried, but I'm not going out with him," Amana Anne says, walking faster to get onto the woods trail so she can lose Wowie. "In fact, I'm going now to meet with his *real* date and Casey."

"You'll see," Wowie says in a sing-songy, know-it-all voice as she makes a turn-around circle at the end of the street, where the woods trail starts. "And *I'll* see you later at the seminar, Sweetie."

"Mom, it's canceled," Amana Anne says, starting on the trail.

"Oh, contraire, see you there," Wowie calls back as she skates up the street. "I'm a poet and don't know it."

Now what? Amana Anne asks herself, looking back at Wowie through the trees. *I'm firing that "manager" of mine if I have to give a seminar for my mother and her matchmaking cronies, who will most likely be heckling me.*

There's no reason I need a manager now anyway, Amana Anne realizes as she starts up the first hill toward the point of their weekly rendezvous.

But that faint little voice of hope in her that never gives up, chimes in as she breaks into a run up the hill:

Unless, of course, God pulls a "suddenly!"

A Most Exciting Day

"Brunch is on me," Eliz says to Quentie as she plops a grocery bag of eggs, multigrain bread, and orange juice on the umbrella table. Quentie's putting a GOING OUT OF BUSINESS stand-up sign on the sidewalk, but her eyes light up at the sight of food.

Eliz had gone to the liquor store last night and returned the champagne so she could use the money to buy groceries, but Quentie had already closed by the time Eliz got to New Beginnings. Eliz scrambled four of the eggs for dinner, downed a few pieces of bread (that she didn't even take time to toast) and washed it down with a good third of the orange juice.

Then she was busy setting things in motion after seeing Casey on the news. She only slept a few hours, and awoke on sheer adrenalin to have the same menu for breakfast. If Eliz was going to pull today off, she was going to *need* her energy.

"And here's a little thank you," Eliz says, lifting a folded T-shirt from the bag and handing it to Quentie. It's a vibrant violet, with *I Got a New Life* stenciled on the front. The "T" in "got" is a beautiful cross with curved and pointed edging.

"I love the message *and* the color!" Quentie exclaims,

slipping it over her tank shirt to see that it fits perfectly.

"I thought royal purple because you're the daughter of the King," Eliz says. "I am, too, but I wanted to match my baby blues." Eliz smoothes her gorgeous teal *I Want a New Life* T-shirt and flutters her eyes comically to make Quentie chuckle.

Quentie shuffles through the groceries with pleasure. "Perfect timing since I'm plumb out of everything."

"You're not going out of business though, as you'll soon see, so you won't need this sign," Eliz says, removing the sign and propping it backward against the door.

"Guess you haven't seen my business records, the ones with all the red," Quentie says, wiping the umbrella table with a cloth. "Still, there sure is a lot of traffic this morning, so maybe you can figure out a way to steer some of it here?" She pauses to watch the traffic backing up the entire length of Blossom Brook Boulevard.

"Done," Eliz says. "Get ready for the overflow. I'll explain more later cause I'm on the run. I need to make a quick stop at Jobe's Funeral Home on my way to meet my *hombres*."

"Did somebody die?" Quentie looks at Eliz with concern.

"Quite the opposite. I'm getting the funeral homes to help people get a new life."

"I love a good mystery, but I'm really confused," Quentie says.

As Eliz takes off up the street, she calls back, "Let's just say that this may end up being one of the most exciting days of my life!"

Anything's Possible

Vibrant yellows and reds and oranges swirl into a lovely apricot-pink as Casey whirls her own version of Zia's RCR energy drink in their blender. Skip actually bought bananas, apples and nectarines in anticipation of her return. No doubt the guys hadn't eaten any, but simply that Skip did it was enough. *And* he was already up and gone, going to work at his new job.

Granted, she didn't return to a perfect world. The moment they got in the house, Wyatt warned her, "Mom, do *not*, like, open any closets." Nonetheless, the façade of a clean home both downstairs and in her bedroom was a good starting point. To find the twins' rooms and the laundry room in untidy chaos was almost comforting lest she think she was in the wrong house. At least she *was* home so that she could try to influence the boys to check out community college or get some kind of work. She could always take off on another mission trip if the guys need another wake-up call down the road.

It's a big, blessed world out there and anything's possible, she tells herself as she opens the front door and lets the brilliant morning sunshine in. She's already dressed in a gorgeous, flamingo-pink *I Want a New Life* T-shirt Eliz had waiting for her, and new, white, Gap shorts Skip once bought for her at a yard sale years ago. The shorts had always been too small but Casey kept them because she was touched that Skip was clearly in denial about her size at the time. Or maybe it was the size he'd *hoped* she'd work into. Now the challenge would be *continuing* to fit in them.

She sips her energy drink, careful not to slop any on her new top, although it does almost match in color. Her sludgie isn't as pulpy as Zia's, or green, but it tastes good and it'll still give her plenty of zip. She'll *need* it for the agenda Eliz has planned for today. Eliz really took the God Stuff and ran with it in the week Casey's been gone. Eliz called early this morning because she was so eager to bring Casey "up to speed." If things came together, it was going to be Indy 500 speed. Especially for Amana Anne. Casey can't wait to see Amana Anne's face when she's "brought up to speed" and can't help but chuckle at the thought.

Still, it isn't going to be any cakewalk for me, either, Casey thinks as she glances at the time on the smiling cow clock over the stove, the one the boys liked since they were little. *I've never done* this *before, either.* She steps out of her slippers and puts on white ankle socks and tennis shoes.

Whatever happens, it'll sure be interesting, Casey decides as she quietly closes the door behind her since the boys are still sleeping.

And maybe, once again, This *is* the day.

The Light of New Life

Eliz is already waiting impatiently on her hilltop for Casey when the brown tip of Casey's head finally juts over the horizon.

"I GOT A NEW LIFE!" Eliz yells, determined to beat her to the punch. Casey laughs that Eliz called it before Casey even saw Eliz.

"I got a new life, too!" Casey yells back.

"I know!" Eliz calls. "And so does the world!"

Amana Anne's finger pointing up to the sky is the first thing Casey and Eliz see over her adjacent hill.

"Believe!" Amana Anne shouts, mostly for herself this morning. At the sight of Casey with her short-cropped hair, tan and weight loss, Amana Anne yells a startled, happy, "Casey!"

They all run down their hills to converge at the base of Baby Bridge, looking like triplets with their *New Life* T-shirts.

"You got a new *you*, too, Casey," Amana Anne says as she hugs Casey.

"Yep, Slim Swanson," Eliz says, hugging over both of them and Casey laughs.

"When I was growing up, one of my skinny friends cried

because she was called Toothpick," Casey says. "I used to think I'd cry for *joy* if anyone ever called me something like that, so thanks."

"And what about big congrats on Toothpick Making a Difference, Bana?" Eliz asks Amana Anne.

"I bet you made a beautiful difference in people's lives on your mission trip, Casey," Amana Anne says, giving Casey's shoulders a little squeeze.

"I take it you haven't been watching the news, Bana?" Eliz asks.

"No, why?" Amana Anne asks when Casey laughs.

"Case-mo was *on* Making a Difference," Eliz says.

"Are you kidding me?" Amana Anne looks from Eliz to Casey.

"It's true," Casey says.

"Casey!" Amana Anne hugs Casey again. "I'm *so proud* of you."

"Eliz got a tape of it," Casey says.

"I can't wait to see it," Amana Anne claps her hands, applauding.

"Toothpick, we're gonna get you the key to the city, but enough about you right now," Eliz says, putting her arm around Casey, who chuckles, to get her moving. "Believe it or not we have something huge on the front burner because of all this, Banaboo."

"Uh oh," Amana Anne says, following them. She should have given Eliz her pink slip earlier. Who knows what's coming down the pike with Eliz *now*.

"I have some time-sensitive info I gotta spit out fast." Eliz starts to speed walk and motions with her arm for Amana Anne and Casey to pick up the pace over Mama Bridge. "First, I am now Slim's manager, too, Bana. You have to share me."

"Well, actually, we won't have to share because..." Amana Anne starts but Eliz cuts her off.

"Shushie, Bana, you're not off the hook."

"Does *hook* sound like a good description?" Casey kids Amana Anne, who moans in reply.

"I got blurbs from Toothpick's tape on all three eleven o'clock local news programs last night and leading every hour on all morning news. Especially the Zia blurb about you, Slim, dropping a load." Eliz pinches Casey playfully at her trimmed-down waist.

"I wish you'd *told* me!" Amana Anne gives Eliz a playful push.

"I've been out all morning," Eliz explains. "And I know you go to bed at four o'clock in the afternoon so I didn't want to call you last night. We need you fresh like a butterfly for your big day. *Partly* your day."

"What're you talking about?" Amana Anne asks with concern creeping in.

"It'll make sense soon," Casey assures her.

"First, I have Quentie and my team selling *I Want a New Life* stuff like those booklets from Jake," Eliz stops and Amana Anne trips over her but Eliz catches her. "Bana, did he ask you for that hot date yet?"

"Whoa, *date*?" Casey stops in her tracks. "And who's *Jake*?"

"A geriatric buffo Banana hit on who did our printing," Eliz explains to Casey, grabbing both their arms to get them moving over Papa Bridge. She's practically dragging Amana Anne because she's a little stunned. "Bana, when I went to the print shop, all he did was ask about you, so I said get the girl out of the nunnery, man, and ask her out."

"Oh my heavens," Amana Anne says, trying to take it all in. But Eliz is railroading on, yammering so fast you'd think she was up for a speed-talking competition.

"Anyway, I've already been down pre-registering the peeps." Eliz knew from crunching the rough numbers that she would have enough to pay the workers, vendors, Amana Anne and Casey, plus donate some to help the tornado victims. With her own share, she could pay this month's rent, with a little left for groceries. *Very* little, but she's been giving thanks all morning that at least she's not like the people featured in Casey's TV segment.

As they take the hill to the library, Casey's surprised that she isn't winded for the first time in all their walks. Must be all the cardio she did at her "fancy-pants" health spa mission. She can faintly hear what must be the gathering people on the other side of the hill. *Hope I'm up for this*, she thinks, then recalls her victories with God in both the little lice and big Killer-man challenges so far this week. *What's the big deal in talking about it to people? Wasn't that the point? To pass it on?*

"What's all that noise?" Amana Anne asks, puzzled. "Is there something going on in town today?"

"I'm getting to that." Eliz looks to Casey on the other side of Amana Anne as they summit the hill. "Let's link arms so we pace together," Eliz says, tucking Amana Anne's arm into hers and winking at Casey as Casey links Amana Anne's other arm.

As they peak the hill, they look down to see hundreds of women in vibrantly-colored *I Want a New Life* and *I Got a New Life* sun visors and T-shirts surrounding the library, and an overflow of women trailing to Quentie's outdoor sale down the street. Jamaica, Ed and Eliz's co-workers busily register people and sell products at the library tables set up in front. The crowd cheers and starts to congregate in front of the podium as Casey, Eliz and Amana Anne come over the hill.

"I'm not speaking in front of a crowd!" Amana Anne digs her heels in. Casey and Eliz are practically carrying Amana Anne, with a hand under each of her arms as they jog down the hill.

"Get a death grip on her, Skinny-ma-rink," Eliz instructs and they both tighten their hold.

"Don't worry, Bana," Eliz says. "Most of the women want to hear about how Toothpick lost ten pounds in a week.

Her seminar's *Making a Difference in Your Life and Others*. I tied it in to the news segment so all the local TV stations would promo our seminar last night and all morning."

"Then Casey's giving the seminar." Amana Anne feels a tidal wave of relief as they round a bend in the path going down the hill.

"One of them," Casey clarifies.

"There's no way we can fit all of the people in one space, so I'm gonna take some of the overflow," Eliz says. "My seminar's called, *From Mess to Message* and I'm giving my testimony about how I became my own boss *and* found God – in a week. Not that *He* was the lost one."

Eliz knew by the swelling registration numbers this morning after the news that there would be well over twice the legal limit the library could hold in its speaker room. So the local funeral homes donated chairs and they set up for two additional seminars outdoors, one in the back grassy area and one on the library's large side yard. Thankfully everyone in town had the good sense not to die and have their viewing today.

"Your seminar's named after your book, *I Want a New Life*," Casey tells Amana Anne.

As they get closer to the podium and Amana Anne can see all the women's expectant faces, she starts breathing like a cornered cat. "I've decided I don't want a new life." Amana Anne wiggles to get loose. "I mean it. I'm going to wet myself."

"Half the gals out there are your age and incontinent." Eliz waves to the crowd. "They'll think you're in solidarity with them."

"You'll be great," Casey assures Amana Anne.

"I said we'd say a word before the walk," Eliz says as they approach the podium.

Amana Anne tries to wrangle free, but Casey and Eliz drag her toward the microphone. Amana Anne's chest muscles tighten like a vise; she feels like a boa constrictor is around her neck. But when she looks out over the crowd, a part of her also recognizes the multi-colored gift God is trying to give her. Amana Anne recalls what the Bible says about "a cord of three is hard to break" and realizes that maybe, with Casey and Eliz at her side, she *could* do this.

"A *word*, not a dissertation, Bana," Eliz smiles through clenched teeth at the weight of dragging the woman.

"Just do your signature move, Amana Anne," Casey says as Eliz and Casey each throw their free hand in the air, pointing heaven-ward.

"BELIEVE!" Casey and Eliz shout into the microphone and Amana Anne yells loudly with them in a sudden burst of confidence. Yet, looking out on the swelling crowd as more women come up the street, and thinking about speaking through a *whole seminar* re-grips Amana Anne with trepidation. She wrestles free of the girls with a surge of strength.

"*This* is my *new* signature move," Amana Anne says to Casey and Eliz as she runs for the hill, mentally offering the briefest prayer for the seminar, the one she always suggests to everyone else when they don't know what else to say or do: *Lord, heeeelp!*

Eliz catches Amana Anne before she's more than a few yards up the hill, with Casey in hot pursuit.

"Let go of me!" Amana Anne can't help but laugh because Eliz is grabbing her in places that tickle. "I don't need you to help me go *away* from them!" The seminar ladies are already taking the girls' lead and starting to follow them for the charity walk.

"I'm not *helping* you, Banaboo, I'm trying to hold you back," Eliz says, laughing as she tries to run ahead of her. "I don't want you to beat me up that hill for the first time in yo life, Granny."

Casey takes advantage of Eliz and Amana Anne pulling at each other, and sprints ahead of them. Eliz lets out an Elizabethan scream that Casey's beating them both up the hill. Eliz and Amana Anne catch up and Eliz grabs Casey's arm, laughing, trying to pull her back, and feels guilty for being so competitive, especially with these women she loves.

Hey, the Promised Land wasn't conquered in a day and some habits die hard. Not to mention the dying-hard habit of wanting a nice, chilled Yuengling on a hot summer day, she thinks, as a frothy beer brought by a cute waiter comes to mind. *I'm trying, Lord, but you're gonna have to help me every step of the way. You can do anything, and I'm the living proof. I'm not where I want to be, but I'm sure not where I used to be, either. I* am *a new creation and I've left my old life behind.*

Then Eliz feels like that still, small voice of the Lord is telling her to look behind her *literally.*

She turns around to see the women streaming behind them, the runners first, weaving up around the second bend already, the walkers threading around the first bend. With their multi-colored T-shirts and visors, it strikes her that they look like two vibrantly beautiful, moving rainbows following her. A tear of both gratitude and happiness comes to her eye, at the sight of her living double rainbow, the double for her trouble, for God's promises, and most of all His love.

Eliz brushes her tear away and turns to see *both* Amana Anne and Casey beating her up the hill. She sprints to catch them until they're all stride for stride, laughing and grabbing and pulling at each other to try to get ahead, until they just hold tight to one another and run together

higher…

and higher…

and into the Light.

Salvation Prayer to a New Life

Lord Jesus, I believe You are the Son of God and that out of love for me you came to earth and paid for every one of my sins on the cross. I'm sorry for all I've done wrong and I ask You to forgive me and come into my life as my Lord and Savior. Thank You for giving me a New Life here on earth and eternal life with You forever in heaven! Amen.

Questions for Discussion

1) In what areas of life – relationships, work, finances, health, challenges – do you most need a new life? What does your vision of a new life look like – and what would change in your current life? How do you act, look and feel in your new life?

2) Which character do you most identify with and in what ways? What specific attitudes, habits or beliefs can you borrow from that character to help you achieve your dreams?

3) Name one main goal for the character who most relates to your own aspirations. What one concrete step can you take toward your own primary goal to help you change your life?

4) Casey, Amana Anne and Eliz are each at different places in their relationship – or lack of one – with God in the opening chapters. Where are *you* in your relationship with God? How can you start or deepen your relationship with God for a new life?

5) God says He knew you before you were born: "Before I formed you in the womb, I knew you." (Jeremiah 1:5) He has a plan for your life. Discuss your partnership with God and ways you can receive His direction and love on your journey. When you pray, do you take silent time to hear how God may be directing you?

6) Amana Anne's relationship with her late husband, Nathan, was honest and open. Is there anyone in your life with whom you can be most honest and most yourself – a spouse, a friend, a family member? Are you open and honest with God about your feelings and your fears as you look at areas in your life that need change?

7) How can two or more gathered, praying, enhance the support and power of a new life? Discuss how your group can help champion new life for each member. How can you help each other achieve your goals and dreams for a new life?

8) In Hebrew, "Elizabeth" means "God is my promise." "Amana" means "believe" and was a popular girls' name in Jesus' time. Casey's name means "brave." God says in the Bible that He knows you by name. Do you know what your name means? Discuss what relevance the meaning may have in your life.

9) Sometimes it's rejuvenating to get away and have a fresh perspective, even if it's just locking yourself in the bathroom and soaking in the tub! But where would you most like to go if you could go anywhere in the world? Where could you realistically go – to a retreat, a Christian conference, a vacation – to help you in a closer walk with God?

10) How can you use *I Want a New Life* to bring people to God or closer to God? Is there someone in your life you might recommend this book to or perhaps give it to as a gift to bring her to a new life or strengthen her faith?

Bible Study

1) The women in *I Want a New Life* all need a new life in different ways. The Bible tells us, *If anyone is in Christ, she is a new creature; the old things passed away, behold, a new life has begun. (2 Corinthians 5:17)*

Have you given your life to God for a New Life?

Why, when and how did you give your life to God?

2) When Eliz has her God Encounter, God tells her of His love for her, the same love He has for you. (See John 15:9)

How do you feel about God loving you so much that He died for you?

What is your favorite Bible passage about God's love for you?

3) It's said that there's a "fear not" scripture for every day of the year.

How does Casey overcome some of her most challenging fears?

How and when have you used a scripture to help you when you're afraid?

4) Amana Anne has been blessed with hearing the voice of God throughout her life. Name a couple incidents from the Bible when God spoke to someone.

To whom do you most relate and why?

Have you ever "heard" from God in any way and what did He say?

5) The Bible says that as a person thinks in his/her heart, so s/he is (Proverbs 23:7). Thinking the way God thinks blossoms your life.

What are you thinking that is not in agreement with God's Word?

How can you change your thinking and use the promises in the Word to bring new life to all areas of your life?

6) God *spoke* the world into existence and says we create with *our* words and will eat of the fruit of our mouths. Choose a Bible quote about the power of your words.

What changes will you make in your life based on this wisdom?

What Bible quotes can you speak to empower you and change your life?

7) The primary power Jesus used in His ministry – and Amana Anne, Casey and Eliz use to change their lives – is the power of belief.

What's your favorite quote from the Word about believing or faith?

How can you daily live it to bring about a New Life?

8) Revisit *I Want a New Life* to pick out your favorite Bible principles.

How did the girls live those principles?

How do *you*?

How will you in the future as you walk into your New Life more and more each day?

Please Share Your Thoughts

Has *I Want a New Life* helped you, or someone you know, along your journey to a New Life?

Write to mmpnewlife@hotmail.com
or
Anything's Possible Publishing
P.O. Box 85
Oakmont, PA 15139
USA

You Can Help

There's nothing more important than sharing God's love to bring help, hope and healing to someone's life. Please consider donating a copy of *I Want a New Life* to a women's shelter, homeless shelter, cancer ward, hospice or wherever you believe it might offer comfort, a smile or bring someone closer to God. If your church is involved in female prison ministry or women's programs, please consider donating copies for your next church project. God bless you as you help other women come to a beautiful new life.

Acknowledgments

Many thanks for excellent input from Jerry Poydence, Lillian Amazeen, Steven Majercik, Mary Ann Mamros, Bruna Riccobon, Linda Hryniszak and Amanda Hryniszak. Gratitude to artist extraordinaire, astute editor and marketing maven Melissa Haas for her lovely cover art, brilliance, joy and inspiration. Thanks to Stephanie Zimble for insights, assistance, sweet enthusiasm and for comparing some of my writing to Steinbeck's (I don't care how remote the reference!) and to Tina Whitehead for helping with a gentle spirit and good humor.

Much love and deep appreciation to Jay and Eileen Poydence for their generosity in helping me find more voice. Special thanks to Tina Stephens Herrmann, Stuart Herrmann and my lovely niece Stephanie Hinkes for being my undercover editors.

Thank you to Chris Poydence and Rick Seigh for computers and computer help, and Craig Poydence for helping to move my writing and hope forward! Special gratitude to spiritual writer friend Eileen Colianni for her valued input and kind-hearted caring, and to Mary Alice (M.A.) Cookson, creative midwife, editor and encourager from conception to birth of New Life, and deep, sweet, fun friend through the ages.

And most of all to God, for giving me gifts to share with the world, unconditional and eternal love... and a bright, beautiful New Life.

Author Biography

Michele Poydence wrote and produced the inspirational television magazine program, *A New Beginning*, which has spanned the globe in over 130 countries and U.S. territories. Along with Bill Cosby, Randy Travis and other notables, her television program won the Angel Award for outstanding positive-value entertainment. She has worked with CBS Television, and with film and tv studios as a writer, producer and director, and has been published in a variety of inspirational magazines. Michele has produced, directed and written comedic plays through her theater company, *We Quit Our Day Jobs*. Her feature film, *Anything's Possible*, has been optioned by a William Morris Agency director.

I WANT A NEW LIFE

is available at

amazon.com & barnesandnoble.com